# Against The Tide

First Published in the UK 2012 by Belvedere Publishing

First edition: 2012

*Any reference to real names and places are purely fictional
and are constructs of the author. Any offence the references
produce is unintentional and in no way reflects the reality of
any locations or people involved.*

A copy of this work is available through the British Library.

ISBN: 978-1-909224-02-5

Belvedere Publishing
Mirador
Wearne Lane
Langport
Somerset
TA10 9HB

# AGAINST THE TIDE

# BY

# ELIZABETH REVILL

# Author's Acknowledgements

This book is dedicated to all those who have supported and encouraged me, especially my loving husband, Andrew Spear, who still puts up with my constant tap, tapping away on my laptop at all hours and my creative bursts. He knows now when to leave me alone!

To my good friend and co-writer in Malta, Ivan Scicluna, who has worked with me on developing the screenplay, "The Outsider," taken from this book and optioned by Lee Levinson. Ivan is a phenomenal and talented screenwriter, so expect to see his name on the big screen in the not too distant future.

To Alexia Miles who did the wonderful photography for the cover and her beautiful model, Crystal Featherstone, the epitome of Jenny Banwen and daughter of my best friend Hayley.

To my sweet Dad, who has provided me with a profound love of all things Welsh and huge pride in my Welsh heritage on both sides of my family.

My son, Ben Fielder who shares my passion for writing and all the excellent discussions and ideas we share together.

To my dear friend, Hayley Raistrick-Episkopos, who constantly encourages and wills me on to succeed. Her tarot readings are second to none!

My lovely FB friends from around the world, who have bought all my books, read them and wanted more.

And as always very special thanks to Sarah Luddington and her brilliant team at Belvedere who made this possible. Thank you one and all and here's to the next...

Future titles will hopefully include, The Electra Conspiracy a fast paced, contemporary thriller and Rainbows in the Clouds the continuing saga of the Llewellyn family.

# Foreward

The year is 1796 and in England smuggling is at its peak. But it is not smuggling as perpetuated, by romantics with images of flashing lights on cliff tops, the moon shining on a gentle sea whilst the boats with muffled oars are rowed ashore, where jovial gentlemen colourfully dressed *a la'* Gilbert and Sullivan are ready to load tobacco, tea and brandy onto the ponies before spiriting them away into the night.

In 1796 smuggling is, even by the standards of the time, nothing more than a violent, vicious and bloody trade, the enormity and violence of which surpasses any form of illegal activity. It is a major criminal undertaking conducted on a colossal scale which penetrates every level of society; from the gentry who finance it down to the ordinary people who actively aid and abet the business.

The smuggled goods find their way into virtually every household in the land. It is condoned by the clergy and supported by corrupt magistrates who fail to convict the few smugglers who are caught. Thus, it is against this background of organized violence, sheer terrorism and even murder that one must judge the actions of the Customs Men. They are dedicated individuals trying to maintain law and order against all odds. They are always vastly outnumbered, universally despised and hated. They and their families live as unwelcome outsiders in communities, which whole-heartedly support the smugglers or, at the very least, are sympathetic to them. They receive scant support from the authorities or the Dragoons and even, on occasions, their own superiors who are in the pay of the smuggling organizations.

Nathaniel Brookes is one such outsider. He is always working, 'Against the Tide.'

# Chapter One

## 1781 - The Oath

The gentle surf softly caressed the beach like a flirtatious lover, fickly enticing back the sand and shingle only to spurn it and toss it back to the shoreline. The shimmering, blood red sun had begun to slip more quickly toward the horizon as two young children played happily by the rock pools watched lovingly by their mother who was enjoying the last of the warmth from the gradually weakening solar rays.

Little seven-year-old Nathaniel Brookes carefully examined a clump of ribbon seaweed secured at the edge of a rocky outcrop leading down to a miniature lagoon. His expression was serious as he probed the fronds of the water plant and watched as a small crustacean darted away to the comparative safety of a tiny crevice. Nathaniel's dark eyes lit up with pleasure as he saw tiny fish swim quickly across pebbles to hide under an overhang. "Naomi! Naomi, come see," he cried out to his little four-year-old sister who toddled to join him at the water's edge. Their pretty mother watched them with love and pride when a shout came echoing down from the cliff top.

"Myah! Myah!"

Myah looked up to see the tall strong form of her husband, Elijah waving from the top of the steep and craggy cliff. She called to her offspring, "Time to go, now, children. Papa is waiting." Myah stood up and picked up the blanket on which she had been sitting and brushed off the sand. She laughed as she saw the children's expressions and promised, "We will return another day."

There were murmurings of disappointment as the children picked their way back to their mother's side on the beach and began to gather their things together. The setting sun dropped more quickly now, and young Nathaniel lifted his face up to the sky where the clouds began to shroud the smiling sun and ominous shadows passed across his upturned face.

A shower of stones and rocks suddenly avalanched down the cliff side and young Nathaniel called out in horror, "Look, Mama. Look!"

Several hooded, brutish men armed with cudgels menacingly advanced on the uniformed Riding Officer forcing him toward the edge of the cliff until he had nowhere to run or manoeuvre. Elijah roared like a trapped animal and valiantly tried to fight his way through the gang of cutthroats. One bestial, bearded smuggler twisted Elijah around and grabbed his hand. He gruffly nodded to another larger member of the gang who jeered and forcibly held Elijah, preventing him from any movement. The first adversary pulled a wicked looking blade from a sheath at his side and raised it in evil glee. He hacked at Elijah's hand severing a finger bearing the distinctive Brookes' family ring, with an ornately monogrammed initial 'B' over a chain and anchor emblem and, then whooped in triumph.

Elijah emitted a tortured growl of agony as he struggled to fight back. His good hand closed on a chain around the ruffian's neck. The rest of the devils converged on Elijah even more threateningly, as if that were possible, crowding him and trapping him. The burly bearded smuggler spun Elijah off his feet and hurled him violently from off the cliff. An anguished cry was ripped from Elijah's belly as he plummeted to his death. The thugs watched in delight as the body bounced off the rocky cliff side and hurtled to the sand below. The wreckers jeered and laughed, commenting that there would be one less Custom's man to hamper their activities.

Myah's tormented cry melded with that of her husband and reverberated around the lonely beach. Her children watched in shock. Elijah's body landed with a sickening thud and Myah raced to his side. She screamed his name in horror and disbelief as young Nathaniel dissolved into tears, calling, "Mama?" Little Naomi looked lost and bewildered. She popped her thumb comfortingly into her mouth.

"Noooo!" Myah struggled to control her sobs and took Elijah's bloodied hand. There in his grasp was a golden ankh, an Egyptian type cross talisman, on a broken chain. Young Nathaniel moved quickly and retrieved the item. He studied it carefully before pocketing it, a fierce expression on his little face.

Myah held on to Elijah's still warm hand and pressed it toward her lips as she whispered, "Goodbye, my dear sweet love. For now, your fight is over." And she laid her face on his chest and wept, before hearing rattled cries of derision echoing on the breeze.

The savage band of murderers continued to watch and jeer from the cliff tops. The family were forced to endure this tortuous display of mockery and the hoodlums congratulating each other on a job they considered had been well done.

Myah was so overcome with sorrow as Elijah's broken body lay before her that she didn't notice the sudden departure of the cowardly thugs from the cliffs who had fled instantly at the sight of a small platoon of Dragoons galloping along the sands. Still crying, Myah looked up at the sound of the thudding horses' footfalls. Relieved, she recognised her brother-in-law, Jeremiah Brookes, Elijah's brother, who had arrived at the scene with his Sergeant and five others. He leapt from his horse and dashed to Myah's side, taking the sobbing woman in his arms trying to still her tremulous cries and comfort her.

Jeremiah barked an order to his men, "Quickly, search the beach, caves and surrounds. *Now*!" The riders began to canter off as instructed.

Nathaniel placed a protective arm around his little sister and they huddled together.

"Rest assured, Myah, I'll not rest until my brother's murderers are found," promised Jeremiah.

"The cliff top. Your men must search the cliff top. That's where they were," Myah pleaded in anguish.

"Sergeant Morris!" shouted Jeremiah, arresting the departure of his second in command.

The Sergeant stopped and trotted back to the family, "Sir?" he questioned.

"Scour the cliff top. Find these fiends."

"But, Sir," protested the Sergeant, "They know these cliffs like the insides of their pockets. I don't think…"

"You heard me. Up that footpath, now."

Sergeant Morris did not argue with his superior officer.

He rounded up his men and ordered them curtly, "To the cliff tops. Quickly, now. Make haste."

The men grumbled, dismounted and gathered themselves half-heartedly and scrambled up the slippery scree.

"Oh, Jeremiah, what am I to do? What am I to do?" Myah wailed.

Her brother-in-law attempted to calm her; "You are my brother's family and now my responsibility. Fear not. I will care for you all. You are under my protection."

Young Nathaniel glared stonily ahead, his face frozen in bitter acrimony. He took his sister's hand. Naomi's eyes were wide and distracted, and she shivered miserably.

"I swear by all that's holy I will find the men who killed Papa, even if it takes me a lifetime to do it. They will pay," swore little Nathaniel, suddenly seeming older than his seven years.

Jeremiah glanced at his nephew and gasped. The sun's rays had escaped the clouds and shone forth dazzlingly, surrounding Nathaniel's head in a halo of light like an angel from a Biblical picture.

Later that night there was much revelry and celebrations in the Black Dog Inn, a dangerous place, renowned for its criminal element where few honest men would dare to tread. A handful of coarsely dressed ruffians guzzled ale in drunken abandonment. They were self-congratulatory, crude and loud in their chatter.

Suddenly, the old oak door creaked open, a sound not heard in the melee, but a blistering wind rushed through the bar, churning the tobacco smoke in the room like a maelstrom. The stinging chill of the gusting wind silenced the occupants and they turned as one body to eye the newcomer as the door slammed shut. The drinkers stared at the silhouette of a man swaddled in a black cloak that covered him from head to foot and thus disguised his identity. The man scrutinised the people present. A hush fell over the crowd of drinkers as they watched the invader stride in. He had an air of confidence about him, an arrogant presence that made people stare.

The cloaked man approached one group of drinkers and

threw down a heavy moneybag onto the dirty tabletop. Gold coins spilled from the open neck of the pouch and chinked onto the grimy surface. A burly, black bearded man, known as Black Bob, crashed down his pewter tankard and licked his cracked, chapped lips. He reached into his jacket pocket and removed Elijah's blood stained ring. He placed it along side the drawstring pouch of coins. The caped man snatched it up and without a word turned and stepped to the stout door. As he heaved it open the wind from outside blew through the bar once more and disturbed the hood of the seemingly anonymous visitor. A shifty, weasily looking scruff gasped and his jaw dropped as the man swept out into the painfully cold night air, and the thug exclaimed, "Bloody hell! The smuggler Knight."

The bar erupted into chatter and Black Bob shouted out, "Friends and fellow drinkers, the ales are on me." There was a rush to the bar as the ruffians shouted out their orders to the overworked Landlord. And Peg-Leg Sam who played for his drinks and supper stretched out his concertina and merry music rang out in the room. It would be a long night.

# Chapter Two

## Newport Fifteen Years Later

Maps of the Welsh coast vied for space on the walls and tables with medical and anatomical charts placed in a very masculine gentleman's bedroom. The room was in disarray with clothes strewn everywhere. Someone was in a frenzy of packing. A black leather doctor's bag waited by the entrance to the room, on the feather bed was a very large carpetbag. Nathaniel, now a handsome twenty-two year-old, scanned his room carefully. He was wearing a long cloak and cocked hat, the recognised garb of a Riding Officer. Nathaniel picked up the last few items and garments and stuffed them fiercely into the voluminous carpetbag. He strode to the door and took one last look around his room. He studied his black, doctor's bag; thought for a moment, then grabbed it and thrust that too, inside the shapeless piece of luggage.

Nathaniel exited his room and firmly closed the door behind him as if he was saying goodbye to his life, as he had known it. He marched purposefully across the landing and approached the elegant grand staircase. The young man had an aura of power and determination about him and he oozed charisma, which commanded attention and with it, respect. He was an imposing and dashing figure in his uniform. He ran down the stairs ignoring the walls littered with family portraits, pausing only at one that was of his deceased father, Elijah. He saluted the painting and spoke quietly in beautifully modulated tones, "Father, I am about to fulfil my oath. Your death will not have been in vain." Nathaniel crossed himself and whispered, "However long it takes."

Nathaniel reached the impressive vaulted hallway and walked along the corridor to the drawing room and opened the door. The room was empty of people but a movement caught his eye through the French Windows. Sitting on a stone bench in the garden, her back to the house was his

6

mother, Myah. Nathaniel opened the garden doors and stepped out onto the patio.

Myah Brookes was sitting stiffly, her eyes puffy and red from weeping. She stared blankly ahead into the yawning emptiness that gave no clue as to why her emotions were bubbling so strongly under the surface, threatening to break free and overflow into abject misery and depression. Her eyes didn't see the magnificent grounds, or the fountains and statues. Her expression was frozen as if her heart had been ripped out.

Nathaniel was filled with deep love and compassion for his mother, and even felt a little guilty, knowing that he was at the root of her melancholy. He lowered his bag to the floor, removed his hat and went to her side, bowing down on one knee. He took both of her fine porcelain hands in his and raised them to his lips and kissed them gently, "Mother…"

"Hush. Don't say a word. I understand. Believe me, I do," she confessed.

"Mother, I know this isn't fair on you." Nathaniel paused.

Myah slipped one hand out of his gentle grasp and ruffled his hair, "I should have realised. You are too much your father's son."

Nathaniel felt a lump manifesting itself in his throat and swallowed, "Mother, remind me of how he was. The years play tricks and I have begun to forget. I don't want that to happen. There is only his portrait on the stairs but it doesn't speak to me of the man inside."

"Oh, Nathaniel. As long as you live, so does he. You only have to look in the mirror. You are so much like him in nature and ways. You have the same sense of justice, his sense of humour and when I look at you I see him reflected back to me in your eyes and voice. You are truly your father's son." Myah leaned forward and kissed him on both cheeks, "I am so proud of you."

"When this is over I shall return and resume my medical career. We will all live in a fine house and not be reliant on Uncle Jeremiah's charity. "

"We?" questioned his mother.

"You, me and Naomi."

"And what of your future wife? Your promise?"

Nathaniel started regretfully with shame and the colour flushed to his cheeks. He hesitated and then bowed his head, "Oh, yes, my wife…"

Myah swept her hand around their surroundings encompassing the garden, the extensive grounds and the magnificent manor house, "My poor sweet generous boy. You had no need to promise yourself out of duty to someone for my sake. Hannah is a sweet girl, yes, but I know that she has an instability inherited from her mother and I fear for you."

"But mother…"

"Hush. You must listen. It is not too late to let her down gently without her losing her family honour. Hannah has bouts of unspeakable sadness and black moods that strike without warning and her behaviour can become erratic and irrational. My son, please pay heed. It is always a worry when close relatives become united. Think of the repercussions for the children of such a union."

"But, mother. I need to secure your future financially, for both you and Naomi. A marriage to Hannah will help provide this."

Nathaniel's mother went on to rebuff him but was interrupted by the sight of her brother-in-law, Jeremiah passing the French Windows with his daughter, Hannah. Myah rose, took Nathaniel's arm and led him further into the garden. She indicated the grand surroundings once more and hurriedly added, "All this means nothing. My wealth lies in you and who you are, in Naomi and the memories of your father."

"You deserved better. Better than to be the wife of a Riding Officer," said Nathaniel bitterly.

"Be under no illusions, Nathaniel. I chose my path. My life was like this before I met your father. I could have chosen to continue to live in luxury, even afterwards, but I decided not to."

Nathaniel looked puzzled, "I don't understand, unlike Uncle Jeremiah, father was not a man of means."

"Neither was Uncle Jeremiah, not until he entered the world of commerce." Myah smiled and turned to face him, she did not wish to explain further and just confirmed, "Yes, he was fortunate; Jeremiah was very lucky." With that she drew Nathaniel into a loving farewell embrace and whispered in his ear, her voice was husky with emotion and her eyes glittered with tears, "God speed, my son. Go now, please. I cannot bear to see thee leave. So, go."

Nathaniel clasped his mother's small frame to him and kissed her one more time before a renegade tear fought to rebel and roll down her cheek and, then he turned away. He left her in the garden. He was feeling responsible for her plight, knowing how bereft she felt. Her words would come back to him another time and he would wonder at what she meant, but for now they were forgotten. He knew he had to get on the road and ride. It would be a hard and long journey.

Nathaniel stepped away toward the stables and Myah sighed, "Be safe, my son. Be safe. You know not what you will face." Sadly, she seated herself once more and watched his powerful frame moving energetically with his strong regular gait, so reminiscent of his father. He would be a force to be reckoned with. This she knew, and she prayed that he would return to her sooner rather than later, and more importantly return alive and not in a casket.

Nathaniel stood, on the steps of the handsome manor house, holding the bridle of his beautiful ebony mare, Jessie. Jessie snorted and stamped her hooves. She was impatient to be off. The animal was at one with Nathaniel's sensibilities and felt that a great adventure awaited. She was anxious to leave.

Nathaniel's first cousin, Hannah, to whom he was betrothed, stood shyly at her father, Jeremiah's side, waiting for her chance to say goodbye. Hannah was the epitome of a fair English rose, with milk white skin, a look of innocence and long, pale corn blonde hair. There was something of another world reflected in her eyes, something of which to be wary. Hannah's troubled spirit so clearly seen by Myah flickered across her face only to vanish and be replaced by an expression of adulation as she studied Nathaniel's face.

Jeremiah grasped Nathaniel's hand firmly and held his gaze, a note of warning entered his voice, "Your mother will not take this well. You know she's not very strong…"

"She's stronger than you know, Sir. She understands."

"But, your medical career?" accused Jeremiah. An uneasy silence lay between them punctuated by Jessie chomping at the reins and chewing on her bit. "It's a dangerous path you have chosen, Nathaniel. Is there nothing I can say to dissuade you?"

Nathaniel remained silent. He steeled himself and his cold, hard eyes were his reply. Jeremiah let go of his hand and acquiesced, "Very well, then. God speed."

Hannah stepped forward modestly, "Come back safely," she said earnestly.

"I intend to," he murmured.

She blushed as she reminded Nathaniel, "The wedding is just ten months away."

Jeremiah muttered, a hint of derision in his tone, "Aye, the wedding."

Nathaniel gently took Hannah's hand and raised it to his lips. His bearing was proud but his manner was stiff, "Milady." He kissed her hand perfunctorily before turning to Jeremiah. "I'll do my duty and fulfil my oath, as I have sworn."

Nathaniel mounted Jessie. He looked magnificent on her back. He touched his forelock in a gesture of respect to them both, kicked Jessie in the flanks, urging her into a canter and he spurred her on down the shingle chipping path.

Jeremiah placed his arm around Hannah's shoulders as they watched Nathaniel fly down the path and into the unknown.

# Chapter Three

## The Journey and Boar's Head Inn

Horse and rider galloped along the uneven stone strewn bridle path atop the craggy cliffs in the breaking dawn. The coastline had changed dramatically and Nathaniel suddenly pulled Jessie up short and skidded to a halt. He paused and gazed down on the sand and pebble beach below. He watched the surf roll in innocently and he remembered that fateful day so many years ago. It was here, in this very spot that his father, Elijah, had been so cruelly thrown to his death by the evil band of smuggling cutthroats that operated in the area; murderers that he determined to bring to justice.

A red sun broke the horizon flooding the sky in a blaze of fire that washed the gathering clouds into a pink haze. Nathaniel reached roughly into his pocket and pulled out the ankh. He glared at it distastefully, his eyes filling with hatred before he thrust it back. His face suffused with colour, and revenge ruled his heart. He took a moment to compose himself and surveyed the scene before him. His eyes swept across the sea and rugged coastline. In the distance he saw a small port and coastal town. It was there he was headed.

A black-headed gull circled and mewled. Its cry a lamentation for lost souls as Nathaniel spurred Jessie forward to his destination. As the decision was made to move on the weather appeared to echo Nathaniel's mood. The glorious dawn changed as the sky turned from its dusky pink hues to a bruised purple and then thunderous black as storm clouds banked up and churned their way toward him finally emptying their load of driving rain, which grew heavier as he rode. The water mingled with the sweat on Jessie's back and soaked through Nathaniel's clothes. Jessie whinnied almost knowingly of what was to come, her back quivered with tension as Nathaniel abruptly turned from the cliff path and cantered toward the small town, which was at least a day's ride away.

Man and horse were almost as one and they progressed through fields and deserted country lanes until they hit the cobbled stone streets of the town. The sun had vanished and the moon's light was often eclipsed by low-slung cloud. Jessie plodded along an empty road that was completely devoid of life.

A battered inn sign, 'The Boar's Head' swung squeakily on rusty hinges attracting Nathaniel's attention. He urged Jessie into a trot as a deluge of torrential rain lashed down from the now coal black sky. They hastened into the cobbled enclosure. Nathaniel quickly dismounted and shouted for the Ostler. His words were almost lost in the wild night and increasingly ravaging storm, but the thickset fifty-year old stable man was keen of hearing and well trained. He ran out into the pebble-paved yard and received the reins from Nathaniel.

Nathaniel took out some coins from his money pouch and gave them to the man whose eyes glinted in anticipation, "Here's three pence. Look after Jessie well. She needs a good rub down after that ride. There will be another tuppence for you, if you do." He patted Jessie on the neck and marched to the inn.

The Ostler sniffed, then jerked his head in acknowledgement and hurriedly led Jessie away to the warmth and dry of the stables.

The busy tavern door opened with a groan and Nathaniel entered with a burst of icy wind following him. He forced the door, unwilling to close, shut, and then stepped toward the roaring fire that was crackling brightly in an inglenook fireplace. He removed his sodden cloak and hat and shook them out before draping them in front of the fire on a guard. The fire complained noisily as the dripping garments spat water into the coals, which sizzled and hissed as if in temper at the wet intrusion.

Nathaniel turned to the bar where the middle-aged Landlord looked up expectantly at the newly arrived stranger who was now attracting some curious glances.

"Evening, Sir. What'll be your pleasure?"

"A quart of your best ale and a room for the night."

The Landlord obligingly poured a dark beer into a large

tankard and placed it before Nathaniel who gazed around at the many patrons savouring their drinks.

"Trade seems good, even on a filthy night like this," observed Nathaniel.

"We don't complain," said the owner. "Is the room just for one night?"

Nathaniel took a gulp of his ale, "I shall be seeking lodgings in the village. Perhaps, you know of somewhere?" he enquired.

"Maybe," replied the Landlord cagily. "Will you be wanting a meal later?"

"The best your good lady can provide, Sir," said Nathaniel heartily.

The Landlord beamed at the compliment and became more forthcoming, "Mrs. Edward at the top of Valley Lane. She has a room vacant. You could do worse."

Nathaniel took another mouthful of his drink and continued, "I'm obliged. I'm also seeking directions to a Mr. Pritchard residing in Mumbles, I believe."

At the mention of Pritchard's name the chatter died down and all in the room stared suspiciously at Nathaniel. The only interruption to the silence was the hissing and spitting of the fire, which greedily devoured the logs and coal, occasionally letting out puffs of smoke as water evaporated from the drenched clothes in the heat. The quiet was dangerous and filled with menace. A chair scraped back and a rough looking man with a cast in one eye, left hurriedly, taking extra care to keep his face hidden from Nathaniel. Someone muttered a goodnight to Silas and Nathaniel's eagle ears picked up the name. He would store it away in his memory for future use.

The Landlord probed further, "Would that be Mr. Samuel Pritchard, the Customs' man?" At this question there was an urgent whispering amongst the drinkers in the bar. They strained their ears and leaned forward in their seats to hear more.

The Landlord added, "He lives over the Customs House by the point," he paused before he continued tentatively, "You'll be an acquaintance of him, then?" The room fell into another deathly hush as they awaited Nathaniel's reply.

Calmly, Nathaniel proclaimed, "Never met the gentleman.

But, I will become acquainted fairly soon." He enjoyed the drama of the situation and wanted to take full advantage of it, he turned and faced the expectant patrons, "I am to be his new Riding Officer." There was an uncomfortable, absolute hush and everyone stared at him, aghast at his announcement. Nathaniel cheekily raised his tankard in a toast and introduced himself, "Nathaniel Brookes, at your service!" and he swallowed down his draught of ale.

# Chapter Four

## The High Seas and Slavery

The umber orange sun burnt down on the hot, dusty, bustling port of Kingston, formerly Santiago in Jamaica. The glorious smell of mace, nutmeg, cloves and other aromatic substances, gathered from the Spice Islands, wafted in the still, heavy air and mingled with that of human sweat as sailors loaded boats with their bounty.

Waiting to board a slaving ship were a line of young muscular Negroes shackled at the neck with stout shafts of wood separating each man. Women, too, were chained and herded onto the deck of the terrifying multi-floored vessel that was to be the transportation for the captives to work in the grand plantations in America.

Further along the dockside, a ring of sailors were laying bets and cheering as a fight was in progress. In the centre of the man made ring, stood a tall, thickset heavyweight, Harry Babb, who was sparring with a shorter bullish man, John Crane, whose veins stood out like cords on his massive neck. The two were well matched and both men had drawn blood. They locked in a fearsome tussle that threatened to spill out of the ring and tumble into the turquoise waters of the harbour. Crane broke free and roared like an enraged buffalo but the sailors tightened their ring and forced Crane back into the fray. Babb raised his iron fist and slammed it into the bridge of Crane's nose, which splintered with a sickening crunch. Blood poured down his face and into his mouth. Crane had barely time to spit it away when another punch landed in his face, dislodging two teeth and the man went down. The sailors went wild and raised Harry's arm above his head as the winner and a challenge went out that anyone who determined to take on the might of Harry Babb and fight, would be richly rewarded.

Crane was tossed into the cool waters to cleanse his wounds and bring him around from his near comatose state.

The man came to in the water and managed to haul himself back onto the dockside and sat coughing and spluttering as he spat out salt water. He puffed loudly as he tried to recover.

Delighted seamen congratulated their champion, Harry. They gave him a bottle of rum and a wad of money. Harry took a swig of the liquor to swill around his mouth. He contemptuously expelled out the alcohol, then guzzled from the bottle and beat on his chest with his knuckles like a demented silverback gorilla roaring in triumph.

Toward the dock entrance traders bartered, and sailors gambled. Some drunkards pawed at women with ebony skins who were selling their charms. A huge giant of a man watched the proceedings silently. The black man stood aloof from the goings on. He was newly arrived in port from across the water and stood head and shoulders above everyone else. He wore the garb of a trader and had bags of nutmegs piled in front of him ready to trade.

One of the captains, Tobias Stone, from a ship bound for Britain eyed the large man with his taut stomach and bulging biceps. Stone grabbed hold of one of his crew weaving his way back toward the vessel, and indicated the Herculean man who looked as if he had fallen from Mount Olympus. "I expect our Harry could handle him, couldn't he?"

"Harry's never been beat. A true champion." The crewman stared at the African, who stood regally waiting to sell his wares. "Mind you, this one is hell of a big. Looks like it would be a close thing. His reach would outstrip Harry."

"Mm. He would be perfect. I could make a fortune from someone of his calibre at home. I wouldn't need to sail no more. Perhaps, we could entice the fellow to fight. See what you can do, Watkins."

"Yes, Captain."

Tobias Stone continued to eye the black giant and his eyes glinted with greed. The seaman, Watkins, headed for Harry Babb and his entourage of fans. They huddled together in deep discussion, occasionally casting glances down the pier at the mighty, statuesque trader. The captain scratched his bristly chin and his eyes wandered to a full-breasted woman in colourful clothes with braided hair. He felt a stirring in his groin and shuffled across to her and began to haggle a price.

The following day saw most ships leave with their cargoes of slaves, spices, rum and other riches. Tobias Stone watched as the last of the kegs of rum were carefully loaded aboard his craft. He began to walk toward a ring of his men that were encircling two fighters. Harry Babb was engaged in a tussle with the black giant from the previous day. Men were shouting and cheering drunkenly whilst others lay bets on the outcome of the match.

Harry Babb was taking a beating. The dusky fighter had already floored his opponent three times only to have Harry hauled up on each occasion by other members of the crew that forced him forward to face the fierce, flying fists of the Negro, once more. Harry Babb was being pulverised, something he wasn't used to. He bellowed like a bayoneted bull and ran at the giant, rushing at him to push his full force into the man, hoping to knock him off his feet but the Titan just as swiftly stepped to the side and Harry hurtled into the crowd and onto the ground. His sailor pals picked him up and tossed him back into the fight. However, the gargantuan gladiator caught him and threw him down. This time Harry didn't rise but struggled over onto his back and groaned. His eyes were puffed up, his cheeks swollen and turning an angry red that gave way to deep purple bruising. The sailors yelled at Harry to continue but his eyes rolled back in his head and he fell into unconsciousness. The cheering continued and the giant was clapped on his back and Watkins raised his arm as the winner. He slapped a purse full of money into the Negro's hand and the watching audience began to drift away. The Herculean strong man started back down the pier. He failed to notice six of the ruffians from the quayside fight following at a discrete distance.

Watkins threw a bucket of water over Harry Babb, which roused him from his exhausted state. Babb shook his head vigorously trying to reawaken his senses and stumbled back onto his feet. Watkins muttered something quietly to him and Babb followed in the wake of the sailors who were in pursuit of the giant.

The Negro headed along the stone path toward the small town. He paused by a building owned by the Dutch East India Company and eased his considerable frame up an adjoining alley where he stopped to count the contents of his purse of prize money.

Six sailors approached the alley and pounced on the unsuspecting champion, who rallied in anger and floored three. But there were too many of them and they gradually managed to restrain the big man, who tumbled to the ground where he was held down by the cowardly ruffians. Watkins and Babb then rounded the corner of the passageway and the ebony fighter was bound and shackled. Harry Babb grabbed the purse of money and pocketed it swearing revenge and the black giant was dragged toward the boat and flung onboard where they tossed him into the hold amongst the rats, goods and other contraband.

A novice seaman, Hywel Banwen watched the events trying to keep the distaste from registering in his eyes as the manacled man was chained to a metal strut. He didn't like the way business was being done. The man had won fair and square and in Hywel's eyes he should have been left to enjoy the fruits of his success, but Hywel knew he didn't dare voice his opinions to this volatile and criminal crowd.

# Chapter Five

## Double Duty

Nathaniel stood before a thickset, balding Mr. Samuel Pritchard, primly dressed in black and white, in the grim and forbidding Customs House in Mumbles. Nathaniel gazed around at the stark décor. There was nothing rich about these surroundings even though the work being done was for the king. There were no favours here.

They had been discussing Nathaniel's lodgings and Pritchard had kindly offered him a room in his own house.

"That's exceedingly good of you, Mr. Pritchard but I have taken a room in Swansea until I can find a cottage to rent. I am viewing one later today. I would, however, like to know my duties."

"Quite. Quite," replied Pritchard in clipped tones as he shuffled his papers. He took a map from a bag of other similar diagrams and geographical drawings, and flattened it out on the desk. He pointed out a pathway, highlighting the journey expected to be taken by the Riding Officer. "This is the route your ride must take. Your patrol is from the Bristol Channel and along the Gower Coast." He handed a wad of papers to Nathaniel, "Your orders. Follow them to the letter. Patrol daily, and at night, too, when you can. Keep a journal and bring it to me each week for inspection. Any written orders you receive from me must be obeyed implicitly. Do you understand?"

Nathaniel stowed the papers into a large canvas bag and affirmed, "Aye." He was slightly perturbed at the inference that he may be disobedient to his cause and the king, which Pritchard picked up on.

Pritchard persisted in driving his point home, "Be vigilant. Things are worse now than in your father's day. He was a good man and more importantly, my friend. Don't let his death be wasted. Learn from it." Pritchard sighed wearily and rubbed his hands across his eyes, "We are pit against a bloody and vicious trade. The smuggling fraternity will stop at nothing to retain their ill-gotten gains and booty. They zealously protect their own. You must be wary at all times." Pritchard warned and, then dismissed him.

Nathaniel nodded thoughtfully and said goodbye. He passed through the outer office where a clerical assistant was making entries into a ledger. He grunted a goodbye to the man and left. He had much to do.

Later that day, after being turned away from two rental houses he stood outside Cliff Cottage, which was a short distance from the town and faced his landlady with whom he had nearly completed a deal. The cottage was in an ideal spot, far enough out of the way so as not to attract unwarranted attention and yet in a position that put him within easy reach of his patrolling duties.

Lily Pugh was a warm hearted, and diminutive Welsh woman in her forties. She had a welcoming, homely manner and Nathaniel instantly liked her.

"There's stabling plenty out the back. Tidy it is, too, and dry. Next farm down has hay and straw. If you run short ask our David. He'll fetch it for you."

"Thank you, Mrs Pugh."

"Call me Lily. Rent's a shilling a week with a month in hand."

"I'll take it." Nathaniel confirmed. He sorted through some coins and handed them to her, "Here's two and a half month's rent."

Lily took the money and fixed her eye on the young and handsome officer. She remarked on his fine tapering hands, "You don't look like you've ever done much cleaning in your life. Do you need someone to do for you?"

Nathaniel thought for a moment, "I might."

"I can help out if you like?"

Nathaniel considered the offer and agreed.

"I'll visit once a week just to keep the dust down, air the bed and so on."

"Thank you."

"Tuppence a visit?"

"Sounds reasonable to me."

"You'll find it difficult to settle round here. Folks won't

20

be none too friendly when they find out you're the new Riding Officer."

"Word spreads fast," murmured Nathaniel.

"It does. And if you don't mind me saying, you didn't do yourself no favours announcing it like that," admonished Lily.

"Then why offer me the cottage?" quizzed Nathaniel.

"I don't have much truck with the village. It was the Wreckers who did for my Bill. Sent me barmy with worry when I was having David. He was born tainted and it's them I blame. Besides, I need the brass."

"Then, Lily, we have a deal."

Nathaniel shook Lily's hand and tied Jessie up outside and followed her into the small, functional but clean cottage. It was reasonably equipped and would suit Nathaniel's needs admirably. More importantly, he felt he had found an ally in Lily in this Godforsaken and hostile place. Nathaniel knew that he would be an outsider and meet with acute prejudice and fear, but hoped that he would also discover the cutthroats who murdered his father whilst serving his King and country.

Nathaniel looked around the small cottage and nodded his approval to Lily who handed him a dish covered by a cloth.

"Being a man, I don't expect you'll have anything in to eat." Nathaniel went to speak, "No, don't thank me. Folks will think I'm daft in the head. It's only a small loaf and some cheese but it will keep you going until you buy in some provisions."

Nathaniel smiled and when he lost his grim expression he had a countenance to light up the world. Lily grunted and took her leave. Nathaniel set about unpacking his few belongings. He built up and lit a fire in the hearth and stoked it up. It soon blazed away cheerfully. The few accoutrements he'd brought from home were sparse but at least lent the house some character and made it more like home.

Nathaniel settled himself at the table and tore into the hunks of bread and cheese gratefully. He put a pan of water on the small range to boil and took out the charts and maps of his route, to familiarise himself and ensure he was ready to begin his patrol in the morning. But now, now he would rest. He wandered to the window and gazed out through the glass.

His eyes searched the land outside and he watched as more inclement weather threatened its approach on the horizon.

Nathaniel woke to more adverse conditions. He readied himself and saddled his horse. The wind was ripping around Jessie and making her skittish as he tried to mount her. He heaved himself astride the mare and pulled his cloak tightly around him, the temperature had dropped dramatically in the night and the ferocious bitter wind stung his face. He set off at a trot whilst calming his steed as they travelled until they reached the cliff tops where the biting air savagely pecked at his face like a persistent bird of prey stripping out a dead creature's eyes. Nathaniel drew his hand up to force his tricorn hat low on his brow as it nearly flew off into the grey drab sky. In the distance he could see a figure, stoically marching along with lengthy raven hair flying in the wind. The figure stumbled and fell and had difficulty rising but then once up doggedly continued on the path although continually buffeted and battered by the bullying, pinching elements.

Nathaniel nudged Jessie to action and as he approached the person he saw it was a young lass with tears streaming down her pretty face. She bore an angry red scar on her right cheek and she pulled her thin woollen shawl about her shoulders as she struggled across the cliff path in the attacking wind.

Nathaniel pulled Jessie up and slid off her, tightly holding her reins. "Whoa Jessie!" He addressed the young woman his voice flying in the bitter chill. "Nathaniel Brookes at your service. Is everything all right?"

The maiden looked at him fearfully. Nathaniel was smitten by her wild beauty. In spite of her scarred face she was an attractive woman. She swallowed before speaking, "I don't know what to do." She had a melodic voice with a pleasing lilt and unusually, Nathaniel felt himself drawn to her.

He continued gently, "If I can help I will, Miss... Miss?"

"Banwen, Jenny Banwen." Jenny gulped again and came to a decision. She spoke with urgency, "It's my father. He's been hurt. I'm afraid he's going to die," and she shivered miserably, her shoulders drooping in the harsh cold.

Nathaniel didn't hesitate, "Take me to him. Where do you live?"

"The cottage on the limestone cliffs above Pwlldu."

"Then Jessie will carry us both."

Nathaniel's strong arms lifted Jenny up onto Jessie's broad back and then he mounted the horse himself. He held onto Jenny's lithe frame with one hand, ignoring the feelings stirring within him at her proximity and spurred Jessie on with the reins in his other hand. Together they raced across the cliff top to Jenny's abode.

# Chapter Six

## Banwen Cottage

Nathaniel slowed Jessie to a trot as they approached a tumble down dwelling on the top of the cliffs. From the outside it looked little more than a hovel. Thankfully the fierce wind had now dropped to a gusting breeze and teased the tangled fringes on Jenny's shawl. Nathaniel dismounted and Jenny slid off Jessie's back without help and ran into the house. He tied the horse to the wooden strut of a storm porch and she began nibbling at the grass and heather. Nathaniel followed Jenny inside.

The cottage itself, although poor, was spotlessly clean and the ill fitting windows rattled, like the bones of the dead in the hands of a witch doctor, in the inquisitive but now moderate breeze.

It was dark in the humble dwelling and the windows let in little light. On a makeshift cot by a meagre fire lay Jenny's father, Hywel. He was feverish and rambling. Jenny knelt down beside him and whispered comforting, soothing words. She took a cloth from a basin of water, wrung it out and mopped his sweat-laden brow. Nathaniel stopped for a moment and watched the scene before him. He was flooded with compassion.

"Dere nawr, Dad. Dere nawr. Bydd 'en well fori"

Nathaniel understood enough Welsh to know that Jenny was telling her father that all would be better on the morrow.

Hywel moved from his side to his back and cried out in pain. Distressed, Jenny began to weep once more. Nathaniel moved swiftly to Hywel's side and felt his pulse, which was erratic. He studied Hywel's flushed face and tested the temperature on the man's forehead.

"He's a raging fever. What happened?" Nathaniel asked softly.

"I don't know, honest. I came home and found him like

this. He was here on the cot with blood on the floor," said Jenny tearfully.

"Here," asserted Nathaniel, taking charge, "Help me raise him. We can try and ease him onto his side."

Together they gingerly lifted Hywel from off his back. He groaned loudly. As he moved they saw his back was encrusted with blood. This was no accident. Nathaniel shuddered and grimaced. "I'll get him a drink. See if you can get his shirt off," he ordered Jenny, "Gently, mind."

The young Riding Officer strode to the door and left the room. Jenny put down her cloth and struggled to remove her father's shirt, her effort was punctuated by his pitiful cries of agony. He whimpered in Jenny's arms and her heart felt as if it would burst.

Nathaniel marched back in bearing a flask. As he approached the cot he saw the full horror of what had been done to Hywel. His back had been lashed until it was raw and had almost exposed his spine. The white bones of his ribs could be seen. Nathaniel gasped in horror and exclaimed, "Good God alive!" He took the rag and poured some whisky from his flask onto it to bathe the painfully sore wounds. Hywel screamed in terror and pain as if being flailed alive again. The treatment was such that he was unable to stand it and he slumped forward barely conscious.

"That should stop the infection," explained Nathaniel. "Help me up with him we need to get some of this inside him." Together they lifted Hywel and forced some of the warming liquid down his throat. "I'll ride to the village. Your father needs aid, now."

"There won't be no one who'll come," murmured Jenny lowering her eyes in apparent shame.

"We'll see. Try and make him comfortable," he saw Jenny's helpless look and added, "As best you can. Here, take this. It's not much but it should help." He handed Jenny a couple of coins.

She turned them over in her hand and looked at him curiously, "Why are you doing this? Who are you?"

Nathaniel ignored her questions and continued, "I'll be back before you know it. Have you any family to help you?"

Jenny shyly shook her head, "There's only me and Dad."

She cast her eyes down again as if she was afraid to be questioned further and that the action would save her from further interrogation.

Nathaniel gently lifted her chin and turned her injured cheek to the little light that filtered through the worn, faded, cotton curtains. "Who did this to you, Jenny fach?" Jenny remained silent. "Partial to using his left hand, is he?"

Jenny raised her eyes in wide-eyed wonder, "How do you know?" she asked breathlessly.

Nathaniel lifted his hand and Jenny flinched. She looked up at him frightened as he mimed slashing her. He explained, "That kind of wound would be impossible to inflict with the right hand."

Jenny said nothing and as Nathaniel turned to leave, he assured her, "I promise, Jenny, I'll be as quick as I can."

Nathaniel swiftly left the cottage and raced on Jessie's back toward his home when he spied Lily Pugh walking and her son David riding on an ass. They were just passing his yard. She was carrying a bundle of firewood. He chased her down and, then reined in his horse, "Quick Lily, I need help. It's Hywel up on the cliffs yonder."

Lily bridled with distaste at the name, "Not Hywel Banwen?"

"Of what consequence is that?" queried Nathaniel confused at the change in the demeanour of his landlady.

"The girl's a bad lot. Her mother died of shame when she found out Jenny was expecting. The village kicked them out. That's why they live there, outside the care of the community."

"But, I didn't see any young ones," faltered Nathaniel.

"Still born... God's punishment. Hywel's had to get what work he could. Last I heard he took to the sea. Always been a bit of a loner. That much we have in common."

The unspoken accusation clear in Nathaniel's eyes was too much to bear and Lily relented, "All right. I'll do my bit, only as my Christian duty, mind."

"If you want to help, hurry into my rooms and fetch me the small black leather bag in the corner of the bedroom. Quickly now!"

"Aye, that much I can do," muttered Lily. She threw down her bundle of wood by the donkey's feet and sprinted across to Nathaniel's cottage. Moments later she emerged with his bag, clutching it tightly to her breast. She turned to her bewildered son, David, sitting astride the bony mule, "Get yourself home, David. Take the firewood and put it in the log store and then see to the cawl on the range. Watch it doesn't burn."

David gave her a lopsided grin, "Right you are, Mam."

Lily turned to Nathaniel, "Give me a lift up then. You'll not be expecting me to walk, surely?"

Nathaniel smiled wryly and jumped down, helping Lily onto Jessie. David plodded away and Nathaniel remounted, dug his heels into Jessie's flanks and spurred her back to Hywel's cottage. Jessie lengthened her stride picking up on Nathaniel's urgency and designed to please her master she ran her heart out to the Banwen's cottage.

The daylight was beginning to fade as they arrived. Lily slid off Jessie and bustled into the dingy but clean house, a fact, which did not go unnoticed by her. She was aware that inside, the place was scrupulously clean. Jenny sat at her father's side. He was rambling deliriously. Odd snatches of words interspersed with groans assailed their ears. Nathaniel's face registered recognition of some notorious smuggling terms but he was more concerned with trying to help Hywel and save his life.

Nathaniel busied himself. He took the bag from Lily and rooted about in it removing various bottles and phials. He jerked his head to her and ordered, "Get some water onto boil. Put it in a basin and add this. We need to make an infusion." He handed Lily a bunch of dried leaves.

Jenny watched curiously and raised her eyes questioningly to Nathaniel. Lily saw the girl's expression and explained, "Comfrey and Valerian. Good for healing."

Nathaniel observed, "So, I see you are versed in healing."

Lily retorted, "God helps those who help themselves… it's certain the villagers don't."

Hywel continued with his dangerous muttering as Lily took in the injuries inflicted on Hywel's back. She grimaced and gasped at the horror of his wounds, but then knuckled down to help Nathaniel make a poultice with paste made from more items in the medical bag.

"They'll kill me. No! Not Jenny… all I got," raved Hywel.

Lily looked sharply at Nathaniel, "You'll close your ears to this if you're wise."

Hywel continued, "I won't say nothing… Pwlldu caves… Meet at inn… ankh… Giant…wasn't me… Not my fault… Thursday, wrecking… New slaves… Black Bob… French brandy… Tobacco."

Lily tried to quieten Hywel aware of the effect his words were having on Nathaniel, "Aisht nawr, Hywel. Cwat lawr." She repeated again in English, "Hush now, Hywel, be quiet."

On hearing feminine tones Hywel's fevered rambling began to question, "Sarah, is it you?"

"Now, now. It's Lily. Lily Pugh your neighbour. You must be quiet, Hywel. Loose words bring danger," she warned.

Hywel fell silent as Jenny returned to her father's side with the hot water infusion.

"I'll do that," asserted Nathaniel, and he began to gently bathe and clean the angry wounds in preparation for treatment.

"The poultice is ready," offered Lily. She rummaged in Nathaniel's bag and brought out another jar of herbs, smelled the contents and added them to a cup of hot water for Hywel to sip. Nathaniel applied the poultice and Jenny was ready with bandages to hold the mess of leaves and paste in place.

Jenny looked up sadly at Nathaniel; "Sarah was my mother, dead now. He hasn't called on her in a long time."

Lily pursed her lips and whispered kindly, "If I find the time, I'll come back tomorrow to change the dressing. Keep him warm and give him lots of liquids." She passed the cup of herb medicine to Jenny. "Try to get him to swallow some of this. It's a tonic made with herbs and flowers. Should help. Now, clear the basin away, make sure it's rinsed thoroughly." She turned to Nathaniel and indicated his bag, "I'll need some more of your preparations. But, a word of warning, don't listen to his ramblings, as I've said, 'close your ears'. Don't tell anyone what you've seen or they'll come back and finish what they started."

Jenny looked from one to the other. She was puzzled and spoke to Lily, "Why? Why are you talking like that? Who is he?"

Lily pointed at Nathaniel and said with trepidation, "The new Riding Officer. That's him."

Jenny gasped in disbelief as she dropped the basin on the floor with a loud clang, and cried, "Then, the Lord save us all."

# Chapter Seven

## Lily's Fear and Hywel's Story

David and Nathaniel sat at the clean scrubbed table in Lily's cottage and looked expectantly as Lily served up three steaming dishes of cawl, a Welsh stew. The tantalising smell of hearty country fare wafted up Nathaniel's nostrils and he breathed in deeply, savouring the smell. Nathaniel tucked in with relish it was clearly very tasty. He praised her wholesome cooking, "There's blas. This is delicious, Lily."

"Aye, Mam, my favourite," spluttered David.

"Where are your manners, David? Don't speak with your mouth full," admonished Lily.

Nathaniel hid a smile and tactfully changed the subject, "Tell me, Lily, how do you know about healing and medicine?"

"Oh, from my mother, bless her, wise woman of the village she was. Could charm warts away and taught me about all the flowers in the field. What was good and what was poison; what would heal and what would mend. Don't know nothing about modern quackery, just natural remedies. She helped many and passed her learning onto me."

"Then she did well. You were a great help with Hywel."

Lily flushed with pleasure, then murmured, "Won't do me no good to have you round often. Tongues will wag and folks will treat us worse than ever."

"I'm renting your cottage, Lily. I could be seeing you about anything."

"I'll just have to be mighty careful. No good antagonising the village."

"I understand, but I have a proposition to put to you although you may not want to hear it now."

David was curious, "What's that?"

"Anything you hear, anything at all… lights on the cliff, cheap brandy in the village or tobacco…"

"You're asking too much. As I have said, loose talk costs

lives. You saw what happened to Hywel. I've lost a husband. I don't want to lose a son. But, there, what would you know or understand about that," she added tartly.

Nathaniel paused and furrowed his brow. His tone became quiet and more serious, "What do I know? I saw my father murdered by hooded criminals. He was a Riding Officer. I was seven. I've never forgotten it. They stole his signet ring after hacking off his finger and one day that act of greed will lead me to his killer."

Lily inclined her head sympathetically and her manner changed, "What happened?"

Nathaniel continued icily as he remembered the events of that day, "My sister and I were playing on the beach with my mother. He was thrown from the cliff by smuggling ruffians. I'll never forget my mother's face as she knelt by his broken body."

"Duw 'elp. There's dreadful."

"In his hand he was clutching this." Nathaniel reached into his pocket, pulled out his fob watch and attached to the time piece's chain was the ankh. "Have you ever seen this or anything like it before?"

Lily studied it and considered, "It's unusual, but … yes… I think I have… once, somewhere."

Nathaniel's eyes gleamed as he caught her words and pressed earnestly, "Where?"

Lily thought hard and slowly shook her head uncertainly, "It's no good. The memory is elusive. But, if I remember, I promise I'll tell you."

Nathaniel nodded grimly, "I've sworn an oath, Lily. I *will* find my father's murderers."

"But from so long ago how do you know those men are still here or even if they're alive?"

"I don't, but there was a large gang of them, someone must remember who was involved. However long it takes, I will find them," promised Nathaniel.

"As long as you don't kill yourself and us in the process," she pronounced.

Those words would come back to haunt Nathaniel but he was so hell bent on his mission, he thought nothing of his own or anyone else's danger. "Now, you must keep up the business of patrolling and riding. You don't want them that's guilty to suspect," warned Lily.

"Aye, I will away, now. What of Hywel?"

"I will see to him today."

"Then I will visit tomorrow. If we take it in turns, it won't become so obvious."

"And I say again, if anyone notices, we will all be done for," chided Lily.

"Then we'd best be careful." Nathaniel picked up his hat and swept out.

Lily stepped to the door, her eyes scanning the countryside in the evening air as David followed her outside to chop logs. Lily raised her hand to say goodbye, "Nathaniel?" He mounted Jessie and looked back enquiringly as she called out, "God speed, my friend."

Nathaniel touched his hat and cantered off into the enveloping dark. The weather was for once being kind and he had a long ride ahead of him. His patrolling duties were exhausting.

Lily watched him go and checked for spying eyes. There were none. She disappeared into her cottage and packed a basket with some fresh bread and a pot of stew. She selected a collection of herbs and some fresh lint. These, too, were stowed in the basket. Lily picked up a warm shawl, wrapped it around her shoulders and exited. "David?"

"Yes, Mam?"

"Once you've done that, stack the log scuttle. Make sure the fire stays in. I won't be long. Let no one in and talk to no one. Do you understand?"

"Yes, Mam."

Lily scurried away toward Hywel's cottage to fulfil her promise of help. She prayed the man would come out of his fever and that those that had so brutally beaten him would not return nor find her there. Gossip spread quickly through the villages; gossip, she knew that could put her and David's life in danger. But Lily had a backbone of steel and a strong sense of right and wrong. She determined that she was on the side of right.

Nathaniel watched the pink tinges of dawn washing over

the skyline as he trotted back from his night patrol. He was weary and hungry. Jessie, too, was footsore and yearned to rest but she would valiantly carry her master wherever he wished to travel. Her heart was faithful and true.

The ebony mare trotted on across the grassy cliffs and Nathaniel soon found himself approaching the Banwen's cottage above Pwlldu. Smoke rose from the chimneystack and curled up into the morning sky. It looked to Nathaniel as if the occupants must be awake and so he dug his heels into Jessie's flanks. She perked up into a canter and headed for the tumbledown dwelling, where she knew she could rest awhile and munch some grass. With luck she may even get a drink of water to fortify her and sustain her after her long night until she reached her own warm stable flush with comfortable straw and a bag of hay to nibble.

Nathaniel pulled up outside the shack of a cottage and secured Jessie. He tapped lightly on the door. Jenny opened it to admit him. Once more Nathaniel was entranced by her beauty and he was pleased to be invited in and be allowed to sit at the table. Jenny placed a hot drink in front of him before sitting opposite him, "Here, you'll be needing this after your ride," she said shyly and continued. "Lily came yesterday. Thank you."

"Thank, Lily. She's a good woman," said Nathaniel as he supped the brew gratefully. Conversation lapsed. Jenny nodded and cast her eyes down finding Nathaniel's gaze unnerving.

His eyes drifted to the cot, where Hywel was sitting up. He was no longer delirious but looked pale in the growing light. He hungrily devoured a bowl of oatmeal and milk that Jenny had given him. Hywel paused mid mouthful and studied Nathaniel's face.

"So, you're the new Riding Officer. You'll have it hard. There won't be many that will give you the time of day," murmured Hywel, quietly.

"So I understand," acknowledged Nathaniel.

Hywel took another spoonful of his porridge and added grudgingly, "Thank you for what you did."

Nathaniel was modest in his response, "A small matter. I am glad to see you looking somewhat brighter."

"Whatever it was you gave me I feel a hell of a lot better."

"Good. It is well. I can prepare some more before I leave." Nathaniel paused. He took another sip of his drink and carefully considered what he wanted to say. "Yesterday…" Hywel looked across sharply. Nathaniel continued, "Yesterday, you said things that interested me."

"Dare say I did. But, there's nothing I'd repeat," and he closed his lips tightly brooking no argument. Nathaniel took another slurp and wiped the back of his mouth with his hand. He didn't wish to press Hywel and force an argument but he needed answers.

Jenny looked back and fore between the two of them and admonished her father, "Dad, if it wasn't for Mr. Brookes you'd be dead."

Hywel bawled sharply, "Caw dy geg, girl!" Telling her to shut her mouth and he bristled further, "If you know what's good for you."

Jenny persisted spiritedly, her face turning red in the exchange, "No, I won't. I've been burning to say a lot more and I fancy, now, that I will."

Hywel blazed back, "You don't realise what you're saying."

"Yes, I do. And you'll not stop me," retorted Jenny.

"While I've breath in my body you'll obey me or be damned," blustered Hywel but the effort of this was almost too much for him and he began to cough and wheeze. Jenny's tone became gentler and she dashed to her father's side and lifted up a cup of dark liquid at the side of the cot and tried to help him take a sip.

"Hush now, Dad. Drink this, come on."

Hywel allowed himself to be helped and took a draught. Jenny mopped up some of the spilled liquid as it dribbled down his chin. "Dad, you need to think seriously. We can help Mr. Brookes. No one has helped us. Who knows what will happen, but if more die or get beaten…" She left the rest of the sentence unsaid and Hywel wearily flopped back on his pillows and shook his head grudgingly, "Jenny, love, I don't know. We don't want worse to come on our heads."

But Jenny turned her dark eyes to Nathaniel and began hesitantly, "I used to work for… an important family…

until their son took a shine to me. He trapped me and tricked me, and forcibly took away my innocence. If I wanted to keep my job I wasn't to complain, and if my parents were to stay in employment I had to put up with it." She took a breath and continued more boldly, "While I wasn't making a fuss it was as well to keep me on. As soon as the baby began to show they kicked me out with three shillings for their son's pleasure. Three shillings for life and me with a baby on my back." She sighed, "It was just as well, he was born dead. Shortly after, my mother caught pneumonia and died. People round here said it was because of the shame, but it wasn't."

Hywel, tried to quiet his daughter, "Jenny, please!"

Jenny grew bolder and ignored her father's pleas and continued, "Dad was forced out of his work, all because of my shame. He had to do whatever he could to earn a crust. That's how he got involved with them." The emphasis was on the word 'them' which was almost spat out with venom.

"Jenny! You're risking lives," Hywel insisted.

"What lives? We haven't got any life and we haven't got any family or friends. No one else has tried to help us," she argued.

Nathaniel interrupted trying to placate, "I'm no stranger to trouble. And I'm not afraid of it… If you can help me…" he left the sentence unfinished.

Hywel said darkly, "Did anyone see you come here?"

"No, I've just returned from patrol, travelling at first light, before anyone was up. Besides folk are used to me riding at all hours of the day and night. They don't reckon me to have any friends." Nathaniel swallowed and pressed Hywel again, "Please, Hywel, who did this to you?"

Hywel took a moment to consider what he would say. He glanced at Jenny who nodded encouragingly at him. He cleared his throat and continued, "Those that did for me are some of those you seek. Smuggling is their way of life I have even heard one say they were above the law. They murdered a Riding Officer some fifteen years ago, it's said."

"That was my father," admitted Nathaniel.

"I heard them talking and one or two boasted they wouldn't ever be caught. The same men tried to end my life."

Nathaniel perked up and questioned, "But why? Why did they want rid of you?"

Hywel licked his cracked lips, "I was on a merchant ship due to come into Bristol with a company returning from the Spice Islands. The Captain had brought with us a prize slave, a huge fellow. He abducted him and was going to train him to fight. Out at sea he had sparring matches with some of the men. He seemed to be adapting to the idea and Captain Stone let him out of the hold and remain on deck as a reward. I was on watch when he jumped ship, shackles and chains and all. Captain was so angry they gave me sixty lashes and left me for dead. If they come looking for me and find you here, they'll finish me for sure."

"How did you get back here?"

"I had one friend, he helped me. Got me home. Least you know the better."

"I promise you, I'll not endanger you or Jenny. But, tell me about Thursday. What's happening Thursday?"

Hywel narrowed his eyes, "You ask too much."

Jenny pleaded with her father, "Help him, Dad, for no other man will."

Hywel rolled his eyes and sighed heavily, and then, he started to talk. Once he began the words tumbled out of him and Nathaniel learned the names of wayward seafarers and the plans for a landing of contraband from France on Thursday, followed by another scheduled landing two nights later. A wrecking was on the calendar, as well. A rich merchant ship was being charted and followed closely. Word had it that once it strayed into these shores it was doomed. The Wreckers would be lying in wait. Nathaniel listened to Hywel in awe. It was as if someone had unblocked a dam and once the words started flowing from him they couldn't be stopped.

It was much later that Nathaniel left the Banwens and Jessie finally reached her cosy stable and was rewarded with warm bedding, a good feed and a pail of thirst quenching water. Nathaniel prayed that no eyes saw him leave the Banwens. He knew how dangerous his newfound knowledge could be.

# Chapter Eight

## Goliath


The sun arose from its slumbers waking the day into life.
Birds began to chirrup and sing heralding the start of a new
day. The soft footfalls of a refreshed Jessie padded gently on
the grassy cliff top coastal path. Nathaniel and his steed
moved slowly and cautiously, not that there was any need to
as the weather was kind to them that morning.

Nathaniel's brow was creased in concentration as he
thought. He had received various bits of information;
information that would help the Crown and the thwarting of
current smuggling activities but nothing that seemed to be
leading him closer to his avowed mission of finding his
father's killers and that thought alone brought sadness in his
heart. He stopped for a minute and gave a deep sigh that left
his shoulders drooped. Jessie as always sensitive to her
master's moods whinnied softly in her throat as if to lighten
his mood and offer some form of comfort. The steed snuffed
the air and pawed the ground as if trying to awaken Nathaniel
from his depression.

Nathaniel raised his head from its downward position
where he had appeared to be studying the horse's neck. He
lifted his tear filled eyes and stared out to sea. There was
nothing to be seen on the horizon or the in the bay. He swept
off his head covering and rubbed his forehead and eyes as if
the action itself would somehow change the vista. He
replaced his tricorn hat and took the reins firmly to move on.
Jessie, however, had other ideas and reared up on her hind
legs and neighed. Nathaniel steadied himself and his steed.
He patted her neck to calm her and cursorily glanced about
him to see if anyone was around to spook her. He glanced
down the cliff face to the beach and his eyes were caught by
something on the sand. At first he thought it was some
flotsam washed up on the shore. He looked again and
breathed in sharply. On closer inspection and adjusting his

eyes in the sunlight Nathaniel recognised the bulk lying on the sand as the form of a man, a body.

Melancholy forgotten Nathaniel encouraged Jessie to the cliff path, which led down to the cove. He dismounted and picked his way carefully down the steep track, not wanting Jessie to slide and break a leg. He eventually reached the golden sand and remounted, then galloped along it until he reached the motionless figure. He slid down from Jessie's back letting the reins fall free in front of her and hurried to the man who was lying on his side.

Nathaniel turned the man over. He was a giant, a huge Negro. He had chains and manacles on his hands. His feet were shackled. Nathaniel placed his ear on the man's chest and then next to the man's mouth. Unable to ascertain any sign of life, he rolled the man over onto his chest and pressed on his back to try and release any water trapped in the lungs. There was nothing. Nathaniel moved him onto his back again and watched the man's chest to see if there was any small movement, any sign of life. He saw nothing. He jumped up and grabbed his black bag from Jessie; he took a small mirror and held it close to the man's mouth and nostrils. The mirror misted ever so slightly.

"Thank God," breathed Nathaniel. It was enough to spur the Riding Officer on and he tore at the man's shirt where he saw a wooden ankh strung around the man's neck. The sight of this amulet stopped Nathaniel, momentarily. But, then with more urgency, Nathaniel forced the man onto his side and pulled back the man's arm. Nathaniel applied firm, regular pressure, in bursts, in between the man's shoulder blades. He worked at the man solidly and was eventually rewarded with a seepage of water and reflexive cough from the giant's mouth. Filled with adrenaline, for there was no other way he could have achieved the feat, Nathaniel battled with the dead weight of the man and somehow managed to haul him up, in spite of the difficulty, and slid him over Jessie's back. Miraculously, he had loaded the stranger. The action left Nathaniel huffing and panting. His muscles burned. He leaned forward his hands on his knees breathing heavily. Once he had stopped puffing from his exertions and he had regained some strength, he straightened up and led

Jessie back along the beach. Her feet left deeper marks in the sand from the huge load she was bearing.

With no eyes to see and no one to watch Nathaniel made his way back to his cottage. There he grappled again with the bulk of the giant and managed to haul him inside. He prayed again that no one was watching his cottage to see this escaped slave and the mammoth, physical effort involved in getting him indoors. Nathaniel hoped he would not have to shift this Titan anywhere else.

He set to removing the giant's chains and restraints. It was hard work but had to be done. He sawed at the narrowest part of the shackles and chains. The Negro never murmured or moved and this made Nathaniel's job considerably easier.

The stranger remained unconscious and Nathaniel made him as comfortable as he could. Now he was in a dilemma. He had to get to the Customs House but worried about leaving the man unattended. He could only trust that the man would stay there until his return but now, now he had to report to Mr. Pritchard. He wondered whether or not to mention his discovery on the beach. He was to wrangle with this question on route to the Custom House.


Nathaniel stood to attention at Pritchard's desk whilst his superior perused Nathaniel's journal. He read and reread paragraphs and went back double-checking Nathaniel's analysis. "The full account's there, Sir," declared Nathaniel.

Pritchard looked grave, "One of the smugglers' gang you say?"

"Yes. And he's feared of losing his life."

"How do you know he's telling the truth?"

"If you'd have seen his back, you wouldn't ask. He confirmed what I'd heard in his ramblings. There's a landing planned a week, Thursday. Rowboats will be waiting in Pwlldu Caves at low tide. A French boat will moor in the bay bringing brandy and tobacco. If you send for more men we can catch them red handed. Talk has it another is to follow soon after."

"Hmm." Pritchard sounded doubtful, "It will be difficult." Nathaniel bit back the recriminations that wanted to fall from his lips and hesitated. Pritchard prompted, "Have you any more to tell me, anything not in the journal?"

Nathaniel not understanding his reasons why he didn't want to respond decided there and then not to reveal anything else. "Er no, Sir. If that's all?"

Receiving no answer he turned to go but Pritchard stopped him, "And Brookes? On no account are you to attempt anything on your own. See me Wednesday. I'll tell you if you are to proceed. It could be a trick or an ambush. Smugglers rarely turn King's evidence."

Nathaniel replied reluctantly, "Yes, Sir."

"Brookes are you *sure* you have nothing else to say?"

The image of the big Negro flashed into his head but Nathaniel remained steadfast. "No, Sir. Nothing more."

Pritchard grunted, "Until Wednesday."

Nathaniel gave a curt nod, turned on his heel and left. Pritchard looked after him scratching his head. He returned to his papers and began to study them once more sighing softly, "Don't be foolish my young officer. Please."

Nathaniel rode home as quickly as he dared without attracting suspicion. As he passed through the town, people shied away from him and ignored his polite greetings. It seemed no one wanted to know or to be seen acknowledging the young Riding Officer. It was no matter. Nathaniel had a job to do and one, which he determined to do well, however, he may be perceived by the public. But, now he had to get home and tend to his houseguest. He hoped that the man had not awoken and wandered off somewhere. Nathaniel kicked Jessie's flanks and she broke into a canter and then lengthened her stride into a full gallop. So accustomed was she to the routes her master rode, there was almost no need to instruct the horse.

Nathaniel and Jessie skidded to a stop at his cottage. Nathaniel peeped inside. The big man was still there and appeared to be asleep; for that Nathaniel was grateful and he led Jessie to her stable to untack her. He quickly rubbed her down and placed a rug on her back to repel any biting flies. With a fresh net of hay and a trough of clean water Jessie was content to munch and relax. She had earned a good rest.

Nathaniel strode back to his cottage and entered quietly,

the big man stirred in his sleep and his limbs twitched. Nathaniel busied himself, warming up some nourishing broth and cutting a chunk of bread for his guest. He placed them on a side table and gently attempted to rouse the stranger.

The giant, groggy from his near drowning, began to awake and Nathaniel attempted to help him to some of the soup. He tried to pour some of the warming liquid into his mouth. The Negro coughed and spluttered and his eyes fluttered open. He began to be aware of his strange surroundings and he started quickly almost knocking the soup from Nathaniel's hand. The man studied Nathaniel's house and furnishings fearfully. He had no idea where he was and gave a small cry of despair.

"It's all right," soothed Nathaniel, "I won't hurt you. I'm a friend."

The response was for the huge man to shrink away from Nathaniel in fright. He curled up into a ball trying to make himself look smaller, which was an impossible task. Nathaniel continued to talk kindly and gently, in low comforting tones to calm his anxious patient. "Been in the wars, you have. I'm going to fix you up, make you well. Here drink. It's safe, see," and Nathaniel took a sip of the broth to show that he was telling the truth. On seeing this the man grabbed at the dish. He threw down the spoon and gulped from the bowl.

Nathaniel took a crust of bread, broke into it and nibbled some, "Bread, see, it's good."

The man snatched the other piece and stuffed it in his mouth as fast as he was able. It's clear he was starving.

"Good," affirmed Nathaniel, "Good. Do you want some more?"

The man looked blankly at him, then in surprise at his wrists and feet.

"No, no shackles, no irons. Free."

For the first time the man spoke in a deep melodious voice. He had understood the word, 'free' and repeated it knowingly. "Free."

Nathaniel nodded, pleased a connection had been made, "Yes, free." Nathaniel tapped his chest, "Nathaniel... You?"

The man didn't respond so Nathaniel tried once more. He

tapped his chest, "Me Nathaniel… Nath-an-i-el." He enunciated every syllable, then pointed at the man, "You?"

The man caught on and tapped his chest, "Hekanefer Barka."

"Heka…?" Nathaniel tried to pronounce the name.

"Hekanefer," reiterated the giant.

"Damn it! I can't say that." Nathaniel studied the huge hulk before him and pronounced, "Goliath. From now on I will call you Goliath."

The man appeared to like the name. He smiled and repeated it, "Goliath."

The odd companions shook hands and affirmed each other's names and then Nathaniel poured another bowl of soup, which Goliath ate with relish.

Nathaniel examined Goliath's injuries and treated them accordingly before he aided him out from his bed and helped him to tentatively walk around the room. Goliath had damaged his ankle and a limp was evident so Nathaniel strapped it up to support it. Goliath tested his foot again and found it was easier to walk. The Riding Officer sat Goliath at the table whilst he prepared some more food and this time he set the table and laid two places. When the meal was served he began to show Goliath how to use a knife, fork and spoon. The man was eager and surprisingly quick to learn.

Delighted with his success with the giant, Nathaniel attempted to teach Goliath a few simple English words. He began with the eating implements. He held up a knife, and then mimed cutting with it. "Knife… cuts…"

"Knife… cuts…" said Goliath, looking pleased.

"Yes, well done!" praised Nathaniel.

They continued like this for some time. Nathaniel then placed the learned items over the table and picked them up at random, which Goliath named.

Nathaniel tried to make Goliath understand that he needed some clothes. The ones the giant was wearing were shredded and worn. He made Goliath understand that he was going to get him some fresh apparel. Goliath was to remain there until his return. "You stay. Goliath stay here. Me go to get," he pointed at his attire, "Clothes, better clothes for you." He pointed at Goliath's dress.

Goliath nodded in understanding. "I stay."

Relieved Nathaniel left the cottage to seek Lily's help in finding garments to fit his visitor. He was hoping she could help. He didn't fancy a shopping expedition that was bound to attract attention and then questions.

# Chapter Nine

### Frustrations

Lily Pugh turned out her husband's good clothes that she had kept. He had been a tall, well built man and Lily felt that these would do for Nathaniel, although why he required them she wasn't sure, but he had paid her good money and as Lily had said she needed the brass. Lily parcelled the items up and called to her son, "David, tend the fire, make sure it doesn't go out. I've put the dough to prove. Check it in an hour, if I'm not back. If it's doubled in size then pop it in the bread oven, do you hear?"

"In an hour, Mam."

"Here," Lily grabbed David's hand and took him to the clock sitting on the mantle. "There," she pointed at the hands on the clock, when this hand touches here," she indicated with her finger, "That will be an hour gone."

"Yes, Mam."

"Now, show me, where must the hand be?"

"By here, Mam," said David pointing to the same place.

"Good, that's right. Now, I'll not be long. Speak to no one when I'm gone. If anyone calls, tell them to come back later. Right?"

"Right," David affirmed.

Satisfied, Lily nodded her approval and left her cottage and walked the short distance to Nathaniel's abode. It was a fine morning and Lily sang as she walked. Her rich soprano voice rang out mingling with the birdsong that blessed the land. There was joy in her heart. She didn't know why but she felt glad to be alive and felt that she was doing some good. She felt useful and needed. This gave her a feeling of great wellbeing and she sang all the more clearly and loudly as she approached the cottage.

Lily, still warbling, dropped her voice a little as she knocked on the door and on hearing Nathaniel's instruction to enter walked in. What she was not prepared to see was a huge black giant in the cottage sitting in a chair facing the door. The notes of her song hit a glass shattering top C and her scream rang out rattling the windows. She dropped the bundle of clothes and would have fled had Nathaniel not guided her to a seat.

"It's all right, Lily. Don't be alarmed."

"Duw, Duw. There's a fright. Shock of my life, you've given me, Nathaniel Brookes. Who's this?" She studied the face of the fearsome giant having never seen a black man before.

"This is Goliath," introduced Nathaniel. "He was abducted and imprisoned on a sailing vessel. He jumped ship, I found him and now he's here." Nathaniel smiled brightly.

"He's going to be a bit difficult to hide," warned Lily.

"I don't intend to hide him. Once he's fully better, he will ride with me as my companion."

"And you just be careful that those that took him won't come back," muttered Lily. "Word will spread like wildfire once your secret is out."

"I'm aware of that. I hope they do come looking, it may help me in my quest."

"Yes, well, I don't know about that. Was it for him you wanted the clothes?"

"Indeed, it was and it looks like you've done us proud. I am sure some of these will fit," said Nathaniel, placing them on the table.

Lily dutifully composed herself. She stood up and retrieved a couple of items from the package. She shook out a shirt and jacket, "Try these. If they fit, then so will the rest."

Goliath rose from his seat. He towered over Lily, who screwed her face up as she stared at the sheer size of the man. "He'll be a useful lookout. See for miles from his viewpoint," she laughed. "Duw, my heart's only just stopped its yammer. Next time, have the good grace to warn me when you do something like that. I don't fancy joining my Bill, not just yet," she winked.

Goliath tried on the jacket. It was a perfect fit. He paraded around the kitchen and now there was no visible sign of his limp. Nathaniel patted Goliath heartily on his back and as he did so the wooden ankh jumped free of his shirt and bounced forward. Nathaniel touched the ankh and Goliath looked puzzled. The young Riding Officer pulled out the ankh wrested from his father's hand and compared the two. As he did so a flicker of fear flashed across Goliath's face, which did not go unnoticed by Nathaniel or Lily. But, Nathaniel felt now was not the time to press him on the meaning of the talisman so he put it to the back of his mind.

"I have to see Mr. Pritchard. Will you be all right here, Lily?"

Lily eyed Goliath, "I'll be fine. How long will you be? David expects me back within the hour."

"I'm not sure," he turned to Goliath, "I go." He mimed riding a horse and Goliath nodded in understanding, "But I will be back."

"You've not said anything to Mr. Pritchard about," she jerked her head at Goliath, "Yon."

"I've said nothing to anyone. You and I are the only souls alive who know he is here."

"I won't be telling no one that's for sure. I don't want trouble landing at my feet."

"Then we keep this just between ourselves for now. It will all come out in time."

"Aye, and I don't want to be around when it does."

"Things may be different then, Lily."

"Maybe," she didn't sound convinced.

Nathaniel donned his cape and hat and hurried out of the door. He mounted Jessie and they were away like the wind. He rode along the cliff path, and down the track to the town. People scurried away behind their doors as they recognised his figure trotting past their homes. One or two braver souls acknowledged him but none would stop to talk.

Nathaniel soon arrived at Mr. Pritchard's rooms. He secured Jessie outside and as he approached the door, it opened, a man ducked out and swirled away attempting to hide his face. There was something familiar about him. Nathaniel knew he had seen him before and the name Silas sprang to his lips, which he muttered involuntarily. The man froze as his name was mentioned but then whipping his cape about him he moved off in an agitated manner. Silas was rattled by the thought that Nathaniel knew his name.

Nathaniel knocked on the door and entered the Customs Office. One of Pritchard's assistants turned to see who had arrived. "Ah Mr. Brookes. Mr. Pritchard is expecting you." Nathaniel nodded cursorily and strode behind the counter and into the office at the back where Mr. Pritchard was waiting.

"Brookes," he acknowledged as Nathaniel took off his hat.

"Mr. Pritchard, I almost bumped into a man leaving here, a man called, Silas."

"How do you know that?" pounced Pritchard.

"No matter how, but I know he does not keep good company."

"That's as maybe, but he won't want you knowing. Silas is a valued informant. He has helped us on many occasion."

"And I expect he is well paid."

"Well enough, but that shouldn't concern you. The less who know, the better."

"What of the man out front?"

"Thomas? He thinks the man's in to pay a fine. No more."

"Ah. And our business?"

"He knows you report to me. What of the questions?" Pritchard's eyes narrowed and Nathaniel felt the scrutiny was uncomfortable.

"Well, do I have the men? Am I to be supported in my bid to stop these brigands?"

Pritchard's face became serious, "I did warn you. Times are tough."

"We do the King's work. Why then do I not have the men I need?"

"There's nothing I can do. I did try. I argued the case. No one will offer us the manpower. My directive comes from the top. You are to stay away. We don't want to lose another good man."

"Like my father?" said Nathaniel bitterly.

"Like your father," agreed Pritchard. "Look, I don't like this either, but this is one we have to miss. And that's an order."

Nathaniel fell silent. His mind was racing. Pritchard lowered his voice, conspiratorially, "Nathaniel, these criminals are the scourge of the King and of those, like us, who do his duty. There is a whiff of corruption at the top, but I have no proof. That's why I need men like Silas in my employ, to try and uncover the friends of these devils. The tentacles of this depraved immorality taints many deemed to be above the law like the gentry and even some of the clergy. I need you at my side to fight this war and I cannot risk your life being taken in this vicious and bloody battle. I trust no one and advise you to do the same."

Nathaniel's mouth set in a grim line, "I have to be there. You must understand that. Even if I cannot intervene, I must be there to watch, just to watch."

Pritchard sighed, "This does not sit well with me. I fear for you. But, you are nothing if not your father's son. He would be proud." Pritchard considered a moment more before saying slowly, "Very well. Observe, if you must, but don't get caught."

"Thank you, Sir."

"Don't thank me yet. We do not know what will transpire."

Nathaniel pressed on his hat and opened the door with a flourish; Thomas almost fell into the room muttering excuses. Nathaniel turned, "You'll not regret this, Sir."

Pritchard waved him away with a hand and muttered under his breath, "I hope not, my friend. I hope not."


A day went and the aforementioned Thursday arrived. The day passed slowly for Nathaniel who was anxious for night to fall and for him to get to the cliffs and watch the goings on in secret. He spent the day with Goliath teaching him some more words and he tried to tell him what was intended that night but Goliath just stared blankly at Nathaniel and surprisingly asked no questions.

Time moved on and finally evening arrived. Nathaniel and Goliath ate their supper of a meat and pastry patty with potatoes. Nathaniel was trying to explain, yet again, what he was about to do. Goliath was silent seeming lacking in understanding. Nathaniel again gave the order for the giant to stay and donning his cloak and hat he disappeared into the black of the night, a night that was further encumbered by an encroaching mist.

Nathaniel rode quietly up the cliff path to the top overlooking the cove. He didn't think he'd been seen and all he had to do now was wait and pray.

# Chapter Ten

## Danger

The night was cool and still. There was no breeze, which allowed the mist to hang in the air like a cobweb veil masking the movements at the bottom of the cliffs and smothering the sounds in the dark.

In the murk of the bay a light blinked three times. Nathaniel strained forward to see in the gloom. He lay face down in the bracken on the cliff side and watched. Jessie was safely tethered to a tree further back. Barely visible in the poor light was a boat, a small cutter, anchored in the cove. The moonlight shrouded in cloud broke free and afforded a little more illumination in the enveloping fog. Nathaniel gingerly crawled forward trying not to disturb the loose stones and heather. He peered down to the beach, a known favourite of the Wreckers.

Two wooden rowing boats emerged from under the caves in the cliff. Nathaniel just discerned the men rowing with muffled oars to dull the sound of their splash as they skulled through the water at Pwlldu. The men seemed to be dressed in dull coloured coarse plain smocks and breeches. All was hushed except for the tiny inquisitive waves that persistently nosed their way curiously to the shore.

Nathaniel watched intently until the boats drew closer to the cutter. Indistinct murmuring of voices travelled weakly to Nathaniel's ears. On the beach waited two donkeys with three men. Nathaniel stifled a gasp as hooded figures emerged below. His heart thumped at the memory of those that had so cruelly killed his father. He felt the grating pain of anger begin to file away at his insides. Encouraged by this and desperate to see more Nathaniel crawled even closer to the edge. He gripped a tussock of grass at the periphery of the cliff edge and his fingers dislodged some small stones that traitorously tumbled down the cliff, gathering speed as they fell in full betrayal to the rocks and sea below.

One of the hooded figures looked up, his head snapped around as he scoured the beach and above him, with his eyes, before muttering something to one of the other thugs. He then began to pick his way toward the cliff path intent on climbing the steep track to search the top. The figure was quickly enveloped in mist and Nathaniel did not see the danger. As the smuggler crept away into the night so one of the ruffians on the sand gave a low whistle and uncovered the lamp he was holding and slowly waved it signalling to the rest of his gang. The soft splash of the oars could be heard as the rowing boats made their way back to shore. Nathaniel took note of all that was happening and how they used their lights to message each other.

The faint whinny of a horse was heard in the deathly still night air. Nathaniel had seen enough. He slithered back slowly through the bracken trying to make as little noise as possible. He continued to crawl back to the tree where Jessie was tethered. Hardly daring to breathe he untied the mare but just as he was about to mount her a hooded figure dropped out of the branches onto Nathaniel's back.

Taken by surprise, Nathaniel was winded but he mustered up enough strength to buck the man off who immediately rushed at him again. They struggled violently rolling this way and that on the springy heather. The attacker shoved Nathaniel's face into the dirt and held him there as Nathaniel struggled for breath, spitting out bits of leaves and other detritus. Groaning with the effort Nathaniel rolled onto his back, dislodging the ruffian's grasp but the thug was back with avengeance and pinned the young Riding Officer tight to the ground, sitting astride him with one hand on Nathaniel's throat who was now seemingly at the hoodlum's mercy.

For a moment the cloud began to lift from the face of the moon and Nathaniel could see all too clearly a hand, wielding a stout cudgel that was raised above his head and what's more that hand was bearing his father's ring. The cudgel was coming down onto his head. Nathaniel's eyes widened as he recognized the ring and he bellowed in anguish. Time seemed to stop but could not halt the progress of the weapon, which crashed down on his skull, knocking him into unconsciousness. The murdering brute began to roll Nathaniel's inert body toward the edge of the cliff.

There was a small, rustling sound behind the miscreant who worried not at the noise believing it to be of no consequence. But, the villain should have paid more attention as Goliath emerged from the murky mist like an avenging spirit from the netherworld. In two strides he was there and placed his hand on the hooded, thickset villain. The criminal turned and shocked by the sight of the Negro giant and his sheer size, he trembled in fear but, filled with adrenaline, he succeeded in twisting out of Goliath's grasp and fled into the night as if all the shadows from Hades were on his tail.

Goliath grunted in satisfaction and lifted Nathaniel as easily as if he were a sack of grain. He lowered him over Jessie's back and led the horse with its precious cargo away from the craggy steep rock face, along the path and back in the direction of Cliff Cottage.

A shout went up from the beach but no one came after them, but now Goliath knew he was a secret no more. He had determined that Nathaniel was a man of honour and he could be truthful with his saviour. He urged Jessie into a trot as he ran alongside and they hurriedly retraced their steps back to Cliff Cottage and safety.

Goliath took Nathaniel from Jessie's back, carried him inside and laid him on the bed. Then he went to attend to Jessie, taking her to the stable where he untacked her. The ebony mare allowed herself to be handled by Goliath and all the while Goliath spoke soothingly to the horse. Once she was settled he returned to Nathaniel's bedside. He boiled water on the range and gently bathed the gash on the Riding Officer's head. Goliath searched about the room until he found a bottle of smelling salts, which he wafted under Nathaniel's nose, who thrashed his head from side to side as he began to awaken from his stupor. The odour from the salts was enough to bring any man to his senses.

Nathaniel pushed himself up and groaned as his head throbbed violently. He studied his surroundings as Goliath's face panned in and out before his eyes.

"You safe now." Goliath had a rich melodic voice.

Nathaniel was full of questions, "But, how did you…? What…? How did you…?"

"I followed you. Needed to know," responded Goliath.

"You … you speak English," observed Nathaniel, amazed.

"Needed be sure you not one of them."

"Them?" questioned Nathaniel, confused.

Goliath fingered the wooden ankh around his neck. "All wear them. Wooden one marks me as Captain's property." Goliath ripped the hated talisman from his neck and tossed it into the fire. He smiled grimly in approval as the flames began to dance with the cross, eventually enveloping it all in its fatal embrace.

"But…"

Goliath stilled Nathaniel's words with an oath of his own, "I am for you. Your devoted servant and protector." He bowed his head.

Nathaniel frowned and the movement opened up a cut above his eye and the blood started to stream down his face. But, Goliath had watched and learned at Nathaniel's side, he took a clean rag and poured some liquid onto it from an earthenware bottle. He gently patted the gash with the cloth. Nathaniel winced, "Ouch!"

"Still, now. Don't want burning water in eye."

"Alcohol… No, I don't want to be blinded. It's al-co-hol," he repeated.

"Al-co-hol," said Goliath.

"That's right…" Nathaniel picked up the bottle and took a swig of the liquor. "Alcohol. Very bad for one's health," he said jokingly.

Goliath grinned as he rinsed the cotton rag in the bowl of blood and water. "There."

"Where did you learn to speak such good English?"

"I knew a little before I captured, then on ship, I listened, learned and kept mouth shut."

"Wise man."

"Not wise enough," returned Goliath.

"How did it happen?"

Goliath began to relate what had transpired on the dockside. "Lured by lying tongues and flattery. I was promised a rich purse to fight boxing champion. I knew I could win. Greed got better of me. After fight six sailors ambushed me, bound me and dragged me to ship. I flung in hold. Rest you know."

"Not quite."

Goliath looked questioningly, "I tell all. Tell truth."

Nathaniel continued, "The ankh, what does it mean?"

"Ankh?"

"Round your neck. The talisman you burned." Nathaniel indicated Goliath's neck and then the fire.

Goliath understood, "Sign of the brotherhood."

"Brotherhood?"

"Smugglers. Loyalty to band. Break it and die." Goliath grimaced.

Nathaniel frowned, and then winced as the movement hurt, "I am getting close. The more I learn, the more I am likely to achieve my quest."

"As long as quest doesn't lead to death, death of Nathaniel," said Goliath grimly.

"That, Goliath is a chance I have to take."

"What you do about second landing?"

"I have done no more than report it. Pritchard will have to decide. I am in no fit state to arrest anyone at present. Those we seek have been alerted to my surveillance and that I know facts they wish I didn't. Much as I hate to say it, but it's best we lie low on that one."

"Yes. Better we wait. They will be watchful, we need surprise with us."

# Chapter Eleven

## Smugglers

The night was perfect, an almost full moon with a comparatively cloudless sky. The stars glistened like jewels. The water was smooth with barely a ripple. There was no breeze and the waves lovingly caressed the shore, fingering the fine sand and drawing small patterns, which were teased away with each successive, lapping wave.

Boats, slung low in the water, were approaching. Muffled oars skulled skilfully across the silky sea and beached onto the sand. They were laden with contraband. Men swarmed on the beach and rolled away kegs of rum and other liquor. Waterproof packs of tobacco were hoisted onto shoulders and carried away to two donkeys patiently waiting to transport the illegal loads.

Supervising the distribution of goods was Silas, the man with a cast in his eye, reputed to be an informant. He spoke in hushed tones directing the smugglers this way and that. Bales of luxurious silk and other cloth were hauled up the sand to be spirited away by the criminals.

Silas reached into a rowing boat and removed an elaborately decorated wooden box. He lost his grip and the casket tumbled from his fingers and the lid flew off revealing a collection of precious French perfume in ornately cut glass bottles in the shape of a half-open rose. Silas swore softly and retrieved the lid. He went to replace it and paused, studying the rich contents. He glanced swiftly around and then surreptitiously removed a bottle and pocketed it before securing the lid and adding it to a stack of goods waiting to be carried from the beach.

They were quick and efficient in emptying the boats and once this was done, hooded men rowed back through the ocean to the main vessel, which raised its anchor and slipped off into the veiled night.

Adept at their skulduggery all was done quickly, silently

and efficiently as had been done many times before. The donkeys and smugglers disappeared up the cliff path and out of sight.

The footprints and barrel marks that had scarred the once virgin sand were left for the incoming tide to trickle over and thus, wash away the evidence of the miscreants' deeds. It was a perfect night for their activities and the whole recovery of this illegal trade was executed to perfection.

Back at Cliff Cottage, Nathaniel recounted the events of his father's death to Goliath who sat listening and engrossed in what Nathaniel had to say. It was almost a picture of master and student such was Goliath's eagerness to learn. Goliath nodded in sympathy and understanding as Nathaniel told his story, "And that is why I must ride this coast. I have sworn to avenge my father's death."

"Then I am with you, my master. Yours is noble cause," affirmed Goliath.

"I am not your master," corrected Nathaniel. "You are a free man. But I thank you, friend and welcome your aid," uttered Nathaniel appreciatively.

There was a knock at the door. Goliath stiffened and Nathaniel put his fingers to his lips to quieten his friend. "Yes?" called out Nathaniel, "Who's there?"

"It's David. Mam sent me."

Recognising the young man's voice, Nathaniel signalled to Goliath to open the door and admit their visitor. Goliath opened up revealing David Pugh standing awkwardly holding a basket covered with a cloth. He looked somewhat alarmed at seeing Goliath but was reassured when Nathaniel bade him enter, "Come in, David, come in. It's nothing to be afeared of. Welcome."

David entered tentatively, eyeing Goliath. He neatly sidestepped around him much to Nathaniel's amusement. Nathaniel invited Lily's son to sit. David scraped back a chair at the scrubbed table and perched on the end, his eyes flitting about him as if the room was filled with swarms of flies. He hesitated and attempted to speak, but his voice came out as a squeak. He cleared his throat and tried again.

"Take your time, David. There's no rush."

David decided the best way was for him to focus on

Nathaniel and only him. He fastened his eyes on the Riding Officer as if locked on a target, "Mam sent this for you. It's fresh baked and there's a note."

"Deolch, thank you. It smells delicious." He inhaled the mouth-watering aroma of fresh bread and removed the cloth covering a number of small loaves and tucked amongst them was a message. Nathaniel took the missive and opened it scanning its contents carefully. He then turned to Goliath and grinned eagerly, "It's from Lily. She has information for me."

Nathaniel began to rise but was stopped by Goliath, "No. You rest. You not fit."

David put his hand up timidly asking to speak. Nathaniel encouraged him, "Yes, David. Go on."

"Mam says it *is* urgent," he said in hushed tones. Clearly, David was afraid of the huge giant.

Ignoring Goliath's complaints, Nathaniel started to get up. He winced as he struggled to his feet.

"No," commanded Goliath.

"I'll be all right. I've suffered worse," mused Nathaniel.

Goliath realised that he'd not deter Nathaniel and added, "Where you go. I go."

Nathaniel, jerked his head at David, "Tell your mother I will be along in a short while."

David didn't hesitate; he pushed back the chair and rushed to make his escape.

"David, the basket."

"Oh, yes." David hesitated. The outside beckoned invitingly.

Nathaniel saved him this anxiety, "Tell your mother I'll bring the basket with me when we call."

David grinned amiably in relief and scooted out of the door as fast as he was able.

"I think he's a little afraid of you," asserted Nathaniel. "No matter, it will be better when next we meet."

Goliath agreed, "Boy have no need fear me."

"I know that, and Lily knows that. He'll understand. We will help him understand." Nathaniel laughed, "But did you see the look on his face? Anyone would think you were a fire breathing dragon!"

"Dragon?" quizzed Goliath.

"I'll explain, but first let's find somewhere to store these loaves."

Goliath rubbed his stomach, "My tummy good place," he said engagingly.

"Mine too," grinned Nathaniel and he tossed one of the small loaves to Goliath and they each munched on one.

# Chapter Twelve

## News

Nathaniel, Goliath and David were seated at Lily's table sharing a bowl of country broth and bread. There was quiet as spoons were scraped in bowls. Goliath picked up his bowl, and drained the last of the contents. He replaced the dish and rubbed his tummy, "Good. Very good," he said appreciatively.

Lily looked up from her meal and eyed Nathaniel. "That's a nasty gash, you have there. Need some of Lily's healing herbs you do. I'll make you a poultice."

As Lily finished her broth, the others helped themselves to more bread. She busied herself at the range boiling up a pan of water and adding herbs and dried fruits and flowers, which she strained. The water was set aside and the rest was mashed into a paste to which Lily added some lard. The mixture was plastered on a cloth and bandaged to Nathaniel's head. She gave him the water to drink. "Here. Do you good. Drink it down."

Nathaniel grimaced at the bitter taste, "All of it. In one go, go on," and she stood there until he had complied. Lily pursed her lips and nodded approvingly trying to suppress a laugh as Nathaniel twisted his face into an excruciating expression and shuddered. "That's it. You'll soon mend. There's no lasting damage."

"I feel stronger already," agreed Nathaniel. "But what of this news?"

Lily looked about her cautiously as if she expected someone to burst in. It was clear she wasn't ready to say anything yet.

"David, finish your soup and fetch a basket of logs from the shed. Keep an eye out. Tell me if anyone comes."

"Aye, Mam," he slurped the last of his broth and rose from the table, grabbing a last piece of bread as he left the cottage.

Lily waited until her lad was clear and then explained, "Don't want him hearing. What he doesn't know won't harm him."

Nathaniel nodded sagely in understanding, "What can you tell us?"

"Cleaning in the Black Dog Inn, I was, wiping down the tables full of spilled ale when the door flew open. A swarthy man, a stranger, came in for a drink. I continued mopping but kept my ears open and risked a few peeks at the goings on. He met with three villagers. Fellow wreckers, I'm sure."

"Is that right?"

"Aye. He showed them one of them things, talismans."

"An ankh?"

"Wearing it round his neck, he was. Certain to be one of them else why bother to show it?"

"Go on."

Lily licked her lips nervously and continued, "I caught a whisper of a consignment. Something about wool being landed later this week. They were also muttering about plans to wreck a big merchant ship due to pass through these waters. That's all I heard. Landlord ushered me out to clean the pots and pans. Didn't want me hearing no more."

"They didn't suspect?"

"No. I was careful enough."

Nathaniel took out his money pouch and tossed a gold coin onto the table, "You have done well. I thank you for that. Tell me, is there anywhere around here I can buy a good strong horse?"

"Merlin in Chapel Vale has three. I have heard that Samson, the shire is up for sale."

Nathaniel turned to Goliath, "Samson? That's a fitting name for a steed for you. Thank you, Lily."

"Don't be thanking me. And remember, I shall deny all knowledge of anything if you get caught."

"Lily, that's a risk I have to take."

As if on cue there was a sudden rush of wind, which battered the door, which flew open and crashed against the wall. Lily jumped in fright. "I hope that's not an omen, a warning to me that I should have kept my mouth shut." She hurriedly shut out the driving wind.

"Or maybe the door opened as a sign of an opportunity?"

"Hm. I'm not so sure. I don't know what to think. You'd best be off before David returns with the logs. I don't want him involved in anything to do with this."

"Of course. Know that we respect your wishes, Lily. We want no harm to come to you or David." Nathaniel rose from the table and walked to the door followed by Goliath. Nathaniel turned at the door, his fingers on the handle, "And Lily?"

She looked at him questioningly, "Yes?"

"Thank you." Nathaniel opened the door allowing the wind to search the cottage once more, prising into every nook and cranny. He closed it firmly after him and took Jessie's reins.

Nathaniel was, once more, on the back of the ebony mare with Goliath walking alongside. They soon reached the cliff top and the wind battered them as they walked, head down and hunched into the persistent attacking gale. Speech was almost impossible.

They approached a lone Hawthorne tree frozen in position revealing years of work of the buffeting wind sculpting the tree to grow in one direction. The tree looked petrified, a visible shriek, as if it had seen unspeakable horrors. Nathaniel slipped off Jessie and held the reins. He shouted above the cacophony of the howling elements. "Do you ride?"

"No," Goliath cried.

"Then now's the time to try."

Nathaniel passed the reins to Goliath who looked at first, startled and then confused. Seeing that Nathaniel was serious he turned his attention to Jessie and spoke soothingly to her in his own language while he stroked her neck. He moved around to the front of the mare and breathed softly into her nostrils. Jessie appeared to respond and stood quietly in spite of the screeching, gathering storm. Nathaniel looked on somewhat surprised at Jessie's calm demeanour.

Goliath tentatively mounted her. Immediately his weight was on her back she reared up and whinnied. Goliath patted her neck and leaned forward. He whispered into her ear and scratched it. Jessie settled calmly and then took off across the cliffs. Nathaniel watched in amazement and rubbed his chin in disbelief.

Goliath turned the mare and galloped back. He dismounted and handed the reins back to Nathaniel, "I thought you said you couldn't ride," accused Nathaniel.

"Never been on horse."

"But…"

"I have way with animals. They like me. Also, I watch you. See what you do, how handle Jessie. Jessie and me we have understanding."

Nathaniel grinned, "Then Merlin's farm it is." He went on and added, his voice filled with wonder, "Jessie has never let anyone else ride her. Ever."

Nathaniel turned Jessie back in the direction they had come from and they trekked toward Chapel Farm.

Before too long they reached a thicket and Nathaniel instructed Goliath to wait. He was to try and avoid being seen. Goliath smiled and indicated a tall spreading oak, "Someone come, I climb tree."

"Don't sit on a small branch. It won't stand your weight."

Goliath laughed and grinned toothily. He watched as Nathaniel headed off into the valley and stepped back into the shade of the trees.

Nathaniel cantered along the country roads and arrived at the end of the lane to Chapel Farm. He trotted up the rough track skirting the potholes and came to the ramshackle farmhouse with its outbuildings and his eyes scanned the area for signs of life.

Merlin Evans peered suspiciously through the stable-gate door from his house. He muttered something in Welsh to his wife and ordered her to stay put. He was also not pleased to see the Riding Officer on his property. Merlin pulled on his hat and coat and went out to face the man in his yard. Jessie stamped impatiently.

"Yes? Can I help you?" asked Merlin gruffly with no welcome in his voice and no friendly smile to grace his face. He spat onto the ground and narrowed his eyes as he perused his visitor.

"I understand you have a horse for sale, Samson, I think."

"I might have and then again, I might not," said Merlin cagily.

"Well, either you have or you haven't. I have the money to pay." Nathaniel took out his money pouch, which chinked. Merlin's eyes glowed with avarice.

"He's not cheap."

"I didn't expect him to be. Then you do have one?" pressed Nathaniel.

Merlin jerked his thumb toward the barn where he kept his steeds, "This way."

Nathaniel jumped off Jessie and tied her to a ring on the barn door and followed Merlin into the musty shed.

Little light filtered through. There were three horses, all Shires and a foal.

"Which is Samson?"

Merlin sniffed again and wiped his grimy hand across his face. He indicated a strong looking black and white working horse.

Nathaniel crossed to the animal and examined its feet and fetlocks. He stroked the gentle giant's soft velvet nose and looked in his mouth. "This is a good horse."

"It is. I wouldn't be parting with him, if I didn't have to."

"Why is he going?"

"Hard times. Things are difficult. I have my two plough horses that work in a pair, and a new foal to be trained up. No need for Samson now although it will break my heart to lose him."

Nathaniel didn't think that the last comment was the case at all. But the animal seemed sweet of nature. "May I lead him into the yard?"

Merlin inclined his head and sniffed. Nathaniel put on Samson's head collar and led the horse out to meet Jessie. The two horses considered each other and then put muzzle to muzzle. They seemed quite agreeable together.

"Do you have a saddle to fit?"

"It'll cost," replied Merlin.

"No more than I expected. And I know you wouldn't be cheating a revenue man, now would you?"

Merlin muttered something under his breath and returned to the stable. He came back out and helped Nathaniel fit the saddle on the animal, and checked the girth. "He's a good animal. What will you give?" asked Merlin taking the reins.

"What are you asking?"

The two men haggled awhile and struck up a deal. Merlin pocketed the cash eagerly and they shook hands before Merlin handed the reins to Nathaniel who gave a one-fingered salute in acknowledgement. Nathaniel mounted Jessie and leading Samson trotted off the farm property.

Merlin stared after him. He walked to the farm gate and shaded his eyes peering into the distance after Nathaniel and mused quietly to himself, "Now, why does he need another horse?" He shrugged, turned around and plodded back to the farmhouse.

Nathaniel soon reached the copse of trees and Goliath emerged from the thicket where he had been waiting. Nathaniel watched Goliath interact with Samson as he had with Jessie before he sprang onto Samson's back. The horse shifted slightly at Goliath's weight but otherwise gave no hint of anything unusual. Together, the two men rode off across the hill.

Ominous storm clouds filled the sky, "Let's try and beat the weather," called Nathaniel and they broke first into a canter, then a full gallop.

As they reached the approach to Cliff Cottage the first spots of rain began to fall. Night would come more quickly with the thunderous clouds blocking the afternoon light. They dismounted quickly and Goliath hurried with both animals to their stabling as Nathaniel entered the cottage. He lit a lamp in the darkening kitchen, which brought a little cheer to the gloom.

Nathaniel stoked up the fire and put some water onto boil. He crossed to the table and noticed a scrap of parchment on the table. He picked it up and read the note and immediately reached for his hat and cloak to brave the outside elements once more.

Goliath opened the door and saw the concerned look on Nathaniel's face, "Where you go?"

Nathaniel pointed at the missive, "It's Jenny. She's looking for me. I fear she'll fall foul of the villagers in her search. I don't want that. You wait here in case she returns."

64

Goliath nodded his agreement and Nathaniel turned back from the door and indicated the fire, "I've put water onto boil. Don't let it boil dry." Nathaniel swept out to the stables.

Jessie was surprised and less than happy at being taken from her warm stable and back out into the ferocious wind. "Whoa, Jessie. Let's get this done now and then the sooner we'll be back. And I must teach Goliath proper horsemanship." He muttered as he glanced at Samson still fully tacked. Nathaniel climbed on Jessie's back, kicked her flanks and cantered off into the wind with his cloak streaming behind him like a trail of scavenging crows. The rolling storm clouds boiled a venomous black turning the rest of the daylight into murky darkness.

The wind raged, tugging at Nathaniel's clothes and whipping Jessie's mane into a tangle but horse and rider valiantly pressed on. They soon reached the crest of the hill and Nathaniel could just make out the figure of Jenny scrambling up the sodden hillside. He nudged Jessie forward to meet her and fairly flew to her side. He dismounted instantly and took the shivering Jenny by her shoulders, a tingling prickling tracked up his arm. He wanted to hug her to him but he resisted the urge and became clinically professional as he studied her face. Her scarred cheek was puffed and bruised and a rivulet of blood trickled from the corner of her eye.

Nathaniel took out his handkerchief in the increasing rain and dabbed at her injury. Raindrops mingled with Jenny's tears and she looked up into Nathaniel's eyes and he felt his heart pound even louder in his chest as if it were fighting to jump out. He took a deep breath to clear the rising emotion bubbling up inside him in anger against the villain who had inflicted the wound. "Who did this to you, Jenny fach?" he whispered softly before the wind could snatch his words away.

"It's best you not know. It will only make things worse for me."

The anger that was ravaging his heart tore at him and Nathaniel could not contain his ire, "Damn it!" he roared. "I'll swing for any cowards who prey on women."

Jenny flinched at his tone and was confused at the passion in Nathaniel's voice. "I'll be fine. It's you I'm worried about."

Almost magically, the wind dropped momentarily giving them some short respite. Nathaniel tilted her chin, and gazed into her wild green eyes, the colour of verdant pastures. His eyes misted slightly at her heart stopping beauty and for a minute, just a minute, time seemed to stand still. Nathaniel tenderly stroked her damaged cheek, "Such a lovely face and such cruel blows," he breathed huskily.

Jenny responded, her voice barely audible, "It may have been once. Not now."

Nathaniel and Jenny gazed at each other as the lull in the storm continued fractionally longer. Nathaniel let his finger trace her scar yet Jenny did not wince or pull away. She closed her eyes and leaned her face into his strong hand.

A shout echoed up from the village and the moment was broken. Five men advanced up the hillside toward them yelling, "Is that the woman? Who's she with?"

Nathaniel wasted no time. He scooped Jenny up into his arms and placed her on Jessie's back. He mounted his horse and spurred her on through the driving rain and countryside leaving the thugs bellowing in fury after them.

Nathaniel was disturbed by the proximity of Jenny and knew that if he was to fulfill his mission he must bury these needling pinpricks of desire that made his heart race. Jenny, too, was confused by the feelings emerging in her at Nathaniel's touch but resolved to put her own longings away, pack them into a box at the back of her mind, especially if she wanted to live. However, she feared that it might be too late for her now for if *they* knew that she was in contact with the outsider, the shunned Riding Officer, she placed her father's and her own life in jeopardy.

Nathaniel rode furiously on to the Banwen's shack but before they reached it Jenny called to Nathaniel, "Let me down here. Please. I'll walk the rest of the way. It will do me no good to be seen with you here."

Nathaniel understood her feelings and halted. He slid off Jessie and lifted her down. "Will you be all right?"

"As right as I'll ever be," she responded.

"You'll stop by tomorrow?"

"I will. As soon as I know it's safe. I don't want to anger the village more than I have to. It's not the ordinary villagers, you understand? It's the few that work with, the Wreckers. They have eyes and ears everywhere."

"Any trouble, anything at all. You know where to find me."

Nathaniel remounted and turned Jessie. He gave a one-fingered salute and cantered back along the track toward Cliff Cottage. Jenny watched him ride away. She found it hard to reconcile herself with the very real feelings that were growing stronger within her each time she met with the Riding Officer. She remained in that spot watching him until he disappeared from view and started down the path to her humble dwelling.

To her alarm she saw a rider ferociously bearing down on her coming from the opposite direction, the man was followed by two more at a greater distance. She froze in her tracks for a moment uncertain what to do and then picked up her skirts and ran as soon as she recognized the chestnut stallion with a white blaze that belonged to her abuser. She scrambled down the slope trusting that the horse would not follow where she now slid and slipped.

Jenny tumbled down, her hair tangling in the bracken and brambles; nettles stung her hands and face. The young squire reared up on his horse, Hermes, and cut a vengeful figure against the skyline. He calmed his mount and jumped out of the saddle. The wastrel looked down at the girl, cut, scratched, and bruised. He jeered, "Run from me, would you? Ha! You will soon have marks to match on the other side of your face, if you do not bow to my will."

Jenny said nothing.

He continued to needle her, "How on earth I thought you were comely. I do not know. But there... your body is still pretty and could satisfy my needs again, if I so wish." He laughed cruelly and Jenny shied away from him, trembling. He caught her around her throat and squeezed, his nails embedding themselves in her skin, drawing blood, "I see the wench is afraid. That only serves to heighten my desire. But not here, it is too chilly for my liking. We don't want you

67

wind chapped, now do we? Nor do we want an audience for whatever I choose to do." He let her go and she slipped down the slope and lay in the grass.

Two other riders joined the bully on the hilltop. Silas and Black Bob looked down on Jenny, "Is she for us?" asked Silas with a leer.

"Not yet."

"Is what we heard true? Word has it, she's fraternising with the Outsider."

"Of that I'm not sure…" he called down to Jenny, "Is that right? Have you been misbehaving? Talking to those you shouldn't? Well?" he demanded.

Jenny was silent. The young man loped down the slope to her and caught her roughly and gave her a stinging slap. "I asked you a question, whore."

Jenny fell backwards and touched her enflamed cheek, already turning blue, "I talk to no one that I shouldn't," muttered Jenny.

"Glad to hear it. I'd hate to have to punish you, here and now. You don't want to give folks the wrong idea." He grasped her arm and hauled her up. "Rumours can be deadly. Make sure you don't invite undue attention. Keep to your own. This is just a friendly word of warning, Jenny. That's all." He moved back up the hillside, remounted and called out, "Sometime soon, Jenny. You and I. We will talk further." He turned his horse away and rode back the way he had come followed by the other two ruffians who guffawed at her discomfort and humiliation.

Jenny bit back a sob and hurried to her house and raced inside, leaning heavily against the door, her heart racing. She tasted something warm and coppery when she licked her lips. She put her hand up and wiped her mouth, she was bleeding. She had suffered a number of grazes and was bruised from her tumble. Jenny was shaking, with shock and fright, from the encounter but she had no time to think further as her father called out for her.

"Jenny?"

"Yes, Dad. It's me." Jenny went into the kitchen where her father was sitting. He looked at her in surprise at her dishevelled appearance. Jenny swallowed her fear and forced herself to smile. "I had a small fall outside, tripped on my skirt. Silly really. I'll be fine."

Hywel didn't press her, but he didn't fully believe her either.

Jenny began to prepare their meal. She gathered flour, eggs and milk together to make some savoury pancakes.

"Jenny, you need to get those wounds attended to. You don't want them getting infected."

"I'm all right, Dad. I'll see Lily later, she'll help."

"Not the Riding Officer?"

"Not unless I can't see Lily." Jenny was evasive with her answers.

"Jenny, Jenny," Hywel shook his head sadly. "We have to lie low. Your involvement with Nathaniel Brookes and his man will lead us all to our deaths. Think girl. Think very carefully."

Jenny attempted a bright smile, "Go on with you, dad. You are being melodramatic."

"Melodramatic am I? It comes to something that even my one good friend is afraid to be seen with me. We are just as much outcasts as your Riding Officer." He gestured to the table. "Lay an extra place, we have a guest coming later. Then you better get onto the Inn to do your stint. Say nothing to no one and keep your opinions to yourself."

Jenny remained quiet and resolved that she would see Nathaniel as soon as she was able. The wind howled its warnings as it buffeted the cottage, playing roughly with the windows and the rain began to fall.

# Chapter Thirteen

## Things Move On

Jenny sat at the worn but scrupulously clean pine table while Nathaniel tended to her cuts and bruises. She tried to speak as he bathed her face, "Shush, first things first," insisted Nathaniel.

Goliath threw another log on the fire and he warmed up some nourishing soup. His face was grave when he saw Jenny's damaged skin. It did not sit well with him, either, to see that a woman had been beaten and intimidated in this way.

Nathaniel finished patching up her injuries and Goliath handed her a mug of the broth as she sat shivering at the table. The wind howled around the cottage occasionally rattling the window shutters and blowing the drapes.

Goliath sat next to Jenny and Nathaniel was opposite her. He urged her to drink up, "Come on now, it will do you good to get something warm inside you after trekking through this miserable rain."

Jenny sipped from her mug and said quietly, "I'm all right."

"But why? What I don't understand is why you would risk the villagers' wrath to come looking for me? Don't you know that anyone associated with me has their life put in danger?"

"You've been good to me… and dad. I had to warn you."

"Warn me? Why?" Nathaniel and Goliath leaned forward in their seats to hear her soft tones.

"Rumours are flying through the village and I overheard something at the Inn. Dad says…" She bit her lip hesitantly, looking from one to the other. Her pulse was racing. Now she was here, she wondered if she should speak.

"Go on…" prodded Nathaniel gently.

Jenny indicated Goliath, "The search for your man…"

"What of it?"

"It's spreading up the Bristol Channel and the North Devon coast."

"So?" Nathaniel was puzzled.

"Dad feels that it won't be long before them that shouldn't, hear about your new bodyguard."

Goliath sat back in his chair, the memories of his imprisonment crawled into his head while Nathaniel paused and considered her words. "Tell me Jenny, how does your father know this?"

"A friend."

"This friend, does he have a name?"

Jenny looked uncertainly at them, "I don't know if I should say. I don't want trouble raining on his head. He's a good man."

"His name will be safe with me."

Jenny made up her mind and nodded knowing Nathaniel was a man of his word. She continued, "Johnstone, William Johnstone." She then pleaded, "But please don't go looking for him." There was a pause filled only by the fury of the wind outside punctuating the seriousness of the matter in hand. "He's the man who rescued dad after his beating when he was left for dead. He's terrified of discovery." Jenny immediately bit her lip again confused by events and her feelings, and that eternal devil on her shoulder telling her she had done wrong. "I shouldn't have said anything."

"I won't endanger him. I promise you that. But it does my heart good to know that there are sympathisers. That good men are out there. It takes someone of strong mettle to act as he did."

"He can't help openly for fear of arousing suspicion, you understand?"

"Of course. It's no use inviting trouble. We need as many on our side as possible, whether that support is hidden or not. But, tell me, what of the news you heard at the inn?"

"A man came into the bar. He spoke with the Landlord. He was a swarthy man with dark eyes and hair. A cruel man if ever I saw one."

"What did he say?"

"It was not so much what he said…"

"Well?"

"He was wearing an ankh." Jenny glanced at Goliath and Nathaniel who both exchanged looks. Jenny continued, "The

71

Landlord sold him some scent... perfume in a fancy bottle. Unusual, in the shape of a rose, it was."

Nathaniel rose from the table abruptly and ordered Goliath, "Take Jenny back. Make sure she's safe. Accompany her all the way to her door."

Jenny protested, "No! We must not be seen together. Best if I go... alone." She caught Nathaniel's hand and raised it to her lips kissing it gently.

Nathaniel was surprised and touched. He wasn't expecting his heart to pound at the action in the way it did. His hand tingled and then Jenny's next words were said with such obvious tenderness that he caught his breath.

"Be careful, Nathaniel. Please. There're many that would... do for you as they did for your father. Men without conscience, who kill for pleasure..." She lowered her eyes quickly before her feelings betrayed her completely. Jenny picked up her shawl now a little drier and went to the door. She opened it carefully and peered around it before vanishing into the night with the words, "Be safe, Nathaniel, both of you."

Nathaniel didn't move. He studied his hands where her kiss had impressed itself and sent electric pulses in waves up his arm. He struggled with the turbulent emotions that rose within him and as he observed the bloodied cloth and bandages on the table he became overcome with guilt, guilt that made him question his mission. He sat down heavily and put his head in his hands and now it was Goliath's turn to look concerned.

"What is it? Why you look like that?"

Nathaniel raised his head and gazed concertedly into Goliath's eyes. "I never thought I'd say this, but..." and he stopped.

"What?" Goliath prompted.

"You know, Goliath, I wonder if any of this is worth-while?"

"You not mean that."

"I'm afraid I do." Nathaniel spoke in measured tones, "I swore as a little boy to hunt for the man that killed my father... Hunt him and get justice."

"Good and noble cause."

Nathaniel said nothing.

Goliath prompted again, "But…?"

"Look how many people I am hurting. Good honest people ostracized by the community because of their friendship with me."

"But they…"

Nathaniel cut him off and ploughed on, "Lily and David, Jenny and Hywel to name a few…" He cleared his throat, "These smugglers, these cutthroats… How could I be so arrogant as to think I could stop them? Me? I'm just one man against a whole band of faceless villains. They have the advantage. They know me but I…"

"You have me. I will stand at your side. Your mission is mine. We will succeed together."

"Noble words my friend. But is it enough?" Nathaniel looked downcast, almost defeated.

Goliath tried to inject some positivity into the discussion, and urged, "You not give up, not now."

"Nor can I reconcile myself with my blind need for vengeance if anything happens to those who help me because of who I am. Maybe it's time to stop, to go home."

"You give up and more will die, more be enslaved, more wrongs done. You need to see what good you do in ridding place of killer wreckers. You need one last fight to see you do right."

Nathaniel didn't answer. His face was grim and his heart sorely troubled. The sickening twisting in his stomach needed settling. He knew he had to get out. He had to do something. He picked up his hat and coat and abruptly left the cottage. Goliath looked anxiously after him, uncertain what to do. He heard Jessie canter away and made up his mind. He would follow Nathaniel but at a discrete distance. He grabbed his outer clothes and went out to get Samson.

The wind had now dropped and the rain abated. The secret night was illuminated by the silver sheen of a nearly full moon that lit the sky with its magical glow. Nathaniel cantered across the cliff top and paused as he perused the village below. Inside his head a fierce argument raged, one that needed to be settled. Goliath's words had struck home. Could he abandon the local town folk and villagers to run in fear from the poisonous rabble that defied the law and ruled with fear? What would happen to those who had befriended him and who would no longer enjoy his protection? More importantly, what would happen to Jenny? Jenny, the mere thought of her stirred something deep inside him, strong feelings that were new to him. His feelings for the young woman sent him into turmoil. He had to do something. Nathaniel made up his mind.

Nathaniel urged Jessie to the slope that led to the village. Horse and rider carefully picked their way down the incline until they reached the cobbled streets. Faint strains of music played on the breeze and Nathaniel followed the sound to the Black Dog Inn where Lily had cleaned. He dismounted outside the hostelry and approached the door. He tied Jessie up outside. The Inn was raucous and alive with music, song, chatter and drinking. Nathaniel pushed open the heavy door, which squealed with the effort, and he stood at the threshold, his bold figure a monolith blocking the moonlight's entry. A hush fell over the occupants as they turned to see who had entered so dramatically. A wizen faced old man scraping a bow across violin strings stopped his lively playing with a discordant screech, his mouth fell open revealing rotting, brown teeth.

The gambling at the tables ceased and all eyes focused on Nathaniel as he strode toward the bar. Nathaniel tossed down a coin and spoke, "A quart of your finest ale and some information."

The Landlord bristled at the inference that he might reveal anything to the young Riding Officer and was quick to respond, "I'll take your money for the brew but I'll have no truck with customs men."

Some locals murmured in agreement as the Landlord poured the ale. Nathaniel turned to the villagers who were stunned into silence once more. He raised his pewter mug to them in a toast. "Your very good health, everyone," and he took a swig of beer. "And a guinea to the first man unafraid to speak to a Riding Officer."

The Landlord baulked at the comment, spat and turned away. But undeterred Nathaniel slapped a guinea onto the counter top. The babble of noise resumed as men doggedly turned their backs on Nathaniel and ignored him. Nathaniel took another mouthful of liquor and leaned against the counter facing the bar. Men buying ale avoided standing close to him and if Nathaniel glanced their way they evaded his gaze. Nathaniel appeared intent on his ale but his ears were open and he caught the drift of conversations around the room. It was surprising what he learnt.

At a corner table near the door a huddle of men played cards. They whispered feverishly together. The group tossed down their cards and exited the inn, all except for one left sitting at the card table. That man, Twm Watkins rose from his seat. He nodded to two other scruffs at the adjacent table who responded to him with a jerk of the head, in the same way. Twm wiped his mouth nervously and tried not to attract undue attention to himself from the rest of the crowd but approached the bar hesitantly and ordered a beer. He eyed greedily the shiny guinea sitting on the bar. He nudged Nathaniel's arm to attract his attention and rolled his eyes toward the yard indicating that Nathaniel should follow him. Twm supped his drink and placed the half full tankard on the counter and nonchalantly left the bar by the side door leading to the enclosed yard.

Nathaniel picked up his coin and waited a respectable time before moving across to the side door. As he opened it the two men from the neighbouring table had closed in on him unnoticed. They shoved him from behind and the Riding Officer was propelled into the courtyard.

Nathaniel found himself facing a group of brutish men. They all bore cudgels and circled him menacingly. Nathaniel struck out at Twm and reached for his pistol, but another thug was too quick and grabbed the gun from Nathaniel's belt. The ruffian cocked the pistol and aimed it at Nathaniel's head. He guffawed in triumph and was about to pull the trigger when the courtyard door from the stabling crashed open. Goliath's huge frame sprang through the doorway. Like lightning, Goliath flew at the villain threatening Nathaniel and wrested the firearm from his hands and tossed it to Nathaniel before the criminal could fire.

Four ruffians then turned their attention to Goliath who roared like a demented demon and floored them in quick succession before they could attack. Goliath easily dispatched the cowards, each with a single blow and they fell like dominoes. Twm looked at the wreckage of men and thought twice about continuing the fight and fled.

The noise from the fracas outside was drowned in the merriment of the men at the bar who dared to prematurely celebrate what they perceived to be their wicked victory. The Inn door opened and the Landlord and locals pressed forward expecting to see Nathaniel's demise. To their horror and surprise Nathaniel and Goliath were dusting themselves down. They pushed through the gathering throng who were peering in astonishment through the doorway to their floored drinking companions. Nathaniel and Goliath returned to the bar leaving the villainous rabble out stone cold in the yard.

Nathaniel picked up what was left of his ale and slugged it down. He stepped to the door, followed by Goliath and the bar room was silent as the patrons looked on in disbelief. Nathaniel turned and announced, "The offer still stands. I will give a guinea to any man brave enough to speak with me. You all know where I am." Nathaniel and Goliath exited proudly, their stature majestic whilst the locals were left feeling confused and afraid.

# Chapter Fourteen

## Getting Close.

Nathaniel jumped on Jessie's back and turned to his friend, "Thank you, Goliath. I'm lucky you were there. Tell me, why did you come?"

"You not you, not yourself. Dangerous when like that. Decisions not sensible."

"Well, whatever it was, I am glad you came. If not for you I wouldn't be here. I owe you my life," said Nathaniel gratefully.

Goliath mounted Samson and followed after Nathaniel. Once they reached the outskirts of the village, Goliath rode alongside Nathaniel and they talked.

"What you learn?" asked Goliath.

"Enough. Drink loosens men's tongues and makes them careless."

"So, what now?"

"I'll report to Pritchard. Surely, we will have the jump on the rogues, now?" Nathaniel replied.

"Not know. It seems these men hard to catch. What of quest?"

"You mean finding my father's killers? I am hoping that someone will talk eventually. If not, I shall have to find the ones at the top. That will take time."

"More time take, less chance. And more danger you be in."

Nathaniel looked up at the sky and frowned, the clouds were sweeping in and hiding the moon. "Looks like rain. We better get a move on."

"I never knew one place could be so wet."

"No, I suppose you don't. You are used to sunshine."

"Where I from, sun shines most times. When it rains, it bad, but it all over and done with and sun comes out."

"Ah, in a perfect world we'd have sunshine in the day and it would only rain when we were all asleep in bed."

"Not perfect world."

"No, my friend, it's not. And no matter how hard we work, we cannot make it so."

The men urged their horses on toward Cliff Cottage as the first drops of rain began to fall from the now glowering black sky.


Nathaniel was perched on Pritchard's desk. He looked relaxed and was clearly more at ease with himself and his superior. Discussion had been heavy on Nathaniel's findings and Pritchard made copious notes. He picked up his papers and browsed through them while Nathaniel waited. Pritchard reached the end of the information he had gathered and looked up, "Is that all?"

"It's enough. Give me the men and I can round up this little band and save money for the Crown. A little expenditure for a rich reward."

Pritchard sighed and considered Nathaniel's words, "You have done well, extremely well and against all odds. As soon as we have the final pieces to this puzzle I'll grant you all you need and more."

"You want more proof?"

"Get the evidence we need and we will succeed in putting these rogues away for a good long stretch."

"Or stretch them by the neck," continued Nathaniel.

"If we are lucky."

"What do you mean?" asked Nathaniel his good humour diminishing.

"I'm almost afraid to say." Pritchard hesitated, "It's no good, you need to be prepared."

"Prepared for what?" questioned Nathaniel his eyes searching Pritchard's face. Nathaniel rose from the desk and towered above Pritchard his stance displaying his strength.

"I have already demanded a sloop to replace the smaller one that was torched prior to you arriving in my service. I have told them how desperately we need something to help us patrol the channel. It cannot be done all on horseback. It tires you and leaves you little time for anything else. I am two Riding Officers down and now that the smuggling activities have increased we have even more need, but..."

"But?"

"I am sorry to say that I suspect this request as with others I have made will be denied."

"But why? Why, when we are so close?"

Pritchard lowered his tone confidentially, "Nathaniel, I am convinced that there is someone in authority, higher up than me who is blocking our attempts to thwart this gang and bring them to justice. It's not the first time."

"I don't understand…"

"Your father was a good man and an excellent Riding Officer. He made a similar request all those years ago and it was categorically denied. As a matter of fact, every time something new breaks, my requests fall on deaf ears. As if… as if the missives never arrive at their destination or only part of the information gets through. Believe you me, a man of considerable power lies behind all this, a man of influence…"

Nathaniel slammed his hand down on the desk and interrupted Pritchard, "Then, I'll not rest until I bring him and all his ilk down. I *will* avenge my father."

"Steady, Nathaniel, steady. This obsession may do for you and I would not want that for you or your family."

"I have lived with this yearning quest for justice all my life. I cannot change now. Do what you can. I will continue to play my part."

"I understand. I pray that you will keep safe."

Nathaniel nodded his acknowledgement to Pritchard and swept from his office. Pritchard watched him leave, a worried expression on his face. He began to peruse the notes once more.

Twilight shadows lengthened and spread along the Mumbles Road leading to the cliffs. Nathaniel and Goliath travelled silently, each lost in their own thoughts. All that could be heard was the faint clip-clop of the horses' hooves.

The tiny stars that pierced the velvet heavens afforded some light and when the moon emerged from behind the ever-growing bank of cloud, silver moonbeams washed the pebble strewn road a pearly grey.

The night was quiet but as they progressed a strange

rumbling was heard. In the distance two figures could be seen rolling what appeared to be barrels along the ground. Nathaniel put his fingers to his lips for Goliath to remain quiet and they nudged the horses behind a small clump of trees leading from the grass verge and there they waited until the figures approached.

The two men seemed to be dressed as Batmen, runners or servants for someone in the military. In Nathaniel's eyes this compounded what Pritchard had told him. The barrels appeared to be full such were their exertions. The men grunted as they rolled, and cursed when the barrel developed a mind of its own and began to travel the wrong way. Nathaniel wanted to laugh. It was comical to watch them, groaning and complaining while the wood on stone rattled along the less than even road.

The men were nearly upon them when Nathaniel and Goliath moved forward to challenge them, "In the name of Customs and Excise, HALT!" cried Nathaniel.

The two batmen were startled and jumped in fright. They turned the barrels on end quickly and removed stout cudgels from their belts. They immediately aligned themselves ready to strike. Goliath slid off Samson and the men's faces looked aghast. Nathaniel was forced to suppress a smile. The men's jaws dropped as they saw the height of the Negro giant and his massive muscular frame. With eyes wide, an involuntary cry escaped the ruffians and they turned tail and fled, abandoning their barrels.

Nathaniel dismounted and joined Goliath who was examining one keg. Nathaniel twisted the tap and opened it up to sample the contents. He swallowed a mouthful and wiped his hand over his mouth after closing off the tap, "Well, it's not sea water." He smacked his lips, "Rum. And a good one at that," he muttered before shouting after the fleeing men, "I seize these goods in the name of the King."

Goliath slapped Nathaniel on the back in victory. Nathaniel scratched his head, "Now, how on earth do we get this lot back for safe keeping?"

"You have rope?" asked Goliath.

"That I do, but is it enough?"

"Won't know, till look."

Nathaniel rummaged in a bag at Jessie's side and pulled out a length of strong plaited cord. They managed to loop it around the kegs and secured one each side to Samson's saddle.

"Can you still ride?"

"Will ride. Samson strong, like me." Goliath grinned showing his perfectly white teeth. He mounted carefully and eased himself into the saddle avoiding the rum barrels and they began to return they way they had come.

"We must get these to the King's store, put them under lock and key and then I think another visit to the Black Dog and one to the Boar's Head. We may just be lucky in finding more illegal goods, if our information is correct."

Nathaniel and Goliath continued forward to the store and Customs Offices. Thomas Lloyd, Pritchard's assistant was still on duty. "Mr. Brookes." Thomas greeted him courteously.

"Thomas, we need you to open up the store."

"What have you this time?"

"Rum, two barrels and a good one," winked Nathaniel.

"Sampled it have you?"

"Not exactly. I had to ensure the contents were spirits not water in the kegs."

"Follow me." Thomas led the way around the back of the offices to the store and opened the door, revealing a small cache of goods seized by Nathaniel on previous raids. They unloaded the casks and Thomas locked the weighty doors behind them.

"I hope to fill the store sooner rather than later. Maybe then the authorities will take us more seriously."

"Planning more raids, are you?"

"Let's just say, I hope to catch out a few unsuspecting thieves."

"Good luck with that," smiled Thomas. "Can I inform Mr. Pritchard of where you are going?"

Nathaniel shook his head, "Nay, the element of surprise must remain with me. Sorry, Thomas."

"No consequence. I'll know soon enough, anyway. Word spreads fast."

"Aye, that's what I'm afeared of."

Thomas laughed and added, "Don't think we've ever had any rider succeed as well as you. Good luck!"

Goliath and Nathaniel gathered some rope and pack bags from the store, bade Thomas goodbye and rode off.

They had a hard ride across the cliffs passing the track to the village and onto the small town. The Boar's Head was to be their first raid. This time they planned their strategy. The word from Lily had been that talk in The Black Dog was of black marketeering. Contraband would be openly bought and bartered for in the Boar's Head that night; other smuggled goods were to be stored at The Black Dog. Nathaniel knew he had not got the men to arrest the smugglers but he could certainly irritate them enough by commandeering their ill-gotten goods. If he was lucky he may even recognize one or two of the men and could then arrest them or persuade them to turn King's evidence. Nathaniel would enter boldly by the main door, whilst Goliath would guard the courtyard door to the inn. At least that was the plan.

The blanket of night concealed nefarious deeds and so too, hid Nathaniel and his man's approach to the hostelry. Misshapen trees with wicked poking branches forced into tortured positions by the winds that ravaged the valley provided the perfect spot to dismount and secure their horses. The rest of the path would be trodden on foot.

The two men stealthily made their way to the tavern. Ribald laughter and raucous chatter intruded into the street interspersed with clanging of tankards and chinking of money changing hands. The rusty Inn sign squeaked eerily on its corroded hinges when caught by the whisper of a breeze. The little lamplight invading the street from the inn was muddy in hue and sporadic. Nathaniel instructed Goliath, "Go round to the courtyard entrance, give a whistle when you are in position and count to ten, then enter."

Goliath nodded silently in understanding and slipped away into the masking dark. Nathaniel marveled at how silently the big man moved, just like a cat, stealthily and yet alert. Goliath was a prime athlete.

Nathaniel waited, his muscles taut, ready to burst through the opening and into the inn. There was a twittering whistle like a disturbed bird that carried on the wind. It was Goliath's signal. He was in position. Nathaniel began to count.

As he reached the number ten the Riding Officer crashed through the Inn door and shouted, "These goods are confiscated in the name of the King."

At first a hush fell over the assembled crowd. As Nathaniel moved further into the bar, pandemonium let loose. Men grabbed at money and goods small enough to carry and tried to flee. But they stopped when they realized Nathaniel was just one man. They turned to watch what the Riding Officer would do next.

Three ruffians had stood their ground and leered at Nathaniel. Another one jumped over a table and began to approach menacingly. He removed a knife from his belt and waved it threateningly, "Come on," he growled. "Take me if you dare," and he inched closer. The other men came to back up the villain and they, too, removed various weapons from their person. "You're just one man. I've dispatched more than you," shouted a rough swarthy man, wearing an ankh, who must have been the one Jenny had described to them. The thug was just about to spring at Nathaniel when the courtyard door buckled and gave way. It smashed down off its hinges revealing the huge frame of Goliath bearing an expression that looked as if it had been ripped from hell itself.

The smugglers stopped advancing and turned to see this new sign of danger. There were gasps of astonishment at the sight of the massive black giant. Some visibly quaked in their boots, others thought better of attacking and leapt back, turning over tables as a distraction before springing over the bar counter and fleeing out the back. The Landlord was pushed to the ground in the manic effort of the rogues to escape. The other patrons sidled back in a cowardly fashion as Nathaniel spoke again. "I repeat I claim these goods in the name of the King."

Goliath blocked the courtyard entrance and folded his arms like a genie from a bottle and the rest of the rabble fled through the back entrance. A few pushed past Nathaniel. He didn't stop them. Finally, the bar lay empty and ruined, with splintered chairs and tables, the floor awash with ale and coins rolling and chinking from a dropped purse.

The Landlord picked himself up and yelled at Nathaniel, "You've no right here. You're not welcome. Get out of my inn, ruining a good man's business."

Nathaniel barked back, "Allowing your premises to be used for illicit dealings I should drag you into custody and lock you up! If, I were you, I would keep quiet before I change my mind."

The Landlord slunk away behind his bar and watched, a fierce scowl on his face, as Nathaniel and Goliath gathered the goods and took them to be loaded onto their horses.

"What of the money?" questioned Goliath as he picked up the money pouch.

"Give it to the Landlord. He will need it to clean up and replace some items."

Goliath tossed the purse to the surprised Landlord who came out from behind the bar and proceeded to pick up the coinage from the floor.

They safely loaded the contraband, returned to the storehouse and deposited the appropriated goods. It was a good night's work and Nathaniel knew that some of the fiends he would recognize if he ever saw them again.

Days passed and Nathaniel was becoming like a festering sore in the smugglers' sides. The Riding Officer patrolled dutifully and caught many of the blackguards trying to sneak, liquor and precious material into the market place to sell. The thieves were forced to leave their goods and run, or else risk being caught and arrested for dealing in contraband. The Custom House Store was getting fuller every day.

Nathaniel went for his usual weekly meeting with Pritchard, and reported his further successes in sequestering smuggled goods. "We have a fine store, Sir, but it will soon be full to bursting point. The goods should have been moved on by now."

"Nathaniel Brookes, oh my friend," Pritchard was equally frustrated with his lack of manpower and thumped his desk in annoyance. "To tell the truth, Brookes I am still having problems securing armed guards to remove the booty for the Crown and escort them to Cardiff." He continued to bemoan that fact and observed, "You know, Brookes, I am even more convinced that someone high up in the Custom Service in Cardiff is responsible for this shilly-shallying prevarication. We can wait no longer. We are inviting trouble. I don't want all your hard work to go for nothing. That would be a tragedy. I will approach the local Dragoon Sergeant myself to ask for help to guard the cache for the King."

"Surely, they will agree?"

"They are but a small platoon and this is not in their brief. But, I know the Sergeant well. He was one who searched for your father's murderers all those years ago. I am sure he will find a way to help us until we can safely move the goods."

"But what if he won't?"

"Then, my friend we will have to begin moving them ourselves, a little at a time and try not to attract any undue attention."

"But that could take months. And what of my duties and patrols, if we are engaged on this?"

Pritchard sighed, "I know not, Nathaniel. I know not." He shook his head helplessly and in despair.


Nathaniel and Goliath decided to continue their clamp down on known houses that hid illegal goods. They didn't want to let up and they didn't want the smuggling fraternity to believe the Customs men had any troubles. So, they made their plans to raid the Black Dog Inn where they knew more contraband was being stored. But they needed to change their approach. The same method of attack would not work each time and they needed surprise on their side.

The mission to ambush the criminal gang and their nefarious activities at The Black Dog Inn was to be enlightening. The night was good with no wind. The felons had their own sentries on lookout to watch for any trace of the Riding Officer and his man. Nathaniel and Goliath circled around the village to the back of the Inn. They tied up their horses out of view and, with the stealth of assassins sneaked into the back yard without being seen.

Sounds of merriment seeped out from the bar. The inn was busy and loud. Music played, drunkards sang and occasional raised voices flew out. Nathaniel and Goliath drew their pistols and with swords strapped to their sides they counted down and furtively slunk to the rear of the Inn. They silently approached the rear door and tried to open it as quietly as possible. They quietly slipped inside. They crept past kegs of ale and other boxes. The door to the bar was ajar and the air was blue and thick with pipe smoke that churned and wisped. They could see the back of the landlord as he attended his bar but some sort of auction was going on. Phials and fancy bottles of oils and perfumes were on display in wooden caskets. Silas appeared to be conducting the proceedings and taking bids on the items.

Nathaniel nodded at Goliath and they rose up and thundered through the door. Nathaniel shouted, "I commandeer these goods for King and Crown!"

There was a roar of anger as the auction was halted. Silas raced for the front door, overturning tables and chairs in his bid to escape. Nathaniel yelled at him to halt but the order was ignored and the ruffian broke through the front door and fled. Others followed him whilst the rest closed ranks and prevented the Riding Officer from pushing his way through. Goliath stood as if on guard at the back and those that had not seen the Negro giant before stared in horror at the sheer size of the man.

No one was prepared to take Nathaniel on with Goliath at his side. The occupants of the inn became surprisingly calm and hurriedly moved toward the door and their freedom leaving money and contraband to be collected by the King's men. It was another notch of success on Nathaniel Brookes' belt.

Word was spreading quickly about the black giant, who stood shoulder to shoulder with Nathaniel. The cache of snatched illegal goods continued to fill the Customs' Storehouse. Patrons of the drinking establishments infiltrated by the Riding Officer jeered at the King's men, but no one could stop them. They travelled through small villages where locals would shake their fists at them or ignore them and hide away in their own homes. They despised everything Nathaniel stood for and they were terrified of Goliath.

Silas sat in the bar of the recently raided, Black Dog Inn with a crowd of rogues and hooligans. "This Riding Officer must be stopped. I have it on authority that whoever takes his life will receive a purse of a hundred guineas." The rabble leaned forward in earnest. That kind of money could set someone up for life.

"What about the giant?" questioned the ruffian who had wielded the knife in The Boar's Head.

"Do what you have to. There's a reward for him, too, but him we need alive. His master Tobias has something special in store for his escaped slave."

The men guffawed together, "How much?"

Silas smirked, "Oh, I think his capture would be worth at least sixty guineas."

"Aye, but there's more risk with him. A blow from him could kill. It'll take more than one of us," complained Black Bob.

"Then you'll have to enlist some help and catch him off guard," replied Silas.

"The last two that tried that were flung in gaol," argued Black Bob.

"Then you had better be inventive," grinned Silas but the grin did not reach his eyes, which were as cold as a dead fish.

"Any money then would be shared. It's just not worth it," exclaimed another unhappily.

"Oh, did I forget to say? Sixty guineas each! But Tobias feels it shouldn't take more than four of you."

The group muttered together as they digested this information. They swigged down their ale and agreed that something had to be done.

"Someone's feeding them information, of that I'm sure," grumbled Black Bob.

"Then we must keep our ears and eyes open. Now, it seems to me that the Customs House must be bursting at the seams. What say you that we relieve them of a few items?" asked Silas with an evil grin.

The men laughed and huddled together. Silas dropped his voice conspiratorially, "Here's what we'll do. The dragoons are standing guard in two's and changing duty every four hours, but I have learned that two dragoons have been sent to collect supplies from Cardiff. That means, Men, that the storehouse cannot be guarded all through the night. They are taking a chance on that and that risk will be their downfall as we will be ready."

The rogues laughed in glee and clapped each other on the back in excitement. They were certain they would score and be back in pocket.

Silas gathered his fellow conspirators and they set up a watch on the Custom House Store and waited. They studied the store with the two dragoons standing to attention outside.

Time clicked on. The midnight hour struck and the dragoons on guard duty shuffled away, yawning. The smugglers held on until a respectable amount of time had passed and then they crept round to the store. Black Bob kept a look out, whilst Silas wrestled with the padlock and broke it free from the door. He wrenched open the wooden door almost ripping it from its hinges and the men waited.

With a growl of approval the miscreants swarmed in and began to clear the store. Other thieves arrived with donkeys, and bit-by-bit, all the contraband that had been secured for the Crown was removed and spirited away. No one saw, no one stopped them and they disappeared in the dead of night taking their ill-gotten gains with them. The bandits adjourned to the local hostelry having stashed their treasures elsewhere and there they devised plans to defeat the persistent Riding Officer.

The next morning the day was bright, and dry. For once, the sun was shining and warming the lad with its gentle golden rays. Nathaniel and Goliath were headed for Swansea town and port. They cantered across the cliffs and were surprised to see what they thought were two heavily pregnant women struggling along the path. Nathaniel galloped up to them, followed by Goliath. In spite of the skirts and bonnets there was something strange about the ladies.

"Good day to you, ladies. Are you in need of assistance?" enquired Nathaniel. One of them tittered and turned her face away; the other stared at the ground saying nothing. "Come now, ladies. You must have something to say to me?"

The women remained tight lipped and hurried on. One tripped and fell and the skirts and petticoats flew over her head displaying breeches plus a quantity of wool and silk bolts. Her bonnet slipped revealing a balding head. The 'she' was most definitely a he. Seeing the game was up the miscreant dropped his load, picked up his skirts and ran. He was closely followed by the second who threw off his bonnet and dropped his linen booty. The pregnancy thus dissolved and they attempted to make their escape.

Nathaniel stopped to retrieve the contraband and load it onto Jessie whilst Goliath ran the two men down, easily apprehending them. He tackled them to the ground and just as a cowboy would lasso and tie up his cattle, Goliath immobilized the squirming smugglers and waited for Nathaniel to reach him.

The criminal's hands were neatly bound and the two men were led on a rope to Pritchard's Office to be brought before him. Thomas Lloyd was inside, "Well, well who have we here?"

"I know not their names. They were trying to smuggle valuable material under skirts disguised as women," asserted Nathaniel.

"My, my," said Thomas, "They are certainly becoming more inventive, eh Walter?" remarked Thomas looking at one of the captives, a beefy muddy haired man.

"You know them?" questioned Nathaniel.

"Aye. That I do. This here is Walter Coffey and his partner is Daniel Macgrew."

"You're a dead man, Lloyd," scowled Walter.

"Where is Mr. Pritchard?" asked Nathaniel.

"He's out at the store. There was a report of a break in."

"What?"

"Aye, you can kiss that lot goodbye," jeered Walter, unable to keep quiet.

"I fancy you've a lot to say for yourself," accused Nathaniel.

"Let's say that those that did for your father, will do for you," threatened Walter and Daniel laughed in derision.

"I'll say. You better look out, Customs Man," agreed Macgrew.

Nathaniel was filled with a blind fury and moved to strike the felon but Goliath stopped him, "No Nathaniel, he just trying to rile you."

Nathaniel stopped and ordered Thomas, "Lock them up. We'll visit the store." Thomas led the two men who cursed and spat at their gaoler into the cells and locked them up tight. Nathaniel watched them go and defiantly swirled his cape about him and left for the Custom House Store whilst Goliath waited with the horses.

Nathaniel arrived out the back and saw the splintered door of the storehouse as Pritchard was closing it. Nathaniel ran up, "What's happened?"

"See for yourself," said Pritchard sorrowfully as he flung open the storehouse door. "Look."

The room was stripped bare. Everything that had been gathered for the King was gone. Nathaniel swore in exasperation and Pritchard turned to him. "We must catch these rogues. All you've recovered for the Crown has been stolen."

"But, what of the dragoons?" blustered Nathaniel. "Were they not standing guard?"

"Pritchard stumbled in his reply sounding thoroughly depressed, "My... Our resources are stretched, Sir! We can only arm ourselves and soldier on. We guarded night and day until pressed for supplies and were forced to have two leave their post. Someone knew, someone informed and someone took advantage of our laxity." Pritchard let out an exclamation of frustration as Nathaniel slammed his fist against the wall.

"But without the contraband as evidence we have no case. Apart from the last two we have caught red-handed."

"What were they carrying?" asked Pritchard, surprised.

"Wool, silk and linen."

"In sufficient quantities to look as if they were for resale?" questioned Pritchard, hopefully.

"No, a bolt of each," replied Nathaniel.

Pritchard sighed in despair, "That could be seen as for personal use. It will be hard to make the charge stick."

"They disguised themselves as women to evade the law."

"Where are they now?"

"Thomas is putting them under lock and key"

"I will question them and see what we can learn. Thank you, Brookes. Although, I fear for your safety even more now than before; you are aggravating the thieves so much they may well come after you. They will want your blood."

"Let them, I'll be ready." Nathaniel doffed his hat and left.

Pritchard looked after him a worried frown on his face, "Stubborn man. When will he stop?"

# Chapter Fifteen

## The Gentry Rear Their Head

The early morning sunlight stretched its fingers to bless the land and gently touched Cliff Cottage in its warm embrace. The azure sky looked combed with angels' wings and tresses of brushed white hair. The wispy cirrus clouds indicated that it was to be a fine day. The gentle breeze that whispered hardly disturbed the glossy leaves on the trees, which rippled, dappling the ground below with stippled shadows.

Inside the cottage the men were already up. Goliath was in his singlet and breeches trying to shave his sprouting bristles with a cutthroat razor. Nathaniel was busy at the range heating up some of Lily's wholesome stew.

Neither men noticed the small piece of paper that was working itself under the door; neither heard the rustle as paper hit paper and it lodged on top of another envelope half under the mat that must have been delivered during in the night. Neither man saw the shriek of white on the old stone floor half hidden by a dark rug.

Nathaniel ladled some of the warming food into two bowls. He opened a cupboard door and took out some bread, which he deposited on a plate and then the table.

Goliath patted his face dry, donned his shirt and sat down. Not a word passed between them as they filled their bellies and tore off hunks of bread to mop up the delicious juices.

Nathaniel pushed back his chair and dumped his dish in the shaving water that Goliath had left. He strode to the door to retrieve his cape from off the door hook and that is when he spotted the paper and an envelope. He picked them up curiously and opened the door. He looked to the left and the right but saw no one, so he closed the door and returned to his seat where Goliath was just finishing his repast. He turned the papers over and studied them. The envelope was written in a fine script and sealed with the Bevan seal in red wax. Nathaniel placed it on the table and turned his attention to the scrap of paper and unfolded it.

The handwriting was clumsy and it read in capitals: 'RUM AND SPIRITS TO BE OFF LOADED AT MUMBLES HEAD AFTER WRECKING THIS WEEK'. There was no signature. Nathaniel glanced at Goliath, "It seems the rumours were right. There's a wrecking this week and consignments of rum and spirits are being off loaded at Mumbles Head."

"Or someone wants you out of way watching Mumbles when real wrecking some place else."

"That, of course, is always a possibility," concurred Nathaniel. He looked at the sealed letter in his hand, "Now this… this looks interesting."

Nathaniel ripped open the flap with the seal. An embossed invitation dropped out requesting the pleasure of Nathaniel's company at dinner the following night at Sir James Bevan's Manor.

"What it say?" asked Goliath.

"I'm invited to dinner with Sir James Bevan and his young bride, Lady Caroline tomorrow night."

"That good?" questioned Goliath.

"I don't know. He's a wealthy squire, or so I've heard. Call it a gut feeling but I think he's connected in some way to our smugglers."

"How you know?"

"I don't but it's the manor where Jenny worked and there she was badly beaten by the young master, Sir James' son. Of that I'm almost certain, at least things that Jenny has said to me, lead me to believe that the Bevan family is involved somehow."

"You going?"

"Yes, and so my friend are you."

Nathaniel was sitting uncomfortably at the long dinner table in Sir James Bevan's Manor. There were twelve guests in all, a mixture of gentry and men of the cloth. Nathaniel was between Lady Caroline and the Baptist Minister John Rhys. Opposite sat the young Charles Bevan, son of Sir James, who sat imposingly at the end of the table as head of the household. The dinner table proverbially groaned with delicious food. It was laden with the best dishes money could buy and shining silver cutlery was at every place setting. Crystal glass decanters graced the table at intervals filled with rich red wine. A more sumptuous feast Nathaniel had not seen anywhere.

The table was alive with chatter, but when young Charles suddenly burst into laughter, he threw back his head and Nathaniel's eye was drawn to a golden ankh around his neck. Nathaniel narrowed his eyes dangerously as he saw the talisman and noted the conversation reverted to smuggling.

The Baptist minister in full reverential dress expressed his view and one Nathaniel observed was shared by many, "What harm is there? A little baccy for the clerk, some rum for the postmaster?" He looked around him and took a sip from his goblet of wine, "I'll drink to that," he toasted.

"But I thought it was a cutthroat business," interrupted Lady Caroline, "Not colourful young scallywags helping the poorer classes."

Sir James' disdainful tone rang out bringing the table to quiet, "How like a woman," his voice became heavily laced with sarcasm, "My darling, it doesn't become you to have opinions. You just need to look beautiful and maybe echo my thoughts on the matter," he admonished.

Lady Caroline was certainly brave after this derision but she quietly determined to have her say; she came back at him, "I do have a mind, too."

Cynicism then entered Sir James' voice as he observed, "Spirited filly, isn't she?"

Charles smirked and added, "I like that in a woman."

This remark was followed by Sir James admitting, "Like father, like son."

Nathaniel listened closely. He studied Charles' mannerisms and seeing Charles' glass was empty he proceeded to take the goblet and fill it from the decanter.

"We have servants for that, Mr. Brookes," Sir James reprimanded.

Nathaniel ignored the comment but placed the full glass close to Charles' right hand and watched with his eyes focused on the vessel, while the conversation blurred around him.

Charles reached across with his left hand to take the drink, this action caused Nathaniel to tense, a pulse began to throb in his temple, and in the depth of his eyes danger surfaced. The chatter in the room returned to normal and Nathaniel suddenly realized he was being addressed.

"We'd best ask Mr. Brookes. What are your thoughts on the subject?" asked Lady Caroline.

"It's a vicious and bloody trade that has taken many good lives, including that of my father."

A hush fell over the assembled company and Lady Caroline continued, "Ah, I see we are back to smuggling. I was referring to women and their place in society."

Nathaniel remained silent and Charles broke in laughing as he looked for encouragement amongst the other guests as if making an excellent joke, "Well, it is his job. He eats and sleeps it, I suppose."

"I see you are left handed, Sir," pronounced Nathaniel confusing Charles on the change of topic.

"And of what consequence is that?" quizzed Charles.

"I'm just observant."

"You would need to be in your line of work," puzzled Sir James.

"I had hoped you could shed some light on the dealings in this area," insisted Nathaniel and the room fell into an uncomfortable silence.

Sir James bridled and spoke again with exaggerated patience as if dealing with a wilful child, "I have invited you to make new friends Mr. Brookes. Not to antagonise my guests."

Lady Caroline attempted to calm the situation and offered in a placatory style, "If it will please you, Sir and reassure you. We have no truck with smugglers, but nor do we advocate their persecution in the name of the Crown."

Sir James raised his eyebrows in surprise and applauded her, "Well said, my love."

There were rushed words of agreement from the rest of the company and Nathaniel rose, "If you will excuse me. I thank you for your hospitality and company but I have a call to make, a late appointment. I will take my leave of you."

Sir James stepped in, just a little too quickly, "Please stay

Mr. Brookes. Things are just getting interesting." He leaned forward meaningfully, "I was hoping to discuss the renowned corruption in the Customs Service."

Lady Caroline tossed her fine head and this time supported her husband; her smile was dazzling, "Yes, do stay."

Charles looked up from his drink and in a mocking tone added, "Yes, do stay. Your manservant is enjoying a meal in the kitchen. Do you wish to take him away from that?"

Nathaniel was nothing if not indefatigable, he courteously pronounced, "I'm sure there will be another occasion…"

There was an almost imperceptible pause before Sir James replied grittily, "Don't count on it, Mr. Brookes. Don't count on it."

Nathaniel politely took his leave and exited the fine dining room, leaving the bemused company to indulge in a burst of excited chatter. Nathaniel stepped past the butler and another male servant, and hastened to the servants' quarters where Goliath was indeed enjoying a handsome meal. The cook and other servants were stilted in their conversation together, each one was wary of the giant Negro. In fact, none of them had ever seen a black man before and his appearance filled them with major alarm.

Nathaniel called his name and Goliath pushed away his plate, he announced courteously before leaving, "I thank you for very fine meal. My good wishes and thanks to all." He bowed stiffly and left with the Riding Officer.

They faced a wild and stormy night. The wind ripped around them on their mounts and the rain lashed down soaking both men who fought to stay on their steeds in the ferocious storm. They plodded along the cliff top and Nathaniel shouted above the fury of the blistering wind, "The young master Jenny spoke of. The one who maimed her? I'm sure it's Charles Bevan." Goliath raised his head questioningly and Nathaniel continued, "He's left handed." The two men surged forward and kicked their horses' flanks to push them onward to Mumbles Head.

The rain continued to drive down like iron bolts as they rode the cliff path. In the distance they could see flickering lights and a fire.

"Come on!" bellowed Nathaniel through the ferocious weather. They both engaged their heels in their steeds' sides and Jessie flew on through the night followed by Samson. They soon reached the cliff head and dismounted. The streaming rain blinded their eyes as they stared down onto Mumbles beach.

A fortuitous flash of lightning momentarily revealed over a hundred men massed on the beach where a wrecking was in progress. A stricken ship foundered on the treacherous rocks. The villains prepared to swarm over the reefed vessel and plunder the cargo.

The agonised cries of the few surviving sailors reverberated in the storm. They were being overpowered and ruthlessly slaughtered. Their screams reached Nathaniel and Goliath's ears above the screech of the wind and the cracking thunder. They are both spurred on by this horror and the two remounted their horses to ride to the beach and stop the carnage. They galloped along the beach path and rounded a bend to be met by a figure in a black cape; her raven hair flew in the wind. It was Jenny. She looked stunningly beautiful in spite of her livid scar.

Jessie reared up and as the lightning flashed again the silhouette of man and horse struck a terrifying pose against the raging night sky. Jenny cried out, "No, Nathaniel! No! They will do for you as others before you. I don't want to see you die."

Nathaniel slipped from Jessie's back and Goliath dismounted and stood at Nathaniel's side. "Jenny right. We are two against many. We need to live and fight another day," agreed Goliath.

Nathaniel stood woodenly still, torn between his desires to help the wretches being brutally destroyed, his own burning vengeance, and the knowledge of the wisdom of Jenny and Goliath's words. He had no time to decide as they were interrupted by a shout from the cliff path. A horde of cutthroats, from the beach, thronged on the track. They snarled as one body and waved cutlasses and cudgels in the air. One of them gave the order to attack and they ran at the Riding Officer and his man, screaming obscenities in the stinging wind and rain.

Goliath hurriedly leapt on Samson's back. Nathaniel scooped up Jenny and remounted placing her behind him. He glanced down at the beach and saw two wreckers holding a terrified sailor whilst a third slit his throat. What was even more sickening was the fact that it was done slowly and ruthlessly and with obvious enjoyment. The two Wreckers flung the still twitching body into the surf, which turned red with the spilled blood.

Grim faced, Nathaniel turned Jessie and spurred her back up the path with Goliath hot on his heels away from the murdering rabble. They rode hard and long, Jenny's cape streamed like ribbons in the wind as Nathaniel's cloak flapped out like the wings of the raven, the harbinger of death.

As they progressed to the outskirts of the village the wind had eased and the bellowing thunder rolled away to conquer new ground. Jenny cuddled into Nathaniel's back and he rested a protective hand over hers and continued to ride one handed. The urgent gallop had now dropped to a trot and Jenny felt safe. She was unable to dampen the burgeoning love she felt for the Riding Officer and Nathaniel's heart still raced not with the remnants of fear from the flight but with the proximity of Jenny Banwen.

Goliath looked at the pair and nudged his mount to pass them and trotted a few steps ahead of them creating a discrete distance between them.

Nathaniel stopped as Jenny tapped his back. "Let me down here. I'll run to Lily's. She'll help to cover for me. If those men know it was me that warned you…" Nathaniel jumped down and helped Jenny from off Jessie. She studied his face wanting to remember every line, every curve, on his face, "You have to get to my father's cottage. There's a man there, William."

"The one who saved your father?"

"Yes, he has important information."

The night whose anger had now abated allowed the moon to leave the shadows of the clouds. The silvery light bathed Jenny's face in an ethereal glow. Nathaniel was drawn to her and fondly stroked her cheek. Jenny looked down shyly afraid her emotions would spill out and betray her feelings.

Nathaniel held his own in check. She paused a moment and when she raised her eyes once more Nathaniel was already seated on Jessie. He touched his hat to her and both men cantered off into the night.

Back at Sir James' Manor the dinner party was over and the guests had repaired to their homes. Lady Caroline was sitting in front of a dressing table removing her fine jewellery. Sir James came up behind her and slid his hand sensuously down her neck and across her breasts and began to caress her. His breath reeked of alcohol and Lady Caroline reacted immediately. She averted her face and stopped his hand movement. Sir James bristled, his demeanor changed and an unpleasant expression manifested on his face. His tone was less than friendly and carried an obvious threat, "As I said before, my sweet," the 'my sweet' was bitterly emphasized. He continued icily, "You are my property and you will do your husband's bidding."

To his surprise, his feisty wife was instantly on her feet and she whipped around to face him, retorting, "And as *I* said before, I have a mind as well as a body."

Sir James sneered, raised his hand, and with the speed of a cobra he struck her hard and sent her reeling to the floor. Lady Caroline gasped in pain and astonishment.

Sir James leaned over her and grabbed a fistful of her hair and ripped her head back. He put his face close to hers and spoke with deadly intent, "A very beautiful body it is but, only as long as I want it. When it comes to opinions you take your husband's part. Is that clear, my love?"

Sir James dragged his wife to her feet and threw her on the bed. He forcibly pinned her arms above her head with one hand and ripped at her bodice with the other. Lady Caroline bit her lip to stifle a small cry. She turned her head to one side and suffered her husband's pawing and pinching hands and her eyes glazed over as she absented her mind from the violation of her body.

Nathaniel and Goliath arrived at Hywel's cottage as the dawn was breaking, painting the sky with an artist's palette of colour. They jumped off their steeds and tied them up outside. "Is this wise? Our horses here? What if people see?" Goliath made a valid point.

"Take them yonder by the copse, tether them there and then follow me in."

Nathaniel sprang onto the porch, tapped on the door and entered while the big man ran with the horses to secure them safely.

Inside the house Hywel was sitting in a wooden rocking chair by a meagre fire that spluttered and coughed as it licked around the damp logs and kindling trying to get a bite on the wood and feast. A terrified William Johnstone sat at the table in an agitated state. He leapt up when he saw Nathaniel and clutched his hat protectively in front of him. "I didn't know what to do," he said almost tearfully, "Jenny said to wait. She'd find you."

"She did. What do you have for me?"

William licked his lips nervously, "If they find out.... Aah!" he cried out in horror as Goliath entered and joined them, "You!" he accused.

"He won't hurt you. He is on our side, if there is a side in these terrible times. Now speak, man."

William's bottom lip began to tremble, his voice was tremulous as he started to jabber, "They'll kill me for sure, just like they did my son. Oh Lord, what have I done?"

"Tell me what you know. There's no going back now. Please help me stop this madness and murder," pressed Nathaniel.

William swallowed hard and his voice faltered uncertainly, "Rhossili. A farmer's barn. There's a large cache of brandy and tobacco waiting to be distributed."

"Who's the farmer?" William didn't respond and Nathaniel pushed him again, "Who?"

William's voice wavered, "I only know the name Glyn. There, I've said too much already. God forgive me," and he raced out of the cottage, clamping his hat on his head and he pushed past Goliath with an involuntary cry of fear. The man was clearly terrified of losing his life.

Hywel stopped rocking and warned fiercely, "You have what you came for, now leave. Else you'll have more deaths on your conscience."

"Thank you, Hywel. It's a brave thing you've done. I'll not forget."

Hywel grunted, "We're even now, Riding Officer. Now go."

"Where's Jenny?"

"Safe, for now. She's working at the inn."

Nathaniel and Goliath swept out of the cottage and made their way to their horses in the copse. "Will he be all right?" asked Goliath anxiously.

"I hope so, Goliath. I hope so."

"You know Rhossili?"

"I think so, we must strike while we can before they get word of what we are doing." They reached the copse and mounted their horses. Nathaniel turned Jessie and cantered into the countryside, followed by Goliath. He hoped to have the element of surprise with him when he found and met the farmer, Glyn.

# Chapter Sixteen

## Vendettas

Nathaniel and Goliath were cantering along a leafy country lane. They stopped at a signpost, which read, Rhossili 3 miles. Nathaniel took a swig of water from a flask and offered some to Goliath. "Thirsty work, a ride like this."

Goliath grunted in agreement and took a draught from the vessel. "Not long now."

"No, I just pray he's not expecting us and even more that our friends at home are safe."

"May their God be with them," murmured Goliath and then kicked Samson to encourage him on. Nathaniel laughed and joined him and the two competed against each other to the next crossroads.

"You know, for a carthorse Samson can move."

"But not as fast as Jessie," answered Goliath.

"No, but Jessie is built for speed. And it's speed we may need." He looked at the signpost. "This way." And the two men moved off at a comfortable pace. There was no need to tire out their mounts.

At the Black Dog Inn, in a dimly lit corner of the bar, the smoke from clay pipes churned up turning the air blue as the smuggling fraternity met. The usual ruffians sat swigging ale in the bar. None of them paid any attention to the supposedly respectable men that were gathered there. It was a motley collection. Amongst the cutthroats were John Rhys, the minister who had dined with Nathaniel, young Charles Bevan and the infamous smuggler, Knight who did his best to shroud his identity from the rest of them. He jealously guarded his personage. He wore a heavy scarf that he pulled up obscuring his face and his hat was pulled low on his head. Just his eyes were visible. They were all deep in conversation. Occasionally an odd word would carry to another table but the drunken patrons paid no heed.

The minister, John Rhys insisted, "He has to go."

Charles Bevan agreed, "The man's become a thorn in our side. He's causing too much trouble. He irritates the hell out of me."

"All our profits are being stolen by the Crown. All in the name of law and order," continued John. "What is the point of us financing deals if we see nothing at the end of the day?"

"We have to get rid of him. Do we not pay enough in taxes? Are we to be bled dry?"

The assembled company confirmed that they concurred with popular opinion and Charles emboldened by the support, lowered his voice to a whisper, "Then do we have a volunteer?" he eyed up his less than savoury companions. "Come now, who is the man brave enough to take on Nathaniel Brookes?"

One ruffian stuck his chin out and snarled, "I'll take him. And I'll enjoy it. My brother, Walter languishes in gaol because of him."

"I'm with you," said another. "He cleaned out our stash from the drapers. How is a man supposed to make a living? Tax collectors are little more than thieves and no better than those who enforce the law. The world will cheer at one less Riding Officer."

John broke in, "The man's clever. He's too damned successful and he won't be bought by all accounts."

"No," said Charles considering his options carefully, "We need to be careful of him and his man."

"Aye," chorused the rest of the rabble.

"Yes, this Goliath as they call him. He could be dangerous," said the minister.

"We also have to find the spy feeding them the information. Get him and half the problem's solved."

"How do you know it's a him?"

"We don't. But, it's more than likely to be. We need to be on our guard. Get rid of the traitor and Goliath and Brookes will be more easily dealt with."

There was a rumble of agreement around the table but Knight slammed his hand on the wood, making everyone jump. "No!" The hand bore Nathaniel's father's ring. They all stopped and listened in awe to what he had to say.

The smuggler Knight previously silent spoke up although his voice was muffled and disguised. "The slave is mine. A certain Captain Tobias Stone has plans for him. I have a purse of a hundred guineas that I'll give to the man who brings him to me, alive." He stressed the word 'alive'. "As for the Riding Officer, I offer another purse, another hundred guineas. I want him *dead*."

"There's already a prize of sixty guineas on the giant's head. Sixty guineas for each of four men, and another hundred on Brooke's head," growled Black Bob. "I did the father, I can also do for the son."

A ripple of glee went through the villains and Charles probed further, "And the spy?"

Knight ordered, "Find him quickly and kill him or he will be our ruin."

Charles added his weight to the orders, "And I'll pledge a purse for the traitor." There was a pause, "So, gentlemen, are we agreed?" There was much nodding of heads and mumbles of agreement.

"Remember," continued Knight. "This one is clever, better than many we've spent and spat out. We can only get to Brookes through those he cares most about. What do we know? We must pool our thoughts and ideas. Is there anyone that speaks to him? Is there anyone he sees?"

Charles called to the Landlord for another jug of ale and the disreputable band huddled together and discussed their options in low tones. They plotted and schemed and the smoke hung heavy in the air like an omen of doom. This was a very dangerous bunch.

Nathaniel and Goliath had now arrived in Rhosseli and it didn't take long to establish that a farmer, called Glyn Owen who lived on the outskirts of the village had been acting strangely. There had been all manner of comings and goings in the dead of night. This was enough information for Nathaniel and he thanked the plump Parson's wife, who had supplied it, for her candour, and followed her directions to Glyn Owen's farm.

The farmer was returning to his farm with his dog, Bess, after seeing to the sheep. He stood aside to let the horses and riders pass and he was staggered when they stopped and assailed him.

"Glyn Owens?"

"Who wants to know?" the farmer said gruffly.

Nathaniel spoke up, "We are the Kings men and I command you to take us to your barn where your illegal goods will be seized by the Crown."

"Now, why do you think I am guilty of that?" huffed Glyn.

"We have valid information. I warn you, if you are not prepared to show us then my man will apprehend you while your premises are searched."

Glyn peered up and his eyes popped wide when he saw the huge giant on the shire. He weighed up his odds and decided to cooperate. "I never wanted to do it. I had no choice," he blustered. "They'd have done for me and my family."

"Show us," Nathaniel ordered.

Glyn Owens half walked and half skipped down the rutted track to his farm. He led Nathaniel and Goliath to the back of the farmhouse and to a big stone barn.

"Here. It's in here." Glyn indicated the storehouse.

"Open it," commanded Nathaniel.

Reluctantly, Glyn lifted the wooden bar and opened up the barn. He propped the door open with a large stone. Nathaniel jumped down and peered into the dusty barn, which revealed a cache of brandy in kegs, bolts and rolls of cloth, bundles of tobacco, and boxes containing other contraband. All that Nathaniel had confiscated and more was stacked in this barn. Glyn shifted uneasily on his feet and made an attempt to flee. Goliath slipped from Samson's back and caught hold of the farmer who squirmed in his grasp.

Glyn pleaded with them, "I was forced to store it. I swear. If they find it gone I'm a dead man."

"And if you don't tell us who forced you to do this, it's prison for you," admonished Nathaniel.

"Oh please, man, no. Please. I've a wife and children, they depend on me."

"Then give us a name. I'll have these goods sequestered and you arrested or you can go free... Or maybe..."

Nathaniel turned to Goliath a wicked glint in his eye and he winked, "It's been a while since you tasted… how do you like your men served?"

Gyn's eyes rolled with fright as he exclaimed, "What?"

Goliath catching onto Nathaniel's intentions, humorously played along, "Boiled with onions and potatoes." He held onto Glyn with one hand and brought his other hand up to his mouth putting his thumb and first finger up to his lips and kissed them. Then he smacked his lips murmuring, "Mmmmm," as if tasting something delicious.

Glyn, now, became filled with terror and he blurted out, "I don't know any names. Please. A group of armed men battered down my door and demanded the space."

"Who was in charge?" demanded Nathaniel.

"I swear I don't know," protested Glyn.

Nathaniel marched up to the farmer and slapped him hard across the face. The blow was sufficient to draw blood. "Damn it, man! Who was it?" he persisted.

"He'll kill me," blubbered Glyn.

"I'll kill you! I'm here and he isn't," threatened Nathaniel.

Glyn babbled in fear, "It was… the Knight, the Knight, and I heard the name Black Bob," he cried before breaking down into sobs.

Nathaniel stopped short, "The Knight? Here? Let him go!" he ordered Goliath and Glyn crumpled to the floor. "These goods are to be confiscated in the name of the King!" continued Nathaniel. "Secure them and wait for the dragoons. If I find these items spirited away, it will be your head on the block," growled Nathaniel. He mounted his horse and turned Jessie away. Goliath followed.

"Who is man Knight?" questioned Goliath.

"The Knight is the most notorious smuggler of all. He was hunted by my father and others, and is famed for being as cunning as a fox and always one step ahead of the Customs Men. He's the one behind many of the wreckings, murders and the looting of our stores, without a doubt, but rumour had it he had travelled up the Bristol Channel and further afield."

"This Knight, bad man?"

"The very worst. I am sure it was him who did for my

father. I believe he ordered it, and this Black Bob did the deed. From everything I have heard I am convinced of it. But now, now we must get back, Pritchard will have to get the guards out for this or we will lose to the felons again."

Nathaniel and Goliath sped back along the lanes and through the valley and hills until they reached Mumbles. They trotted to the Customs House and Goliath waited outside with the horses. Nathaniel strode in with his news and as usual Pritchard made copious notes.

"We're in luck, Brookes. The men have returned with fresh supplies and thus we have enough dragoons to make the trip." Pritchard momentarily gentled his grim expression, a rarity for him.

Nathaniel's boss took out some parchment and made out a warrant for the goods held at Glyn Owen's farm and he signed it with a flourish. He called a guardsman from the outer office and presented it to him, "Here, your orders, take a platoon and cart. These goods are to be claimed for the Crown. Hurry now, there is no time to lose." The guardsman acknowledged his command, saluted and left.

Pritchard gazed at Nathaniel who stood before him, "You have done well. The goods are to be sequestered and removed to Cardiff under armed guard." For once Pritchard allowed his countenance to change further and he broke into a smile and he praised Nathaniel, "Your father would be proud."

The steel glint in Nathaniel's eye softened as he acknowledged, "Sir." The remark served to bolster Nathaniel's resolve and the hint of emotion he initially felt was now chased away by unfettered determination to continue on his quest. He knew what he had to do next.

Nathaniel took his leave and left the Customs House. He stood tall outside and breathed in the country air and was filled with pride, in his job and his mission. He mounted Jessie and they began to make their way back. He informed Goliath that they would stop on route at The Black Dog. As they travelled through the busy little village people scurried away, and ducked inside houses and shops. To be a Riding Officer was to be an outsider, to be ostracized, and hated for everything the job entailed. But this reaction was much stronger than anything Nathaniel had ever experienced before.

Occasionally, Nathaniel addressed some folk by name, they responded with a gasp of horror at being singled out and dashed away. These reactions were not unusual but much more intense than before. This raised questions in Nathaniel's mind and seemed somehow to fill him with a new energy. They soon reached the Inn where he dismounted and then handed Jessie's reins to Goliath. As he turned to enter the inn a man rushed out and crashed into him. He looked up at the Riding Officer and muttered, "Can't be seen talking to you."

Nathaniel grabbed him by the arm to prevent him leaving and asked, "Why? What's got into folk round here?"

"Unhand me and leave me be," snapped the man, "I'll not end up like William Johnstone." The man squirmed out of Nathaniel's grasp and Goliath slipped down from Samson and blocked the man's escape.

"Let him go," said Nathaniel and the man ran away down the street. Nathaniel stepped up to the Inn and pushed open the door.

A hush fell over the locals when they saw who had entered. Nathaniel walked to the nearest table and tossed down two gold coins, "Those are for the man who tells me where I can find William Johnstone."

A ripple of consternation passed through the assembled men. The Landlord stepped out from behind the bar and addressed Nathaniel, "You're not welcome here, nor will be again, ever."

"My money's as good as the next man's," argued Nathaniel.

"But with the trouble you bring, it's just not worth it," grunted the Landlord.

"Give me the information I seek and I'll leave with good grace. Be difficult and then…" The threat was left hanging in the air.

The Landlord scrutinised the men in the bar to see if anyone would speak. Hearing nothing he moved forward and snatched up the coins. "There will be no one speaking to William Johnstone ever again." All eyes were now focused on Nathaniel and the Landlord.

Nathaniel's eyes narrowed, "And why may that be, Landlord?"

The landlord stared about him and egged on by a few nods of agreement from the drinkers said, "Let's just say, take your search to Mumbles Head."

Nathaniel paused and the patrons whispered feverishly amongst themselves. The word, 'body' was mentioned. Nathaniel set his mouth in a forbidding line, spun around and left with urgency in his step.

The Landlord watched him go and spoke again. Someone better get to the doctor and report this. They may be something on the body Brookes shouldn't see." The statement brought a murmur of agreement and the doctor's assistant, Joshua Meredith, a chubby man, rose, "I'll get Dewi," and he dashed out after Nathaniel.

As Joshua exited he saw Nathaniel had jumped onto Jessie's back and taken the reins. He also heard him say, "Mumbles Head, Goliath. Now." Joshua knew he had to be quick and ran as fast as he could to the doctor's house.

Goliath didn't comment or question, he kicked Samson in the sides and followed Nathaniel and Jessie. They rode swiftly to the cliff top, along the cliff path and out to the beach road. Both reined in the horses at the cliff edge and studied the beach. As they looked down onto the sand and rocks they spied the form of a man.

"I fear the worst," sighed Nathaniel.

"Maybe not," countered Goliath, "You found me and I lived."

"Come on." Nathaniel urged Jessie forward and they made their way down to the cove and cantered along the beach to the body. The ever-encroaching and greedy tide was already nipping at the feet of the man. The sea was relentlessly rushing in and like a hungry lion was devouring the sand. Its jaws were eager to eat the land away and fill the gnawed rocks with surf. They had to hurry, in a few more minutes the still form would be covered and dragged out by the predatory ocean and they too would be cut off from the beach road to the cliffs.

They both slipped from their saddles and Jessie reared up as the waves attacked her feet. Goliath held both horses, now skittish in the rolling waves and Nathaniel turned the man over. It was William Johnstone. He felt for a pulse. There was none. He shook his head sadly and studied the scene of crime when there was a shout. Trundling through the surf on horseback was the local doctor, Dewi Price and his assistant Joshua. The horse was dragging a stretcher of sorts that was getting battered by the water and Joshua was aiming to keep it safe and as dry as he could.

"Step aside," ordered the doctor, "I'll take over from here."

"We'll have to hurry," urged Joshua. "Or the tide will do for us all."

"How did he die?" questioned Nathaniel who refused to move.

"I shan't know that until I get him back to my rooms. By the look of him he's been in the water a few days. It's drowning, I suspect."

"You won't mind if I accompany you to observe," pressed Nathaniel.

"Are you questioning my authority?"

"No. Just ensuring the correct protocol is adhered to."

"How dare you, Sir!" shouted the doctor red-faced.

"I can get a warrant," Nathaniel persisted.

"That won't be necessary," said the doctor grudgingly.

Joshua piped up, his eyes filled with alarm, "We'd better hurry. I don't want to drown like him."

Goliath and Joshua levered the body of William Johnstone onto the stretcher and the horse began to trawl it along the beach. Nathaniel remounted a nervous Jessie and followed behind, leading Samson as Goliath and Joshua struggled to keep the stretcher upright in the rising surf.

The short stretch across the sand was perilous as the savage sea drove in. Dewi spurred his horse on. He, too, was frightened of the rising water. Goliath and Joshua managed between them to control the stretcher and the sea was now mid-calf. It was with huge relief that the motley collection reached the rocks, and then they were able to get a foothold and step onto the path. Difficult as it was, with the wind now beginning to pick up and whip around them, the troop began their trek up the treacherous track to the beach road.

The horse hauled its precious cargo guided by Goliath and Joshua to the summit. Samson, plodding behind Jessie, stumbled and sent rocks and stones cascading down into the foaming water. Nathaniel looked back grateful that he was out of danger from the angry sea. It seemed to be bellowing at them such was the noise, as if it felt a sacrifice had been stolen and snatched from its jaws and it joined with the wind, growling its disapproval and screeched for revenge.

It was no easier traveling the cliff path where the wind gusted more strongly and tugged at hats and capes trying to prise them from off the men's heads and shoulders. But at last they reached the road to the village and Goliath could remount and ride, with only Joshua walking warily behind the stretcher.

People stopped in the street and watched the spectacle. They were unabashed and stared, some crossed themselves in fear and others seeing the Riding Officer scuttled away like cockroaches. The sight of Goliath filled many with abject terror for few had, if ever, seen a man of this size and colour.

The odd procession continued on and the party came to a halt outside Dewi Price's rooms. Goliath aided Joshua in carting the body inside and onto the mortuary slab. Nathaniel bade Goliath to leave and he went to tend to the horses, whilst Joshua disappeared back to the Inn, no doubt to tell tales on what had transpired at Mumbles Head.

Nathaniel and Dewi perused the still dressed body of William Johnstone lying on the marble slab. Nathaniel watched professionally as Dewi made a cursory examination of the dead man.

"It seems clear to me that the man drowned. The sea did for him," pronounced the doctor.

"No doubt that's what the town folk want to hear," said Nathaniel icily.

"What else could it be?" blustered Dewi.

Nathaniel grabbed the doctor by the arms and forced him to look at the body. "Use your eyes, man. Look at the way he's dressed," ordered Nathaniel.

Dewi studied the man's attire before he realized what Nathaniel was referring to, "So, he's careless when he buttons his shirt. Zounds, we've all done that."

"His shirt maybe, but his jacket as well? And look at his belt."

"What of it?" asked Dewi feeling more and more uncomfortable.

Nathaniel pointed at the worn mark in the leather, "It's clear the man does his belt up on *this* notch. But now it's done up three notches too loose."

"Meaning?" questioned the doctor in a puzzled but intrigued tone.

"It's obvious. The man's been dead awhile. He died stripped and was then redressed. The gaseous decomposition blew his stomach out and so his belt had to be fastened on a different notch. Then, he was slung in the sea to make it look like drowning."

"You can't prove that," derided the doctor who was now feeling uncertain of his ground.

"When we undress him for a complete examination and open him up, the contents of his lungs and stomach will reveal the truth. If water is present he drowned. If not, he was murdered," affirmed Nathaniel.

The doctor looked dubious, "There may be another explanation."

"Open him up and we will see," declared Nathaniel.

Dewi, nodded, "All right. Help me with him."

The two men worked as a team and began to remove William's clothes. The doctor gave a sharp intake of breath as the body bore violently livid marks and bruising. Nathaniel examined them and pronounced, "These wounds are pre-mortis."

"Couldn't the lividity of this bruising just have accumulated where the body has lain?"

Nathaniel pointed out some vicious cuts on the side of the ribs, "Here, look at these. These are different."

Dewi took a closer look and his voice filled with admiration, "You know, you could be right."

"Let's proceed. Open the chest cavity."

Dr. Price picked up the scalpel and sliced into the cadaver's thorax. He peeled back the skin and they examined the lungs and then the stomach's contents. There was no water present.

112

# Chapter Seventeen

## Truth

Villagers and town folk had congregated at the steps of the Town Hall. To the side of the building were a small group of dragoons, idly listening to the proceedings but taking no part. The locals were eager to hear what Sir James Bevan had to say. A sheepish looking Dewi Price was at his side and Sir James waved a sheaf of papers. Sir James was just finishing up regaling details of the death of William Johnstone and he concluded, "So you see, the simple fact is that William Johnstone lost his life through drowning." A murmur of approval rippled through the crowd and many looked infinitely relieved.

Nathaniel and Goliath approached on horseback and before the crowd could disperse Nathaniel called out above the chatter, "Pardon me, Sir James, I didn't quite hear the verdict on William Johnstone's death."

At Nathaniel's words, Dewi flushed with embarrassment and looked down at his feet. The crowd stopped their mutterings and watched with interest.

"It's quite clear, Mr. Brookes," pronounced Sir James. "The man drowned."

Nathaniel persisted, "And are you privy to the details of the Post Mortem?"

"I don't have to be. The good doctor here came up with these findings."

Nathaniel fixed his piercing gaze on the doctor, "Is that so, Doctor Price?"

Dewi shuffled his feet uncomfortably and remained silent, turning redder in the face.

"Come on, man. Speak up!" ordered Sir James.

Dewi could only stutter. The words stuck in his throat and he was becoming more agitated, "I... er..."

Sir James demanded again, impatiently, "Well?"

Excited whispering spread amongst the throng as they saw

clearly Dewi's discomfort. They realized that there was more to hear and strained forward to listen.

"Then I believe that I am more able to judge than you. I was present at the autopsy," announced Nathaniel.

This produced a collective gasp of astonishment from the crowd. Sir James turned frostily to the quivering doctor, "Is that so, Doctor? You didn't inform me of this."

Dewi floundered, "I …"

Nathaniel dismounted and led Jessie through the mob, which parted theatrically and he stood at the foot of the steps. Nathaniel was totally calm and as he walked up onto the steps he cut a dramatic figure against the starkness of the Town Hall building and the shrinking doctor now studying the ground in shame.

Nathaniel raised his voice and addressed the community; "I conducted the procedure with the doctor here. I am staggered that he doesn't remember our findings."

Sir James attempted to interrupt but a voice from the crowd rang out, "Let him speak. We have a right to hear this."

There were many shouts of agreement to encourage Nathaniel who ploughed on, "William Johnstone was subjected to horrific torture and left to die. The man had been stripped and flogged. Whoever perpetrated the deed attempted to redress him but didn't take proper care and his clothes were not fastened correctly."

"That proves nothing!" sneered Sir James.

"His body had so filled with the gases of decomposition that his belt was done up three notches bigger than he normally wore it," continued Nathaniel.

Sir James gave a snort of derision but the crowd was listening intently now and Nathaniel gave his pronouncement, "The man had no water in his lungs or stomach. He was already dead when his body hit the water."

There was absolute silence whilst folk digested the words. A few people moved away in acute discomfort and one called out, "Is that right, Dewi?"

Sir James ordered curtly, "Don't answer that."

But, Dewi raised his head miserably and affirmed with a nod of his head before adding, "If I don't tell the truth now I shall never be able to hold my head up in public again."

Sir James, his anger rising turned on Nathaniel and in a tone attempting to belittle him said scornfully, "And what gives you the right to pronounce the cause of death? You're a Riding Officer not a medical man."

Nathaniel calmly responded, "In truth I am both. I first trained as a doctor and practiced as a surgeon in London before I took up my post here. I have the certificates to prove it."

A rumble of confusion rushed through the villagers and an older woman in a bonnet bravely spoke up, "William Johnstone was a good man. He didn't deserve this."

A volley of voices joined her, "No. Nor anyone else."

"There's been too many losing their lives," screamed a young woman with a child.

"Too much secrecy," growled an old man.

"The wrong people are being protected," shouted another.

James looked wildly about him. He was losing control and the rebellion in the masses was growing. He blustered, "Come now, can't you se what this is?"

The woman in the bonnet retorted, "Aye! We can see!"

Nathaniel decided this was a good time to press home his advantage and he strode back to Jessie and remounted, and addressed the angry throng, "You all know where I am. If anyone has any information it will be treated in the utmost confidence."

Nathaniel set off followed by Goliath whist the mob swelled forward toward the cringing doctor and furious Sir James who was frantically trying to justify what he had said. The dragoons, now more alert at the growing tide of complaints mounted their horses and watched carefully.

Nathaniel and Goliath cantered off ignoring the rising hullabaloo behind them. "Let's hope this might prod someone to do the right thing and turn King's evidence."

"Hm, maybe. Me hope it don't get us killed."

"Come on Goliath, they wouldn't dare."

"They dare. They very bad people."

Nathaniel nodded sadly in agreement with Goliath's words before turning his horse to the cliff path and the two continued on their way to Cliff Cottage.

The afternoon sun gently pervaded the room at Cliff

Cottage and dust motes flew in the air like tiny midges. Goliath and Nathaniel were sitting at the table with a huge Bible and Nathaniel was attempting to teach Goliath to read.

The Great Tome was opened at Psalms and Goliath was struggling with Psalm twenty-three. He hesitantly intoned, "The Lord is my shep… herd, I shall not want…"

Nathaniel purred encouragingly, "Good, good."

"I don't understand." Goliath complained.

"Understanding will come later. You're doing well. Continue."

"He make… eth me…" There was a tentative tap on the door. Nathaniel and Goliath looked up and, then at each other. They weren't expecting anyone, and it wasn't like Lily's familiar knock.

Nathaniel called out, "Come in."

The door swung open and Jenny entered looking windswept and in Nathaniel's eyes beautiful. He drew a sharp intake of breath, and then steadied himself to control the turbulence awakening within him. Jenny's face was clouded with sorrow.

"Why, Jenny, what's wrong?"

Jenny's eyes filled with tears, "Haven't you heard?"

"Heard what?"

"No, I don't suppose you would all the way out here."

"What's happened?"

"It's the doctor."

"Dewi? Dewi Price?"

Jenny nodded, "He's dead." She began to cry.

"What? How?"

"Suicide, they say. He shot himself. Some said because of the shame he'd been forced to bear, others mooted that the gun was put to his head to stop him saying anymore."

"That's all very sudden, very sad and very wrong." Nathaniel rose and took Jenny's hand, "Come, and sit a while. I'll get you a drink." He led her to a seat and busied himself with boiling a pot of water. Jenny half smiled at Goliath and looked at the big Bible.

"What is it you do?" she asked indicating the huge book.

"I read," answered Goliath. "Nathaniel teach me to read."

"Oh."

116

Nathaniel handed Jenny a warm drink and knelt at her side. "We must be extra vigilant. I can take no more risks with dear friends' lives," there was a barely imperceptible pause, "Especially yours."

Jenny quickly lifted her eyes and saw something in Nathaniel's eyes that registered in her own heart, but it was fleeting and she was afraid to interpret the signs in case she was wrong.

"Now tell me, Jenny, tell me everything."

Jenny sipped her drink gratefully and said, "After you left the Town Hall, the locals were in a mutinous mood. They threatened Sir James, and the doctor took the opportunity to slip away from the angry crowd. Sir James called on the dragoons and they rode through everyone and used batons hit some to the ground. It was awful, innocent people beaten because they spoke out against injustice. Oh Nathaniel, I am afraid, sore afraid."

Nathaniel removed her drink from her hands and placed it on the table in front of her. He put his arms around her shoulders and hugged her to him and tried to quell the emotions rising within him as he comforted her. "Worry not, Jenny. You have my protection. Mine and Goliath's. We will do our best to see no harm comes to you. You have my word."

Jenny nestled in Nathaniel's strong arms. Here she felt safe but her eyes held a haunted look and a stray tear rolled down her cheek. Goliath stared at the two of them and smiled. He could sense the growing feeling between the two of them.

Nathaniel released Jenny he took her face in his hands, "Jenny, the doctor, Dewi."

"Yes? What about him?"

"What is the family planning? When is the funeral?"

"I heard say it was to be soon. They were talking tomorrow."

"What's the rush?" questioned Nathaniel.

"Sir James said, it would be better for the family to help get over the stigma of suicide. He promised to arrange it all for Dewi's wife."

"I bet he did."

"You don't believe he committed suicide, do you?" asked Jenny as she studied Nathaniel's face.

"Do you?"

Jenny sat upright, "What are you going to do?"

"I'm not sure… yet. But I am not standing by while Sir James Bevan whitewashes the whole affair."

# Chapter Eighteen

## Repercussions

The day was grey, and drab as the rain drizzled down its unrelenting mournful tears. The sky lacked any hint of blue as all colour had been washed away. At the cemetery the gravestones stood stark and miserable against a melancholy church. The atmosphere was bleak and unforgiving.

A sizable crowd had gathered for the funeral of the doctor, Dewi Price, who had been well liked in the village and town. Unusually, both men and women were at the graveside, usually a male domain in Welsh families, but no one sang. No one was in the mood after this sudden and terrible tragedy. A plain casket rested on trestles at the newly dug grave while the pastor performed a basic, no frills ceremony.

Nathaniel stood to one side of the throng, alone. His brow was furrowed as he thought what to do. He scanned the faces of the people closest to the graveside and settled on Sir James who wore his sorry very lightly with the hint of a barely perceptible smirk. He felt Nathaniel's penetrating gaze and looked across at him and they locked eyes.

If Sir James was apprehensive he didn't show it. There was cockiness in his stance, an arrogance belonging to someone who had got away with murder, Nathaniel thought. This was enough to further antagonize the Riding Officer who waited for the simple service to end. He needed to choose his moment carefully.

The service ended and the undertakers prepared to lower the casket into the ground when Nathaniel lunged forward through the mourners and attacked the casket, upending it, tipping it off the trestles. Amid gasps of horror the lid flew off the coffin and the body of the doctor slid out with half his face missing. There was a roar of disapproval at this sacrilegious act and a woman fainted at the sight of the mutilated corpse.

Sir James, exclaimed, "What in hell...?" but he was unable to stop Nathaniel who leapt to the body and swiftly turned the now grotesque looking body face down. Right in the nape of the neck was a round bullet hole and it was plain for everyone to see. Nathaniel announced in triumph, "A strange way to commit suicide." As if to illustrate his point he tried to mime shooting himself in the back of the neck. It was clearly clumsy and virtually impossible.

One man yelled, "That's not suicide. That's murder!" The congregation murmured again and the man continued, "I'd say there's questions to be asked *and* answered," and he threw a dark, challenging look at Sir James. Others then joined in the accusations, whilst Sir James became more uncomfortable. It was then Nathaniel chose to slip away and return to Cliff Cottage where Goliath and Jenny waited.

The soft footfalls of horses' hooves were heard outside and Jenny gathered herself and began to prepare a drink for them all, as they were both eager to hear his news. Nathaniel strode in and acknowledged them with a smile. He began to recount what had happened at the graveside. When he finished Jenny delivered everyone's beverages and sat fearfully, "Never? This is bad. Oh, Nathaniel. I am frightened they will come after you, especially after everything that you have stirred up."

"At least the villagers know the truth and that knowledge alone may bring some folk to my side," responded Nathaniel.

Jenny continued, "We can but hope. In the meantime you will need to watch your back."

Goliath grunted, "I have that. I will let no man hurt Nathaniel."

"But you may not always be there," warned Jenny.

"Enough doom and gloom," pronounced Nathaniel. "I will do what I have to and I feel I am getting close. Today has been a turning point. You will see."

"But at what cost?" murmured Jenny quietly.

Nathaniel drained his mug, "I will not be drawn on this. Suffice it to say, we are gaining support. People are beginning to learn that smuggling is a vicious and bloody trade, not just a bit of extra help to the poor. Now, Goliath," he swiftly changed the subject, "Another lesson?"

Goliath fetched the Bible and placed it between them and searched for Psalm twenty-three. He began reading aloud.

Jenny sat attentively, sipping her drink as she watched and listened to Nathaniel as he taught Goliath how to read. She was in awe of him and his teaching skills.

Goliath stuttered on the word, 'Trespassers' and asked, "What that mean?"

"It's someone that does you wrong," interjected Jenny. "Sorry, I didn't mean to interrupt."

"That's all right," smiled Nathaniel. "Was there something else?" he asked as he saw the earnest look on her face.

"I was wondering, would you teach me? That is, if you are willing."

"You can't read?" said Nathaniel, surprised.

"I never learned. Dad thought it was a waste of time for a girl. Mam was instructing me before she died."

"Then, yes. I would be delighted to teach you."

Jenny flushed with pleasure and rose up from her seat to peer over Goliath's shoulder as he followed the text with his finger. "I have books at home. I will bring them," she said excitedly. "And now I must go. I will stop by tomorrow."

"Please do, at this time, we are usually home. And now we must gather ourselves for patrol. One more verse Goliath and we'll ready ourselves and away. And Jenny?"

"Yes?"

"Be careful. Try not to be seen leaving here. Wait!"

Nathaniel rose and opened the door. He looked about him in all directions and then nodded back at Jenny, "All right. Now hurry. Get yourself away from here as quickly as possible."

Jenny pulled up her shawl and slipped out. Nathaniel watched her back until she was out of sight.

One hour later Nathaniel and Goliath were riding through the streets of Mumbles, headed toward the cliff path. There was a noticeable change in the air. People, who would have been too afraid to speak to him before, politely acknowledged both the young Riding Officer and his man. Gentlemen doffed their caps and the villagers and town folk addressed him respectfully. Few turned away from him.

Nathaniel remarked to Goliath, "I was right. We have reached a turning point," and he dug his heels into Jessie's flanks and they cantered away toward the path, when a man stepped out in front of them and stopped their journey. Nathaniel reined in his horse and halted. Jessie reared up at the abruptness of the stop.

It was the man who had been at the Town Hall and had demanded Nathaniel be allowed to speak. Nathaniel slipped from Jessie's back and listened to what he had to say. The man spoke in low tones and Goliath could not hear what was said although he strained to listen.

"Mr. Brookes, first may I say I don't like what's been happening in our village and neighbouring town. And I am not alone. You are gaining support here, Mr. Brookes."

"Thank you, Mr....?"

"Davies. Bryn Davies."

"You have something for me?"

"Aye, I have." His tone dropped even lower and even Nathaniel struggled to hear. "I heard that Black Bob has got a band of rogues together. It seems that someone in the Harbour Master's Service has informed them that a very rich merchant ship on route from France is due to call at ports this side of the coast. By the time it reaches our waters it will be laden to the brim."

"And?"

Bryn Davies licked his lips and looked about him anxiously, "The ship is supposed to be granted safe passage, but nothing is being done to help."

"And how do you know all this?"

"My brother, Noah, works for the Harbour Master. He says that the information was suppressed. The Harbour Master doesn't know. Noah only found out by accident when he overheard a colleague talking with another ruffian, name of Silas." At this Nathaniel snorted. "Noah daren't report it or he'll be killed. And not just him, these fiends would think nothing of striking at his whole family. Is there anything you can do, Mr. Brookes?"

"When is this to happen?"

"I'm not certain, but Noah thinks it's happening later this

week, but you need to be ready, as it could be any night, even tonight or on the morrow. Can you do something? Those poor sailors."

"I promise you that we will try, Bryn."

"Aye, thank you. There's enough dead already without more blood being spilled."

Nathaniel shook hands warmly with the man who retreated back down the path. Nathaniel remounted.

"What he want?" asked Goliath curiously.

"A merchant ship is going to be travelling through our waters and we are to ensure their safe passage. Word has it the scoundrels are going to attempt another wrecking but I swear, this time they won't succeed. Goliath, we have friends out there. At long last, we have friends."

Nathaniel went onward to the Customs House. He marched inside and was greeted by Thomas, "Good day, Mr. Brookes."

"That it is, Thomas. That it is. The tide seems to be flowing our way. Is Mr. Pritchard in?"

"He's in his office. Things must be improving judging by your excellent humour," said Thomas, smiling.

"And I am hoping things will get even better." Nathaniel strode past Thomas behind the counter and knocked on Pritchard's door.

"Enter," Pritchard instructed.

Nathaniel swept in and spoke earnestly to his senior. "Mr. Pritchard, we have something. At last we have something."

Pritchard looked up from his paperwork and gestured Nathaniel to pull up a chair. "You have your report?"

"More than that, Sir. I have information."

Pritchard's eyes gleamed and he ordered, "Speak."

Nathaniel began to unfold his tale but was careful to omit the names of the people who had informed him. He was determined the names would stay only with him, that way there could be no mistakes.

"Are you sure of this? The information is reliable?"

"I am as sure as I can be. Sir, we have to do something or many men will die."

"If what you say is true…"

"It is, Sir," interrupted Nathaniel.

Pritchard studied his Young Riding Officer's face and pronounced, "I believe you. And fortunately, this time I can do something."

Pritchard began scribbling his orders on a warrant and hardly raised his eyes as he spoke, "I'm arranging for a platoon of dragoons to be on duty on the beach later tonight. In fact I will order them to be there each night this week. Ever since the debacle with the storehouse the powers that be are letting this small platoon remain with us for our exclusive use. Things are changing, Nathaniel and you are reason for this big change."

"So, there is no opposition?"

"No and I am more than happy to be able to provide the men that you require. I will meet you here at six this evening."

"Very well Mr. Pritchard. Six it is." Nathaniel rose from his seat and there was a newfound spring in his stride. The tide was definitely turning. Nathaniel afforded a rare smile and made his way back to Goliath. He remounted and the two men trotted through the village toward the cliff path. They were surprised but delighted to see so many villagers being civil and daring to exchange a few words with them.

Nathaniel and Goliath returned home to find Jenny waiting clutching a pile of books. They dismounted and Goliath took the steeds to the stables whilst Nathaniel went in and settled at the table with Jenny and they began to read.

Goliath entered as Jenny was struggling with a word. He walked behind her and peered over her shoulder. Jenny pointed at the problem word and Goliath said, "Laugh. The word is laugh." Jenny smiled her thanks and carried on reading. Every now and then Goliath would chip in with a word when she became stuck.

Nathaniel then made her go back to the beginning and start again. Her voice was clear and sweet as she recited aloud. Nathaniel was entranced as he watched her face as she read.

Goliath stood back and nodded solemnly in approval of her progress. He shivered slightly and noticed that the fire was on the wane and so he removed himself to fetch some more logs from the wood store.

Soon the sound of chopping wood filtered through from outside and Jenny completed her page of script. Nathaniel applauded and reached across to take Jenny's hands in delight and congratulated her. Her book slipped from her lap to the floor and together they reached down to retrieve it and their faces almost touched. Encased in a bubble of love they did not hear that the chopping of logs had ceased.

Nathaniel held Jenny's gaze with longing and a burning that suddenly met in a blaze of passion. The door creaked open and Goliath strode in carrying logs for the fire. The couple sprang apart guiltily but Goliath smiled knowingly. Feeling embarrassed Jenny gathered her books and hurriedly left, muttering her thanks and goodbyes.

Goliath stacked the wood on the hearth, "Why you not admit it?"

"What?" asked Nathaniel defensively.

"You… Jenny. You meant to be her man and she your woman."

"It's complicated."

"It's natural."

"No, you don't understand." Nathaniel frowned and put his head in his hands, "I am betrothed to another."

"Betrothed? What that mean?"

"I am to marry someone else and have *her* as my woman," explained Nathaniel.

Goliath paused while he considered this, "And you love other woman?"

Nathaniel sighed, "No. But I am duty bound."

"That not right. Why duty?"

"It's expected of me. She is my cousin."

"I think duty in this case is bad thing," pronounced Goliath. "Jenny is for you. She right woman." Goliath proceeded to stoke up the fire. Nathaniel's thoughts whirled in his mind. He knew Goliath was right and he somehow had to deal with it. He knew it would be hard. He had to either explain to Hannah or forget Jenny if he was to follow through on his promise. For the moment he didn't trust himself to make the right decision and he didn't want to tangle with another's emotions. Time was stampeding on and he had to meet Pritchard at six. He took Goliath and they made their way back to the Customs House where Pritchard was waiting along with the dragoons.

"The men have their orders. They are to guard the cove through the night, tonight and each night this week. They are to stand watch to ensure safe passage for any ships that pass. Any movement, any sign and the sergeant here will send a man for me. You meanwhile will continue your patrol. If you spot anything untoward ride back and we will progress from there. Is that understood?"

"Mr. Pritchard, Sir." Nathaniel nodded with satisfaction and urged Jessie forward. Goliath followed and they set off on patrol.

Night fell and drinking was heavy in the Black Dog Inn. Tucked away in the corner was the notorious smuggler Knight who zealously protected his identity. He always dressed in a thick and heavy cape, wore his hat low on his brow and had a scarf that covered most of his face. His identification to his gang was Nathaniel's father's ring with its distinctive monogram. No one ever dared to question the smuggler Knight who spoke in a hoarse whisper to disguise his voice. There were some suspicions amongst the fraternity as to whom this man really was, but no one was inclined to push to find out the truth, as they feared that would result in their death. It didn't pay to be curious. One man did know his identity and that was Sir James Bevan, and he guarded the Knight's secret just as fiercely. The conversation at the table was earnest. Knight and his fellow conspirators guzzled their ale and set their plans against the damned Riding Officer who was damaging their pockets and their freedom to act.

"He must be stopped," rasped Knight vehemently.

"We've said that before," grumbled Silas.

"Aye, on at least two occasions," complained Black Bob.

Another drinker raised his head to pronounce his own judgement. It was Sir James Bevan, who obviously believed himself above the law and despised the humiliation heaped on his head by Nathaniel Brookes, "Get to those he cares most about and he'll be defeated. Of that I am sure. They are the weakness, the chink in his armour."

The others considered his words carefully, Silas, looked slyly about him, "You may be right. It could be a good move. Now let's think, who would he consider a friend?"

"There's Lily Pugh," offered one man with thinning straggly red hair and a scar on one cheek.

"And her imbecile son," smirked Sir James.

Knight grunted in acknowledgement, "That might do the trick. What about Jenny Banwen? I hear she's been seen speaking with him."

"Leave her to me," grinned Sir James, his smile widening cruelly like the grinning maw of a shark, "I have something special planned for her. Something I will enjoy, as will my son."

Silas leered and guffawed. The Knight raised his tankard and the men clashed their pewter mugs together in a toast. The conversation became more raucous and Knight and Sir James rose to leave the rest of the ruffians gorging on liquor. Sir James slipped out of the inn. The Landlord looked curiously after them but Knight halted in the doorframe and glanced back at the Landlord, and stared, willing the man to face him down in a stare, his eyes were glowering like a soul possessed. The Landlord quickly averted his gaze and busied himself wiping down the bar and washing glasses. He did not want to be singled out for scrutiny by the Knight. A thin sheen of sweat broke out on the Landlord's face and he wiped it away nervously. Relief flooded through him when the Knight left the bar.

The Knight joined Sir James outside, who was already mounted on his steed. The night sky was filled with a thousand stars and a wind was beginning to gust rustling the leaves of the trees like a baby's rattle.

"Come to the house, we can talk safely there. The inn has too many ears, and you will be able to enjoy a proper drink," observed Sir James with a jerk of his head at the Knight's scarf disguise.

The Knight agreed, and murmured, "The Landlord, too. He must be watched."

"No. He's no threat. He's just curious about you, as many are. Your very anonymity attracts attention."

"And that inquisitiveness could cost him his life. If I am threatened then so are we all." The menacing truth of his remark sunk home and Sir James kicked his horse in the ribs and sped off into the night toward his manor.

Sir James rode as if the devil was hanging on his shirttails. He clattered into the stable block and shouted for his groom who raced to take the reins and attend to the horse. Sir James forced his way through the rising wind and disappeared into the house. A little while later, the smuggler Knight trotted into the yard and dismounted. Again the groom rushed out and took the reins from this visitor. Knight flipped a coin at the man and growled, "Take care of her."

The groom nodded and hurried the horse away. The outside door to the house opened and Knight was admitted. He didn't see the face from the window upstairs watching the comings and goings in the yard. Lady Caroline stepped back into the shadows her expression thoughtful.

Lady Caroline tiptoed to her bedroom door, opened it a fraction and sat at her dressing table brushing her hair. She paused as she stared at the bruise on her neck from the imprint of fingers that had clutched her throat and her eyes swum with tears. This was not how she had imagined her newly married life would be. She had many accomplishments and was loathe to be treated as a pretty plaything. She began to brush more vigorously as her anger began to build. The rumble of low voices travelled up the stairs and she replaced her brush. Lady Caroline edged to the door to hear the click of another as it shut. She opened hers wide and heard the footsteps of a servant taking refreshment into the drawing room. She stepped back inside her bedroom and pondered a moment before checking the time on the clock. It was nearing midnight.

Reluctantly she disrobed and donned her nightwear. Silently, she stepped out of her room and crossed the landing to the top of the staircase. She paused as the drawing room door opened and her husband emerged with Knight, already pulling up his scarf. Lady Caroline stepped back to avoid being seen and strained her ears to listen.

In the hallway Sir James shook Knight's hand. She could just perceive Knight's muffled tones, "Then we're agreed?"

"Of course," came Sir James' confident answer.

"And your wife?" questioned Knight.

"Let me worry about her," asserted Sir James.

"But if she's a threat…" pressed Knight.

"I lost one wife. I can always lose another," affirmed Sir James glibly.

Lady Caroline shuddered as she heard the words. She prayed her husband would not seek her bed that night. She slipped back to her room and closed the door firmly. Lady Caroline waited by the window until she heard the stride of a horse leaving the yard and saw the man and rider leave. She hastily scrambled to her bed and closed her eyes tightly willing her husband to seek his own room.

Footsteps could be heard mounting the stairs. They paused outside her room. The door creaked open and light spilled in from the lamp on the landing. Satisfied his wife was indeed asleep, Sir James closed the door quietly and headed for his own bed. As the door clicked shut, Lady Caroline opened her eyes wide and sighed with relief. She thought quickly. She knew what she had to do.

The dragoons were assembled on the cliff tops watching and waiting. All was still. The moon was out and the heavens were filled with stars. One of them spat on the grass and grumbled, "This is a waste of time. There'll be no wrecking tonight. The air is too calm and still. The sea is hardly moving."

"That's right," complained another, "And there is no sign of a ship on the horizon or anywhere in view. A wasted night."

"We have our orders," muttered the sergeant.

"Aye, are we to have a week of this? Standing about and doing nothing?"

"And as I said, we have our orders. We move back at first light," continued the sergeant.

The dragoons continued to stamp their feet and mutter disagreeably as they longed for the shift of duty to end.

# Chapter Nineteen

## Friends in High Places

Jenny sang happily as she prepared and cooked a meal at Nathaniel's range. Her eyes shone brightly with the expectation of love and hope for the future, hope that had been denied her for too long and she was feeling relaxed and easy within her self until there was a frenzied knocking at the door, which startled her almost making her burn herself on the cooking pot. Her easy demeanour vanished and she approached the door apprehensively.

A burst of urgent knocking came again and Jenny took a deep breath and opened the door to reveal Lady Caroline Bevan's, Lady–in–Waiting, Martha, who looked as surprised to see Jenny as Jenny was to see her.

"Oh… I was looking for Mr. Brookes," stuttered Martha.

"I am afraid Mr. Brookes is on patrol," Jenny responded nervously, half expecting someone else to burst past Martha and into the cottage.

Martha stood there awkwardly uncertain what to do.

Jenny felt a little more confident and noticing the maid's agitated state inquired, "Can I help, Martha?"

"Um… I have a message, a very important message for Mr. Brookes."

"I'll see he gets it," said Jenny extending her hand.

Martha shifted uncomfortably from foot to foot, "But, Jenny, I have strict instructions to give it to no one except Mr. Brookes himself," she muttered nervously.

"And I repeat, I'll see he gets it," said Jenny more forcefully and she took the envelope from the reluctant woman.

Martha apologized, "Oh Duw, if only I didn't have to be back. It's just… just… I daren't be missed." Her eyes searched about her anxiously.

Jenny stepped forward and took Martha's hands. She said gently and reassuringly, "I promise you, Martha. This is in safe hands. Honest. Now go. Hurry back before anyone notices your absence. And don't mention you have seen me here. Promise?"

The Lady-in-Waiting nodded submissively and made her way back down the path and hurried away, pulling her shawl about her. Jenny peered about her and watched Martha's retreating figure before returning inside. She turned the sealed message over and fingered the red wax crest of the Bevan Family before placing it on the table and continued with her cooking.

It was late afternoon before Nathaniel and Goliath returned and they were both ready for the wholesome meal that Jenny had prepared. They sat at the table and Nathaniel, picked up the letter, "What's this?"

"Martha, Lady Caroline's Lady-in-Waiting delivered it. She was under strict instructions to leave it with no one but you." Nathaniel raised his eyebrows questioningly. "She was terrified. Terrified of being missed. I persuaded her to leave it with me."

"Best see what it says, then." Nathaniel broke the seal and began reading the missive. Jenny and Goliath watched with concern.

"What it say?" asked Goliath.

"Apparently, the lady fears not just for my life but also for her own."

Jenny gasped, "I have never met the new bride, but I have heard she's a good woman. If she's afeared then she has good reason. I know Sir James and his son, only too well, devilish brutes that they are. We all thought he did away with his first wife by his own hand...What are you going to do?"

"I don't know... yet."


Later that night an angry mob of mutinous men gathered in the village with their faces hidden, like the Knight, disguised by heavy scarves, brandishing fiery torches. The man with a cast in his eye, recognized as Silas, was stirring the ruffians to anger.

"Are we going to put up with our income stolen for the Crown? Are we going to tolerate our friends tossed into gaol? Are we going to accept informers in our midst that put our lives and livelihoods in jeopardy? We must do something about it. Do something about it, now! As we speak, dragoons wait in the cove giving safe passage to our future. Are we going to put up with it?"

The rabble shouted their agreement vociferously. Carried along with the sway of the crowd they yelled in anger and Silas nodded, pleased at their reaction. He turned to the throng and raised his hands to quiet them, "Then, *what* are we going to do? Who are we going to seek out? Remember, we need to root out The Riding Officer's friends; that's how we'll get to him. That's how we will break him."

One burly thug with a bushy beard threaded with gold shouted out, "Lily Pugh. She gave shelter to the man. He rents from her."

There was a babble of agreement. "Yes, I'm sure he counts her as a friend."

"Aye, some say she takes food to him," roared another.

"And her boy. He shouldn't ever have been born. We'd be doing them a favour," screeched a short stocky ruffian. There was more nodding of heads and shouts of agreement.

The cultured voice of Sir James broke through the babble, "Then what are you waiting for? Let's get rid of the traitors and do away with Nathaniel Brookes. We'll have no more Riding Officer."

The unruly crowd clamored their support and surged forward. The lynch mob started down the road their torches blazing and pushed forward to the mountain path leading to Lily Pugh's cottage. They were bloodthirsty for revenge and like a mindless stampeding herd of cattle, they came together as one body, and they marched on.

Sir James fell back from the group and watched them parade up the hill and smiled superciliously. He was delighted to be striking a blow for the smuggling fraternity. He retreated to his horse and sped off to his manor. He needed to be home whilst this pillage went on.

As Sir James rode off and the brutish thugs had marched on, three villagers stepped out from the shadows. They had heard the cry for vengeance. All were angered by this brawling pack of marauders and wondered what to do.

"It's not right," whispered Dai Meredith. Lily Pugh is a good woman, good and true."

"Aye," agreed Joseph Evans, "It was them that did for Bill Pugh, them's the ones that made her David simple."

"You're right. And he's not a bad lad, just a bit twp," agreed Talfryn Jenkins.

"What do we do? We are only three. I can't risk my family by wading in."

"No, more than likely they'd do for us, too."

"Only one thing for it."

"What's that?" asked Dai.

"I'll rouse the villagers. There's safety in numbers. Get a group of us together. Get to Lily's," pronounced Talfryn.

"The Riding Officer. We have to warn him," urged Joseph.

"You do that, I'll start here," said Talfryn.

"But we'll have to pass the Pugh's," warned Dai.

"No, we'll approach from the other side," asserted Joseph.

"Then we may be too late."

"That's a chance we have to take, come on." Dai and Joseph hurried away to get their horses as Talfryn began hammering on the doors of those he thought he could persuade to help.


The lights on the hill flared and flickered dangerously. The crowd became more agitated as they neared Lilly Pugh's cottage. They were now chanting and shouting together, "Death to the traitors! Burn them out! Death to the traitors! Burn them out!" They screamed it out over and over again.

Inside the cottage, Lily and David were having a bit of supper at the table. David looked up from his meal as he heard the rumbling roar of voices, "What's that, Mam?"

Lily stopped and listened, "I don't know, bach. You finish your food and I'll go and see."

Lily stepped up from the table and walked to the door. She opened it and peered out into the night. She could see the flaming torches coming up the track and hear the chanted threats closing in on her dwelling. Lily retreated inside, drew the curtains and bolted the door. She looked about her anxiously.

"What is it, Mam?"

"I'm not sure. There's a pack of murdering thugs swarming up the track. I don't know if they're headed for Nathaniel's cottage or us."

"If they are after Nathaniel, we must warn him."

"No, we don't have time. Best put out our lights. Let them think there's no one home."

David scraped back his chair and turned down the oil lamps. They crouched down by the table hoping the mob would pass them by. To their horror the throng congregated outside her cottage. The light from the torches flickered through a chink in the curtain. David began to wail, "Make it stop, Mam. Make it stop. I don't like it."

"Hush now, be quiet, there's a good boy."

David began to rock back and fore on his haunches crying quietly. Lily crept to the window where the glow from the fire seeped through. She saw the gang of ruffians, their faces hidden, brandishing the flaming torches. She tugged at the curtains to close the gap but not before one of the rabble saw her frightened face at the window.

"She's there. The traitorous bitch is inside!" yelled Silas.

The vicious mob began to shout and hurl obscenities at the two of them inside, who cowered down on the floor.

A tall figure stepped forward carrying a beam. He and another man used this to bar the door. The bearded smuggler and another stocky brute did the same at the back of the house. Now, there was no escape.

Lily wrapped her arms around her son and cradled him to her as the mob surged forward and used their torches to light the kindling stacked on the verandah. The flames greedily devoured the wood and danced devilishly up the wooden porch in demented fury engulfing Lily's cottage.

Screams could be heard above the crackle of the flames.

Dai and Joseph rode their horses hard as they could across the cliffs to Nathaniel's abode. Dai leapt off his horse and ran to the door and frantically hammered and called, "Mr. Brookes, Sir!"

The door opened and Goliath filled the frame, Joseph slipped off his mount and joined Dai at the door. "Please, Mister we need to speak to Mr. Brookes."

Dai turned to Joseph, indicating the skyline, "I fear we may be too late."

Goliath called back, "Nathaniel!"

Nathaniel came to the door and saw the two villagers. Dai shook his head sadly and pointed to the glow in the distance.

"Lily?" questioned Nathaniel.

"We overheard a gang of men. They said they were going to torch Lily's house."

"Aye, with her and David in it," added Joseph.

"We didn't know what to do," muttered Dai.

"So we came to you," finished Joseph.

Nathaniel and Goliath exchanged a look, "Get back to the village. Get help. We need men brave enough to come and fight the fire," ordered Nathaniel.

"Talfryn's already doing that," said Dai.

"Then follow us." Nathaniel and Goliath rushed to the stables. Moments later they were astride Jessie and Samson and they galloped off toward the red light in the sky. Dai and Joseph sped off after them.

# Chapter Twenty

## Outrage and Revenge

A mass of villagers bravely swarmed up the hill toward the cowardly thugs who on seeing the approaching army of people tossed some of their torches into the thatch. They hurled their fiery lights at the porch. One window smashed and flames quickly snapped at the curtains and began to eat them away. Seeing this as victory the mob hurriedly scattered into the night.

The villagers struggled valiantly to douse the out of control fire that licked the thatch, that was spluttering and cracking as the straw first smouldered and then fiercely blazed. One brave soul tried to get to the front door and move the beam to get in and rescue the couple but the searing heat beat him back. His hair singed and his skin burned and it was to this chaotic scene that Nathaniel and Goliath arrived. Nathaniel cried out in horror and anguish, "Noooo!"

Nathaniel jumped down from Jessie and he too, tried to break into the house but was knocked back by the flames. He managed to dislodge the beam across the door, scorching his clothes and hand in the process.

Nathaniel's agony at his friends' plight was plain for all to see as a cry ripped from his belly, "Lily!" Then the rest of the windows blew out. Glass shards flew and people ducked.

The misery of the courageous villagers was obvious as they watched helplessly whilst the unrelenting fire gleefully destroyed Lily's home.

The first light of dawn mingled with the smoke and fearsome, raging glow of the arson. No one moved, no one spoke; the desperation and hopelessness was etched on the faces of everyone there.

They watched, as timber became charcoal and one wall crumbled. There was nothing more to be done. The cottage was a charred mass of glowing embers. The villagers who had worked so hard to defeat the flames were in total despair.

Nathaniel and Goliath stepped forward into the cottage and gazed in sorrow at the remains of Lily and David lying in a blackened, petrified embrace. Nathaniel's head bowed in abject misery, "They didn't stand a chance." He looked up at Goliath and swore vehemently, "As God is my witness I'll stand no more."

Goliath's face registered alarm and he searched the faces of the villages, standing with faces downcast. Nathaniel eyed him questioningly, "What is it?"

"Jenny," muttered Goliath.

"What? Where?"

"She not here."

The meaning behind the words became clear and Nathaniel's brows knitted together, his jaw muscles tightened and a pulse began to pound in his cheek. As one the two men made a sprint for their horses and set off at a thunderous gallop. The mourning villagers watched in confusion as the Riding Officer flew away with his man stride for stride.

Nathaniel and Goliath filled with urgency and trepidation sped along the road skirting the cliff tops. The horses' hooves pounded along the ground in a regular rhythm accentuating the dire need to race at an almost excessive pace.

The Banwen cottage came into sight but even from a distance something did not look right. The windows had been shattered and the door half torn off its hinges. They leapt out of their saddles even before the horses had stopped moving. For a man of his huge size and bulk, Goliath moved very nimbly. He outpaced Nathaniel and arrived at the splintered door first. He spun around with the agility of a gymnast and caught hold of Nathaniel preventing him from entering the broken hovel.

"Let me go, man. What's got into you?" blustered Nathaniel.

"Please," Goliath pleaded, "Me go in first."

Nathaniel started to question, "What?" And then as realization dawned he understood that Goliath was stopping him from entering because he was frightened at what they might find. Nathaniel sobbed out his agony, "Noooo!"

The two men struggled together. Nathaniel's efforts to thwart Goliath were futile.

Goliath grasped his friend by the shoulders and shook him to make him listen, "Please!" he bellowed.

Nathaniel appeared to nod in acquiescence and Goliath albeit slowly but foolishly released his grip, and started for the broken door.

Quick as a lightning bolt Nathaniel lunged forward but Goliath was faster. He reached out swiftly and grabbed his friend by the collar and stopped Nathaniel where he stood.

Reluctantly Nathaniel submitted, "Very well then."

Goliath approached the threshold, pushing aside the remains of the shattered door.

The silence was eerie as Goliath crossed the door durn. He gazed about him in horror. Everything around him was destroyed, shattered and torn. The scene of devastation filled Goliath with cold dread. The cooking pot had been kicked off its hook and was lying in a pool of stew. The fire in the range was all but dead.

Nathaniel was at Goliath's back and he cried out in trepidation, "Jenny?"

A faint groan was heard from another room. Nathaniel called again, this time an element of hope had entered his voice, "Jenny!"

The friends rushed in and discovered Hywel, half sprawled and half propped up against the wall. There was blood everywhere. A low moan whimpered out as Hywel clutched his stomach with both hands as his life force ebbed away. His blood spurted weakly from between his fingers.

Nathaniel and Goliath hurried to his side and gently attempted to lift him onto the bed. Goliath grimaced as he saw Hywel's stomach had been ripped open and his intestines protruded. Goliath shuddered in disbelief. "They opened him up," he said incredulously.

As they laid Jenny's father down, Goliath covered the dying man with a quilt and pulled it up to his chest.

Nathaniel questioned gently, "Where's Jenny? What happened?"

Goliath shook his head, "He lost too much blood. He can't speak. Not even understand you."

"I must know," pressed Nathaniel. "Please Hywel. Where is she? Tell me."

Hywel shuddered in agony, his body gripped with the rigor of approaching death. He began shivering involuntarily and let out a pitiful yelp. Nathaniel lifted the quilt to inspect the injury and saw clearly again that there was nothing he could do. His head dropped. Goliath replaced the cover and laid his ham-sized hands on Nathaniel's shoulders kindly offering him some comfort.

"He in God's hands now, Nathaniel. Let him be. Let him die in peace."

"But his daughter…"

At the mention of this Hywel struggled to breathe Jenny's name, "Jen…"

Nathaniel, persisted, but gently, "Hywel, Where is Jenny?" He cradled Hywel in his arms.

Hywel sighed, "Fy merch gwael."

Goliath looked puzzled then Nathaniel translated, "My poor girl." He focused on Hywel, "Tell me, Hywel, what… what has happened to Jenny?"

"Yn yr ogofâu, Wreckers Way" he wheezed.

"The caves? What about the caves?"

Hywel coughed and took a mouthful of air, his eyes opened wide and he grabbed Nathaniel's hand, "Bevan… get the bastards for me…" His voice trailed off and he sighed his last. The light went out of his eyes and he flopped forward.

Nathaniel choked back a sob as Goliath murmured softly, "How many more must die?"

Nathaniel steeled himself before closing Hywel's eyes and swore, "Two more, for sure. If they harm a single hair of Jenny…."

Goliath rose and stepped through the debris of broken furniture and turned at the door. "Come. Leave. We can do no more."

Nathaniel reluctantly rose from Hywel's side and followed Goliath, the front of his shirt and hands were now smothered in blood.

# Chapter Twenty-One

## Abduction

The musty smell of damp assailed Jenny's nostrils as she began to come round. The caves walls were dripping with water and ink black; they rose up to disappear in the darkness. The mouth of the yawning cave was lit up by the morning sun. A group of men silhouetted in the gaping maw of the cavern shuffled along the sand and shingle as they half dragged, half carried a squirming Jenny as she gradually regained her senses and struggled against her captors. She remembered that they had dragged her to a narrow path on the cliff face, which led to the mouth of the cave about a hundred feet above the sand; a wisely chosen spot that was difficult to access. She recalled being struck on the head and the taste of blood in her mouth. Jenny was very afraid. Her fear grew as she remembered what had happened at her house.

Violent images thrashed through her mind as her father's screams resounded in her head and when she flew out from the back room to Hywel's defence she was forced to the floor and a boot thudded in her back pinning her down. She received a vicious kick in the ribs and a dirty rag was shoved in her mouth. Then her hands were bound and she was bludgeoned on her head until she passed out.

Now, she could see she was trapped in the Wreckers' Cave and terror gripped her heart. She wondered if she would ever see Nathaniel again. That thought alone was enough to bring a sob to her lips.

The wreckers flung the trussed young woman to the sandy floor and she screamed in pain, a scream that reverberated and echoed in the rocky hollow. Silas stood over the cowering young woman and laughed cruelly, "You can cry all you want in here, girl. There's no one to hear you."

Jenny snatched a breath and spoke defiantly, "Where's my father? What have you done to him?"

Silas sneered, "Don't you worry yourself for your dad.

He's rejoined your crazy mother by now or gone to hell." He laughed cruelly.

Understanding washed through her and she spat forcefully, "Bastards!"

Silas' hand came crashing against her cheek and a pitiful wail escaped Jenny's lips.

"No need to cry. We'll reunite your whole family before the day is out," he uttered scornfully. "And your passing will be none too pleasant. You'll be begging me to finish you by the time we're done."

The hooded Knight stepped out from the shadows with a curt warning to all the wreckers assembled. "I'm not denying your fun with the wench but leave enough of her for the Rider to identify her. That's how we will break him."

The men began to converge on Jenny as the Knight turned away.

Silas threatened, "Well, my beauty. Well, we'll not do away with you yet. We have manners." The rest of the rabble roared in excitement as Silas added, "One at a time boys, one at a time. We're not animals." He laughed and Jenny screamed as one fat, sweating wrecker began unbuckling his belt.

Her terrified cries mingled with the shriek of seagulls that flew on the wind outside the cave and her cries disappeared into the air and the ether.


Nathaniel and Goliath thundered along the cliff path their cloaks streaming behind them in the wind, the urgency was apparent in the lengthening horses' strides. Gannets and other sea birds mewled and called above as they circled in the sky.

"Where are these caves?" shouted Goliath.

"I don't know. The coastline is littered with them. We need local knowledge. With Lily and Hywel gone we will have to ask the villagers."

"If they speak to us. They may be too frightened," called Goliath.

The two riders soldiered on and eventually reached the outskirts of the village and meet an old wizened farmer dragging a small handcart. They pulled up abruptly and Jessie reared up and whinnied. The aged farmer raised his arm as if to protect himself.

"Whoa, Jessie, whoa!" Jessie snorted and stamped her feet. "Sir, no harm meant. Please can you give us directions to the caves?"

"The old man scratched his head, "Now you're asking something. Caves? There's many along this coastline, Pwlldu, Mumbles, which do you mean??"

"I'm not sure. Old smuggling caves, I think," replied Nathaniel.

A flicker of fear glimmered in the old man's rheumy eyes, "Can't help you then. Sorry," he muttered and dragged his cart on, ignoring the two riders.

Nathaniel sighed long sufferingly, "When one won't speak, another might," he proclaimed resolutely.

The continued on their way and met a group of the villagers who had desperately tried to help extinguish the flames at Lily's cottage. They were reverently wheeling a covered wagon toward the village cemetery. A gust of wind ruffled the blanket covering the charred remains of Lily and David; one of the women hurriedly rearranged the covering to make sure decency was maintained. She shouted up to Nathaniel, "They deserve a proper burial in a church yard."

Her companion looked up and nodded agreement, "Aye. Pyres are for heathens not God fearing people like us."

Nathaniel's bearing stiffened and he promised, "Whatever the cost for the funeral, I'll cover it with my own coin."

"She was a good woman, Lily. She was," continued the woman.

Nathaniel tried to use the moment to help him in his quest, "Tell me, where would the wreckers hide out around here? Caves maybe? Close by?"

The crowd fell silent. There was much shuffling of feet as they averted their eyes and faces. Nathaniel became more incensed at their continued silence and avoidance and rasped angrily, "Speak! Have you not had enough of the bloodshed and slaughter? Do you want more?"

The woman at the wagon blustered, "We have our own families to care for. We cannot risk…"

Nathaniel interrupted her, "Soon there will be no one else left in the village except for them. They've also slaughtered Hywel and taken Jenny. I have to find her.

142

Please." Nathaniel's sincerity of his plea was plain for everyone to see.

A man stepped forward and removed his hat. He was unable to hold Nathaniel's gaze and kept looking away, he said sheepishly, "They could be anywhere. The fiends roam the cliffs and coves even in the darkness of night. They know this coast and every nook and cranny like they know the insides of their own houses. It will be hard."

"I know," said Nathaniel in agreement, "But, where… where would they be likely to take a prisoner or hide someone? Please think."

The man spoke again grudgingly, "Well, I have heard…" He stopped.

"Go on, man, don't stop now."

"Look, and you didn't hear this from me." He looked about him nervously, "William Johnstone."

"What about him?"

"The last anyone saw of him alive was Yn yr ogofâu. Wreckers Way"

Goliath jumped in excitedly, "That what Hywel said."

"Where is this place? How do I get there?" pressed Nathaniel.

"In the caves? I'll show you," offered another called Ben Beynon. "I've had enough of the murderous goings on. It's not right that innocent people are dying."

The crowd made encouraging supporting noises, "Ben's right. Something needs to be done and quickly."

"Best go prepared," shouted another.

"Aye. He's right," agreed Nathaniel. "We need to arm ourselves. Come on."

Nathaniel, Goliath and Ben made their way to the Customs' House and raided the arms store. They each equipped themselves with a sword and a pistol and Nathaniel signed the book, for checking out firearms, waved at them by a blustering but insistent Thomas, who was still on duty as the overworked Mr. Pritchard had retired for the day.

Ben led the way on his wagon, "You'll have to leave the horses. Tie them up safely. I'll tether my horse and wagon by here, too. The way down is narrow and treacherous for those that don't know it."

143

"Best take strong rope if way as difficult as you say, we don't want us to fall," urged Goliath.

Nathaniel nodded agreement and took three coils of rope from Jessie's pack and together the three men began their trek to the cave.

Nathaniel and Goliath followed on Ben's heels. Loose stones kicked by the men rattled down the side of the cliff to the heaving waves a hundred feet below.

"Careful now," warned Ben. "We should see the entrance beyond this next bend."

"They could not bring anyone down this path against their will," observed Nathaniel.

"No. They would have used a different way that's much too exposed, even though it's easier. We'd have been spotted had we taken that way and been picked off one at a time. Then they would have won the day."

Impatient, Nathaniel squeezed past Ben. The man was telling the truth. Nathaniel looked furtively around the bend. The cave entrance looked like a monstrous gaping hole, slightly lopsided, a hundred feet above the rolling waves and about thirty feet from the top of the cliff. The path to the cave was little more than a ribbon and hugged the side of the cliff right up to the entrance. Two of the armed ruffians stood guard at the cave entrance.

Nathaniel stepped back and muttered, "This is going to be difficult. What now?"

Goliath closed up to Nathaniel and peered over Nathaniel's head to take a look. "Difficult? No, not possible, I think. Look, see, even weak man standing on own could see off entire army coming down path. We don't stand chance, be picked off one at time."

"But, what about Jenny? ...Goliath, we have to try," insisted Nathaniel.

"There must be way to get in," decided Goliath and craned his neck. His eyes searched along the top of the cliff above the cave entrance.

Ben interrupted their thoughts, "There isn't. It's either down this path or up the Wreckers' Way."

Goliath began to grin and asked, "You ever hunt for sea eagles' nests?"

Puzzled, Nathaniel responded curiously, "No, why?"

"Because if had, you learn fast how to 'run' across cliff face. Come. I know what we need do." Goliath turned back down the path and beckoned Nathaniel and Ben to follow.

Ben looked incredulously, "Run across the face of a cliff? The man must have lost his reason!"

"No," said Nathaniel slowly. "I trust him and if he has another way, then I'm prepared to try. Come on."

Sounds drifted up on the wind that emanated from the cave. This spurred Nathaniel on as he could only imagine what was happening inside and he didn't like what he could hear. Ribald comments and much jeering were carried on the breeze.

Inside the open mouthed gap, Wreckers were passing a large earthenware jug around. They each took copious swigs of rum. Every now and then they broke out into drunken laughter. At the back of the cave lay Jenny. She sat there pitifully, hardly recognizable as the winsome girl who had caught Nathaniel's eye. Her clothes had been torn, and were in tatters. She clutched what remained to her trying to cover herself up as best she could. Her face was a mask of blood where she had been battered cruelly by the thugs. What could be seen of her milk white body was bruised and cut. Jenny had drawn her knees up protectively to her chin and she shivered miserably.

The shadow of a wrecker fell over her. Jenny felt his presence; she lifted her eyes and cowered and whimpered as he loomed above her. Jenny couldn't help herself and began to cry.

One of the wreckers on duty at the front of the cave retreated inside and stood to watch what humiliation Jenny was to suffer next.

Nathaniel, Goliath and Ben had now reached the grass on the top of the cliffs. Ben looked down at the steaming surf, "You must both be crazy," he lamented. "To run down the cliff, it's impossible."

Goliath finished tying the thick rope around his own waist and turned to tie another around Nathaniel. "You don't want come, you stay. But three is better than two," he addressed Ben.

"You *are* mad," exclaimed Ben, his eyes widening at the thought of them swinging over the cliff into the air and then trying to gain a footing on the cliffs and walk down them.

"My thoughts exactly," pronounced Nathaniel.

"Desperate things need desperate ways deal with them," proclaimed Goliath.

"Who taught you that?" questioned Nathaniel.

The reply came hurtling back, "You did, friend. Now," he looked Nathaniel in the eye, "You ready?"

Nathaniel swallowed hard, "As I ever will be," and fiercely nodded. "Let's do it. But remind me, a little knowledge is a dangerous thing that's if I live through this!"

Goliath laughed heartily and winked, "Right. We go, now! Count five then follow."

"I hope my counting is better than yours," said Nathaniel cheekily remembering the night at the inn.

Looking braver than he felt Goliath swung over the cliff face and using the rope to brace himself he virtually ran along the cliff face toward the top of the cave. Ben gasped in astonishment having never seen anything like it before and then Nathaniel pronounced, "Five!" And he, too, dropped over the side of the cliff.

The now very drunken wreckers were still swigging rum and turned every now and then to look at Jenny, threatening her with lewd comments and gestures. Jenny was terrified but a glimmer of her fighting spirit was still present. The wrecker who had begun to torment her by pawing at her clothes, received a swift kick in the groin from Jenny in a last ditch attempt to save herself.

He roared in anger and pain and fell back on the floor. Silas rose unsteadily to his feet and swaggered toward her.

Jenny cried out, "No! Please, NO!"

Her plaintive voice filtered out through the cave entrance and Nathaniel stopped short. "That's Jenny. She's alive. Quick, hurry!"

Silas staggered forward and paused as he eyed their captive. "Well, well Jenny Banwen. Not so pretty now. Some of the men have been a bit rough with you. Tell me," and he reached down and forced Jenny to look at him gripping her cheeks and pulling up her face with his calloused hand. "Are we not good enough for the likes of you, girl?"

Silas pushed her back on the cave floor and his hands went for his buckle to undo his belt. It was not clear if he intended to beat her with it or to use it and bind her to his will.

Jenny frantically scrambled away from him. Other wreckers watched the proceedings and laughed viciously. Silas spurred on by his ruffian friends growled, "I think I might sample some of what the gentry had. You can tell me afterwards if I am as good as them or any of the others when they have their turn."

Jenny feeling the fight drain out of her, feebly tried to crawl away when a warning shout came from the cave entrance.

The wreckers turned to see the reason for the alarm and saw Goliath swing into view. He took a running leap into the cave with the rope trailing behind him. One sentry lunged at him but Goliath's huge arms blocked him. He threw the brutish guard head first into the wall of the cavern.

The wrecker's head made a sickening crunching sound and left a swathe of blood and brains on the rocks as he slid lifelessly to the sand. With an effortless swing of his other arm Goliath threw the second sentry, who had rushed back to the mouth of the cave, over the ledge and down the cliff face. The second guard screamed all the way down until his cry was cut short when he reached the rocks and threshing ocean below. The surf sprayed up as his body was sucked under with the current.

The smuggling thugs, befuddled by drink and not in complete control of their sensibilities shook their heads in disbelief and scrambled around the cave to arm themselves, searching the sandy floor for their weapons.

Nathaniel suddenly appeared swinging across the entrance. His legs were pumping as he continued to run but he found nothing solid under his feet and he swung back out again into fresh air. Goliath turned and on Nathaniel's return swing he grasped him around the waist and pulled him into the cave. They hurriedly worked to free themselves from their restraining ropes and brandished their swords preparing for battle.

147

The smugglers, by now, had grabbed cudgels and swords and rushed forward. A wild melee ensued with some wreckers inadvertently turning on their own in their drunken confusion. Blood flew wildly and the sound of steel clashing on steel ripped through the cave as limbs were hacked through with the sharpest of blades.

Silas felt the end was near and he was determined that if he was to lose his life then he would first press home his point and make Nathaniel suffer. He threw down his cudgel and pulled out a pistol and aimed it at Goliath but he couldn't get a clear shot as two of his men were in the way. He then switched targets and turned the gun on Nathaniel but such was the fracas that he was unable to fire off a round at the Riding Officer. Infuriated, Silas pulled himself up to his full height and roared like a demented demon and spun around leveling the pistol at Jenny. His mouth twisted into a cruel grin and he rasped, "So, it seems I am not to taste your bloodied flesh after all."

Silas cocked the pistol and Nathaniel hearing the action saw Silas' intention. He bellowed, "Noooooo!" With a final surge of strength Nathaniel lunged forward and impaled the drunken adversary that he was battling against with his sabre. He let go of his weapon and ran at Silas, who on hearing the cry turned to see Nathaniel bearing down on him.

Silas leered malevolently, "Big mistake Riding Officer; big mistake," and he fired at Nathaniel.

Jenny screamed, in anguish, "Nathaniel!" and was horrified to see Nathaniel had fallen to his knees.

Silas dropped the still smoking pistol and fled. He managed to avoid Goliath's swinging fists and he ran out taking the treacherous ribbon path.

Jenny struggled to crawl to Nathaniel's side. The effort was too great and she murmured, "Oh, Nathaniel, I knew you'd…" She stopped short as she saw the blood seeping rapidly through his shirt.

Goliath dispatched the last of his attackers and ran to Nathaniel's side. Now he was in a quandary: Jenny was clearly in a bad way but his friend was losing too much blood, too quickly.

Jenny bit her lip and tried again. She fought her way

through to Nathaniel and tried to staunch the flow of blood from his wound, and attempted to remove some of the little clothing she had left to stop the crimson tide and forgot her own modesty. Goliath's eyes filled with tears and he said gently, "No, Miss Jenny, no," whilst he tore off his own shirt. He prised her hold from off Nathaniel and placed his shirt over her head to cover her body. The garment looked like a veritable dress on her. Goliath ripped open the front of Nathaniel's shirt to inspect the wound. A small round bullet hole about three inches below his heart welled with bright red blood.

Jenny looked up at Goliath anxiously, "Will he... will he live?" Jenny took Nathaniel's ashen face in her hands and cried.

Goliath shook her gently, "Can you walk?"

"No, but I can crawl if you carry him."

Another shadow flitted across the mouth of the cave as Ben swung in and out of the cave repeatedly before he found his footing and landed safely inside the cave. He laughed, "That wasn't half bad..." Then he stopped as he saw the carnage that lay before him.

"Over here," called Goliath. "We need help here."

Ben rushed to their side and instantly understood the seriousness of their situation, "You carry him," he ordered Goliath, taking charge. "I'll take care of Jenny. Get back. Take my wagon and ride as if the devil is after your soul."

Goliath shook his head, "No," then he looked about him and saw that some of the ruffians he had knocked senseless seemed to be coming round. He indicated everyone, "We go, all of us, or not at all."

Goliath's words made sense and they galvanized themselves into action to escape the deathtrap of a cave that threatened more bloodshed. Goliath swung Nathaniel onto his shoulders as Ben lifted Jenny as gently as he could. Now they had to get out and quickly.

Goliath and Ben were uninjured and now speed was of the essence if they were to save the lives of the young couple and escape the clutches of the murdering vermin that were set to chase after them once they were able.

"Go," shouted Goliath. "Go now!"

# Chapter Twenty-Two

## Race Against Time

Goliath scrambled to the top of the cliff using the same technique, as he had to scale down the cliff. But travelling up was much harder work. Ben had helped secure Nathaniel to his rope and now Goliath had to haul his friend up the cliff side already aware that some of the wreckers would be coming round and would soon be in pursuit.

Goliath recovered the horses and Ben's wagon and braced it against the cliff edge. His face was a mask of sweat as he hauled on the rope and grunted with the extreme exertion. Nathaniel swung precariously in space and Goliath tried not to let his body smash against the cliffs. He didn't want his friend to suffer any more injury.

Nathaniel grimaced as he was tugged up the rock face and Ben was only able to guide him part for the way from below. Goliath bellowed with the effort that seemed to give him extra strength and he tugged hard. Nathaniel's feet found the wall and he tried to pump his legs as if walking. This small movement helped Goliath who with hand over hand on the rope finally brought Nathaniel to the top. He quickly undid the rope releasing Nathaniel and threw it back down for Ben to help Jenny. Nathaniel however didn't move. He lay still on the grass. "No, no, no!" Goliath roared. Finding new energy he picked up his friend and laid him in the back of the wagon.

Goliath ran to the cliff edge and began to pull Jenny up to safety. Jenny was conscious and able to use her feet to walk up the cliff, and being much lighter she was soon on the grassy cliff top. She was able to scramble, albeit painfully, into the wagon to be with Nathaniel, and Goliath threw the rope down again for Ben.

Ben fiddled and twisted with the rope trying to tie it. His hands were shaking and he bore rope burns from trying to hold the strong cord taut for Nathaniel. Sounds of shouts and groans emanated from the cave and Goliath urged, "Come on, Ben. Hurry, please." The urgency was apparent and Ben hurried to tie the knot.

A shout broke out from the cave mouth and a ruffian waved a cutlass at Ben and began to charge up the narrow path, closely followed by another thug. Panicked Ben fumbled even more and then yelled. "Haul, just haul and I'll hold on."

Goliath tugged on the rope and Ben lifted from the ground, another heave and he moved further up the cliff but was still in reach. The thugs ran to get their quarry and just as one reached out to grasp Ben's leg Goliath with a huge grunt of exertion yanked harder on the rope and Ben hung on desperately lifting his feet out of the way of clutching hands and a slicing cutlass.

Nathaniel was safe in the wagon with Jenny and he was being tended to as best as Jenny, in her battered state, was able. Nathaniel began to regain consciousness. Goliath gave a final cry and let out a huge gasp as with a final heave Ben was pulled to the top of the crag and he clambered along the cliff edge until he found somewhere to stand. Shouts and cries of frustration came from below and the thugs turned to the ribbon path that led to the top.

Ben was at first quite jocund, filled with adrenalin from the adventure and joked, "That wasn't half bad either," before he doubled up and retched violently as the realisation of his close shave with death hit him. The yells from the wreckers drew nearer. Goliath picked Ben up and deposited him in the back of the cart none too gently. Time was of the essence.

Goliath jumped onto the wagon and cracked the whip fiercely. The horse leapt into action. The wheels spluttered as they turned and spewed gravel and soil behind them. Jessie and Samson ran alongside the cart. They needed to get back to the village, urgently and get help.

The two thugs could only look after the fleeing wagon and curse.

The cart raced along the track and path like a chariot in gladiatorial combat. It travelled swiftly and in a less than safe manner. Goliath was like someone from Biblical days competing in an arena.

Finally, the cart rattled into the village and Goliath turned to Ben, "Where? Where we find help?"

Ben shrugged, "Now Dewi's gone... Wait, his assistant, Joshua. He's trained in first aid. This way." Ben issued directions to Goliath who turned the cart and hurtled to Joshua's abode.

Goliath raced against time and skidded to a halt on Ben's shout, "Here! We're here!" Ben ran to the door and pounded on it. Bethany Meredith, Joshua's wife answered the door and ushered them in. Goliath lifted a barely conscious Nathaniel and carried him into Joshua's consulting rooms whilst Ben took Jenny inside.

Joshua studied the Riding Officer's wounds, "I can remove the bullet. It won't be easy and I can clean him up, but it won't be safe for him here. He will need rest and recuperation away from here. He needs to be safe. He's lost a lot of blood and will probably fall into unconsciousness. I cannot promise anything."

"Do what can," urged Goliath.

Ben questioned, "What of Jenny? She, too, is in a bad way."

"Bethany!" shouted Joshua, "See to Jenny. Clean her wounds."

Bethany Meredith scuttled in at her husband's bidding and husband and wife did what they could to save the couple. Bethany frowned when she saw Jenny's battered face and body. "The poor lass is barely alive. No one deserves this. I will do what I can. You must take Joshua's advice and get them away from here. If it's discovered we've helped, we'll be next," she told Goliath.

"Where can you go?" asked Ben.

"I know not," replied Goliath.

"His home? Where does he hail from?" questioned Joshua.

"Another part of Wales, methinks," answered Goliath.

"Who would know?" pressed Bethany.

"Mr. Pritchard," pronounced Goliath. "Mr. Pritchard would know family address."

"I'll go," volunteered Ben. "I'll be back. You can use my wagon to transport them."

"That's if they survive the journey," advised Joshua gravely. "Away then, Ben. See what you can do."

Ben nodded in agreement and swiftly left the premises. Nathaniel was now almost comatose and Jenny was faring little better.

Bethany observed, "The child has been raped. She could be with child."

"What's to be done?"

"I'll douche her, hopefully it will wash anything away," she said meaningfully.

"Do it," said Goliath and Joshua together.

Bethany didn't need to be asked again and prepared the shivering Jenny. "I'll find her some clothes, too. She can't be sent away in these rags."


Charles Bevan poured a brandy for Sir James, Minister John Rhys and the Knight, who even in this trusted company still maintained his disguise of a heavy scarf in case a servant noticed what he or she shouldn't. The remains of a celebratory dinner was on the table. The only light in the room was that of the burning fire in the grate that flickered and threw shadows over the assembled company's faces and from a single candle on the table that was slowly burning down.

Sir James raised his glass and addressed the others, "I really think we should drink to this moderate success." He smiled at the others before taking a long draught of his fine French brandy.

His son, Charles, was more cautious in his assessment and added, "Forgive me, Father but I believe the success will come once the Rider is dead. As it is now, his resolve will be all the stronger, of that I am sure."

The minister did not partake in the toast and protested, "Gentlemen, I pray you, please. This talk of death and killings is not for me. It goes against my beliefs. I want no involvement with this."

Charles laughed scornfully, "Minister, Minister," he said derisively; "You cannot make an omelette without breaking a few eggs. You must understand this. If we are to succeed then our will must be done."

Sir James jumped in, backing up his son's comments, "I find your logic, Minister, quite strange to say the least. You have no qualms in drinking contraband brandy, for which people were killed, but find it objectionable to discuss the manner by which we have all become rich."

The Knight interrupted, his voice still muffled. He appeared to placate the men, "Gentlemen, gentlemen, please. The Minister has his reasons and we have agreed that we will all respect each other's opinions in this venture. Besides, the rider may not return. We will have won the day after all, without the use of bloodshed."

John Rhys was more than happy to take this proffered attempt at acceptance of his words, and raised his glass, "Sir, I thank you." And he took another sip of his brandy. "Whatever you need to do, you do, but I wish no part in these actions." John Rhys drained his drink and stood. "I will not hinder your discussions and plans, Gentlemen. I bid you all a good night." He walked to the door and turned, "I thank you for your kind hospitality, Sir James. Fare thee well."

The Minister left the room. Sir James and Charles turned to the Knight and looked quizzically at him. The Knight raised his finger to his lips and waited until the front door had opened and closed. He listened for the sound of the trap leaving the courtyard.

Then, without a word, the Knight picked up the sputtering candle and walked to the window. He signalled three times waving the candle across the window, waited for an answering light, then returned it to the table and turned to his companions. "Gentlemen, as of now our profits will increase substantially, as we now have one purse less to fill."

Sir James lifted his glass to the Knight and smiled. Charles was now on the edge of his chair, eager to show his loyalty to the group and announced, "I can do this, let me... I will deal with the minister."

The Knight calmly pronounced, "Not to worry. It is already done. As for the Rider, I will make similar arrangements."

Charles pouted in disappointment as he toyed with his brandy, swooshing the contents around the glass and smelling its bouquet before taking another drink.

The Knight sat, "Another brandy, I think, Sir James." He held out his glass and relaxed his scarf. Sir James duly poured another large one, which the Knight swirled with relish and added. "It is good we keep company tonight, very good."

The unsuspecting minister climbed into his buggy and rattled away across the cobblestones toward the village church and his home. The night was reasonably clear and the heavens lit by a myriad of stars. The face of the moon shone malevolently, its leprous surface pitted by one wispy cloud that floated across its face. An owl hooted and was answered by the screech of a vixen on its nightly prowl.

The minister's pony snorted uneasily. He pulled up in the courtyard outside his house and alighted. He patted the pony before walking up the steps to his door, his gait somewhat unsteady due to his large consumption of brandy. Hearing a sound behind him he called out over his shoulder, "Give her a good rub down and some extra hay, it's been a long night for her," and a whistle rose readily to his lips as he fumbled for his keys.

A figure silently stepped up behind him. The minister's head was roughly yanked back and before John Rhys had time to murmur Silas quickly sliced his dagger across John Rhys' throat. The minister dropped to his knees with a gurgling sound as his blood spewed out. He twitched in his death throes and bled to death on the Parsonage steps.

Silas coldly cleaned his bloodied blade on the Minister's cloak and disappeared through a gap in the hedgerow and the night swallowed him up. No one heard and no one saw. Night, secretive night had masked the deadly deed.

Ben drove wildly through the cobbled streets to the Custom House. He ran around the back and hammered on the door of Pritchard's house.

"Pritchard, for God's sake Mr. Pritchard!"

He heard a shuffling and footsteps, the door opened slowly and Ben babbled uncomprehendingly. Pritchard rubbed his bleary eyes that looked bloodshot from lack of sleep or possibly the odd brandy.

"Slowly, man, slowly. What are you blathering about? Do you know what time it is?"

155

Ben took a deep breath, "Nathaniel Brookes, Sir. He is hurt and in urgent need of treatment. I must get him home, away from here to try and help him recover."

Pritchard was suddenly alert, "Brookes you say? What happened? How is he?"

"Sir, I don't have time for discussion. He is near death's door. I am looking to save him. His family's address, his man and I will strive to get him there."

"Of course, of course. Wait a moment." Pritchard retreated from the hall to his drawing room his nightshirt flapping around his ankle and boots. Ben waited anxiously stamping his feet.

Pritchard emerged with a scrap of paper with the Brookes' family address. He passed it across to Ben. "Here. God speed, I wish you well. And tell him he has done enough. I will not expect him back after this."

Ben nodded his acknowledgement and hurried away. Pritchard watched him thoughtfully a worried expression on his face and then he heard the sound of the wagon's wheels on cobbles and horses' hooves racing away. He sighed and closed the door wearily. There he kicked off his boots and mounted the stairs to his bedchamber.

Ben rushed to Goliath waiting at the wagon and gave him the address. He made to jump up, "No, you have done enough. I take it from here and please believe we will return your wagon."

Ben nodded in grateful understanding and Goliath sprang into the driver's seat and shook the reins shouting encouragement to the horse to gallop on. Jessie and Samson kept pace as they ran by the wagon. Jenny cried out, "Careful. This jolting is not kind to him. Please, Goliath slow down."

"Me slow down, may not get him there alive," called Goliath.

Jenny struggled to hold Nathaniel to her and steady him. He was still unconscious and his blood still seeped bloodying her bodice front. Jenny was in a poor state herself but she remained strong for Nathaniel and eventually she, too, fell into semi consciousness.

The stalwart pony's feet pounded on and gouged away the

miles. Goliath was relentless in his urging the steed on. Dawn was breaking. He had driven the horses hard through the night and was now rewarded with the first flush of the breaking day. The sun slowly raised its head from sleep and made the way easier to follow. Goliath examined the signposts and the address he held in his hand, thankful that Nathaniel had taught him to read. He powered recklessly on into mid Wales hurtling wildly along the quiet country lanes until he saw the sign to Llangammarch Wells. He stopped at the edge of a small village where a young farm labourer emerged from a small cottage and began to walk toward a neighbouring farm. He stopped abruptly as the wagon and horses pulled up alongside him. His face filled with fear as he saw the huge giant.

"I mean you no harm. Not be afraid. Lake Manor, which way please?" His voice was mellow and polite yet had urgency.

The young man, clearly astonished, stuttered a reply, "Turn left at the crossroads then left again."

"That be Brookes' home?"

"The same," admitted the man. He watched in wonder as Goliath spurred the horse on again and the wagon rattled away. He quickly turned tail and fled back to his house calling out, "Mam!"

Goliath had run the wagon and horse like an Olympian. He turned into the long tree lined drive that led to the imposing and impressive Lake Manor House. He passed a large expanse of water where swans swam and ruffled their feathers at the beginning of the day, a small coach house and elaborate gardens with statues and fountains, the like of which Goliath had never seen before.

He pulled up at the front of the house and ran up the stone steps. He jangled the heavy bell outside and waited. No one came. Then more persistently, he didn't hold off but continued to ring and ring. Eventually the door opened and a smartly dressed solemn faced servant solemnly appeared on the step. His jaw dropped when he saw the huge Negro and moved to shut the door. Goliath stopped him. "Help, please Nathaniel Brookes is here," he gestured to the cart. "Badly injured."

"What's that?" Myah appeared on the stairs. "What's going on?"

"Nathaniel Brookes, he injured, here in wagon. Please, help."

Myah pushed past the butler and ran to the cart. She shouted back at the manservant, "Quick, help him in. Now."

"He lost much blood," added Goliath.

The butler hastened down the steps and aided Goliath in removing Nathaniel from the wagon and carrying him inside.

"Into the drawing room, quickly now."

Goliath laid him out on the huge chaise longue and then he returned for Jenny. Myah took charge, "Caleb, send young Redfern for the doctor. NOW!" she shouted alerting the poe faced butler to action, who hurried away.

"Thank you Mr... er..."

"Barka, Hekenefa Barka. Nathaniel call me Goliath."

"I can see why," she half smiled but then Myah was at Nathaniel's side, she stripped off her dressing gown and placed it over her son. She indicated Jenny. "And who is this?"

"This Miss Jenny, good friend."

"What happened?"

Goliath began to relate the events at the cave, and Myah listened, appalled at the tale of violence and murder. She stroked her son's forehead. He was now deathly pale and her breath caught in a sob. "Please, Nathaniel, my son. Hold on. Dr. Cunningham will be with us shortly." She clasped her hands together and began to pray. Her voice whispered the words of the Lord's Prayer and she added her own words, "Please, God, grant my son the gift of life, help him to live, to recover. I will forever be your devoted servant, Amen." She looked up and indicated the bell pull, "Mr. Barka, Goliath, please ring the bell."

Goliath lumbered across to the huge fireplace and pulled the braided cord that hung down. A bell jangled below stairs, the kitchen maid heard and ran up to the drawing room, and entered, "Ma'am..." her hand flew up to her face as she saw the bloody spectacle before her.

"Milly, get blankets for Nathaniel and the young lady," she indicated Jenny Banwen. "And then prepare the guest room for Mr. Barka, here."

Milly's eyes opened wide and she stared in incredulity at the hulking form of Goliath.

"Milly, stop staring. It's rude," she reprimanded. "You will need to air young Mr. Brooke's bed and prepare another room for Miss Jenny. Hurry now."

The maid bobbed a courtesy, "Yes, Ma'am," and gratefully fled the room.


Nathaniel's bedroom at home was unchanged and just, as he had left it. The maps and charts were still adorning the walls and tables. Nathaniel lay comatose in his bed with heavy bandages bound around his chest. Goliath was sitting on the floor his head rested on his arms that were supported by his knees.

The door handle moved slightly. At the sound, Goliath's shoulders bunched up, his muscles taut, tense and ready for action. Slowly, the door opened with a grating squeak. Goliath clenched his fists, his knuckles turned white. He lifted his head and turned to see who had entered. Nathaniel's mother, Myah stepped into the room and Goliath heaved a huge sigh of relief.

"I'm sorry. Did I startle you?" Myah asked gently.

Goliath stood up and bowed to Nathaniel's mother, "No, Ma'am. I not asleep."

"Come now, you should. You need to sleep. It's been three days and two nights that you have been sitting there in vigil at my son's side. You will make yourself ill."

"I feared for him," Goliath responded.

"We all did. Were it not for you... Well, I dread to think."

"What I did no more than he did for me. How Miss Jenny?"

Myah did not respond but something in Nathaniel's brain stirred him to consciousness and he repeated Goliath's question, "Jenny. How is Jenny?"

Myah rushed to Nathaniel's side, tears coursed down her cheeks. Goliath looked over Myah's head to his friend Nathaniel and nodded encouragingly.

Nathaniel's eyes fluttered open and he sighed, "Hush mother. I am well rested if just a little sore. My mouth is dry. I would love a drink."

"Water for you only," laughed Myah. Then concerned once more she asked tentatively, "Are you in pain, my son?"

"Only when I breathe," replied Nathaniel with a wry smile.

Delighted at the interchange Myah fussed over Nathaniel and offered him some food and water. Nathaniel pushed away the food but sipped the water gratefully.

"You need to regain your strength," his mother advised.

"I will eat later. Now, I would like to see Jenny," requested Nathaniel.

"No, not yet. You shouldn't move around yet. Dr. Cunningham is with her changing her dressings," admonished Myah.

But Nathaniel wasn't listening. He pulled himself up and called Goliath. "Help me, friend. Take me to her."

Goliath strode across and helped his friend to his feet and together they shuffled to the door. Myah bit her lip anxiously and followed them out, before hurrying away to Hannah's room.

Myah knocked on the door, "Hannah, Hannah I have news."

Hannah opened the door and gazed questioningly at Myah. "Nathaniel is awake."

Hannah's face lit up with delight, "I must see him."

Myah hesitated, "No, leave it a while."

"Why? It is only right I should see my beloved."

"He has gone to see how Miss Banwen fares. Wait until he is back in his own room. We must be thankful that he is at last awake and shows signs of healing. Dr. Cunningham has done well."

Hannah looked crestfallen, "I must thank the good doctor myself."

"Certainly, certainly. But, first let us be assured that he really is fit to see his family and friends."

Hannah persisted, "You see him," she said accusingly, her eyes turning dark with anger.

"I am his mother."

"And that black man sits with him night and day."

"It is thanks to Mr. Barka, Goliath that Nathaniel lives. If it were not for him, he would have returned in a box. We

160

must afford him our respect and thanks. I for one will make him welcome at any time."

Hannah was suitably chastened and pursed her lips. She turned away from the door, "Very well, I will see you at dinner and await your instruction." Myah closed the door quietly and sighed with relief. Hannah was going to be difficult to deal with, and unpredictable, of that she was sure.

Hannah's face hardened. She was suspicious of this Jenny Banwen and the place she held in Nathaniel's heart. She determined to watch and observe, and at the first opportunity she would see Nathaniel. She would see him sooner rather than later.

Jenny was lying on her bed, blood stained dressings lay on the table. Dr. Cunningham was examining her poor battered countenance. The whole of one side of her face was one huge swollen purple bruise. Her eyes were puffed shut where she had been struck so many times and the livid scar on her other cheek was gaping open and oozing blood.

The door opened slowly. Goliath helped Nathaniel to hobble into the room. An involuntary cry escaped Nathaniel's lips as he saw the mess that Jenny's face was in, "My God," he gasped.

The doctor continued his ministering and remarked, "Mr. Brookes, you should be in bed."

"I had to see her," floundered Nathaniel, shocked at the image she presented.

"You need more rest. You are lucky to be with us. A fraction higher and to the left and…" He didn't complete the sentence.

"Tell me, doctor, please. What of Jen er… Miss Banwen?"

Goliath helped Nathaniel to struggle to a chair by the bed. Nathaniel lowered himself into it and grimaced in discomfort. He watched as the doctor prepared to place fresh dressings on Jenny's face before ordering sharply, "Stop!"

The doctor halted and turned enquiringly to Nathaniel who manoeuvred himself in a better position to study Jenny's face. "Please doctor, look," he indicated the oozing scarred cheek. "There is some necrosis on the edges of this wound.

161

With some careful surgery the scarring could be reduced to a minimum."

"You're not alone in thinking this. They were my thoughts exactly. The problem is that my hands are too old for such delicate surgery. With a master surgeon, however … Now then it would be possible, perhaps…"

Nathaniel interrupted and spoke slowly as he considered Jenny's injuries. "Not necessarily, a master surgeon. Using a very fine needle, tiny sutures and with a delicate hand…" he peered more closely at her cheek.

Dr. Cunningham turned to him and mused over his half moon glasses, "You had that touch once, Nathaniel."

Nathaniel leaned across and softly brushed Jenny's raven hair away from her face.

Footsteps thudded past the door as Hannah flew toward Nathaniel's room and burst inside. Her eyes were puffed red from crying but she was smiling happily with the news from Myah that Nathaniel was now conscious but she stopped in her tracks when she viewed the empty bed. Enthusiasm forgotten she left his room, her heart heavy with disappointment and returned to her own chamber unaware that Nathaniel was in Jenny's room.

162

# Chapter Twenty-Three

## Recuperation

Nathaniel was bundled up against the cool chill in the air and seated very comfortably in a wing back armchair that has been dragged out into the Manor House gardens. Both his mother, Myah, and sister, Naomi fussed over him delighted to have him back in the bosom of the family and clearly healing well. Goliath was sitting impassively on a wooden bench watching and observing. His eyes rose up to view Hannah as she breezed out through the French Windows into the garden and hurried to Nathaniel's side.

Goliath noticed the secretive, knowing look that passed between Nathaniel's mother and sister, Naomi before they moved away to allow Hannah through and he continued to assess the proceedings.

Hannah fairly gushed, "Oh, Nathaniel, my dear. I nearly died when I heard what had happened and learned how you have suffered." She leaned across to kiss him but he pulled back, the movement causing him to wince in pain. "Oh, my sweet. I am so sorry." Undeterred, Hannah tried once more to plant a kiss on his lips but Nathaniel turned ever so slightly and received the brush of Hannah's lips on his cheek. If she was affronted she didn't show it.

Further comment was prevented by Myah, "Hannah! Good afternoon. Would you like some tea?"

Hannah nodded eagerly, "Yes, please." She pulled a garden seat close to Nathaniel's side and pressed him, "Nathaniel, how worried we have all been and how anxious am I to hear your story. Please, my love, do tell us what happened," she pleaded.

Again, Myah intervened, "Hush! None of that for the moment. He will tell us all in his own time. Let the boy rest. He needs to hear pleasantries and engage in inconsequential chatter not unburden his heart with tales of smugglers, wreckers and other murdering scoundrels."

Nathaniel laughed, "Then tell me, Mother, what news will you shower me with," teased Nathaniel.

Naomi clapped her hands delightedly and burst in, "Oh, Nat, it's about me. Mother has news about me."

"I do wish you wouldn't call him that. His name is Nathaniel," admonished Myah, then she laughed. "Go on then tell him," purred Myah.

"I may not have to," responded Naomi as a blur of red and white passed behind the French Windows.

Goliath still watched. He saw Hannah's frozen expression and her mouth set in a grim line. He saw the depression marauding in her eyes and then the moment was broken by the entrance of a tall, handsome officer entering the garden. Naomi leapt to her feet and skipped to the side of the dashing, Philip Chapman. They kissed briefly, Naomi's eyes were lit up with love and Philip gazed more than fondly at her, with an undeniable passion that bubbled under the surface.

Naomi took Philip's arm and led him to Nathaniel. "Nat... Nathaniel, this is Philip, *my* Philip."

Second Lieutenant Philip Chapman first turned to Myah in greeting, then to stone faced, Hannah before he finally offered his hand to Nathaniel. He introduced himself, "Philip Chapman, Forty First Welsh Foot. Mr. Brookes, it is an honour. Naomi is always talking about your exploits." He took Nathaniel's hand and shook it firmly.

Nathaniel smiled, "Unfortunately, I cannot say the same about you. I never knew that Naomi could keep a secret. A very pleasant one, too, I might add." It was clear the two men had taken an immediate liking to each other and the assembled company laughed together, all except for Hannah who remained quiet and still, her face devoid of emotion.

Myah walked across to the young officer, "Lieutenant Chapman, you will, of course, stay for dinner? Do say yes."

"Yes, please do, Philip and you can become better acquainted with my brother."

He nodded affably and smiled, "Mrs. Brookes, it will be a pleasure."

Naomi laughed delightedly and took Philip's arm, "Come, I think I would enjoy a turn around the garden."

Philip patted her hand and they set off on a stroll through the grounds.

Nathaniel called to Goliath and indicated his chair, "Goliath, help me up, please. I think I would like to return inside now. And Mama will need help returning this beast to the drawing room."

Goliath stood, crossed to his friend and grabbed Nathaniel's arms. He assisted him to his feet. Together they went indoors. Hannah stared after them, feeling confusion, anger and hurt building inside her. She tossed her head and glided to the French Windows and went indoors. No one stopped her and no one spoke. She felt neglected and craved a kind word or look but there was none to be had; stifling a sob she ran from the drawing room and moved up the stairs just in time to see Goliath and Nathaniel enter Jenny's room. Her eyes dulled with despair and she dashed to her own room.

Hannah threw herself on her bed and sobbed. Suddenly, she stopped and sat up. She brushed her tears away and looked at her betrothal token, a small gold ring inset with tiny pearls and a central ruby stone. "I must believe," she told herself, "Or... I wonder if anyone would notice if I wasn't wearing it? That would speak volumes." Hannah tugged at the ring and removed it. She placed it wistfully in a tiny pot on her dressing table, before calling her maid to help her dress for dinner.

Once suitably attired she powdered her porcelain skin and pinched her cheeks to give her some colour before brushing her corn blonde hair and styling it in tendrils and curls piled high on her head with ringlets framing her face.

Hannah sat and studied her reflection in the looking glass. She examined her profile critically. The gong for dinner sounded, she gathered herself together and took a deep breath to calm herself before going downstairs to the dining room. She fixed a small tight smile on her face and entered.

She waited to be seated and watched the faces of the others as they entered and politely addressed her. Goliath, dressed to the nines, and feeling slightly uncomfortable, followed Nathaniel and stood behind his chair. It was the first time he had entered the dining room since their arrival as he had refused to leave Nathaniel's side and ate small snacks there whilst he watched over Nathaniel. He looked around him. The surroundings were a sharp contrast to anything that Goliath had ever been used to but there was a garishness about some of the furnishings that hinted at new money. Goliath continued to stare about him. It was the first time Nathaniel had been into dinner. He appreciated the fact that Goliath had sat at his bedside until the moment he had awoken.

Myah, Naomi, Philip Chapman and Hannah sat at the table with Nathaniel but the chair at the head of the table remained empty, although the place was set. The door was thrown open and Jeremiah Brookes strode in. He took his seat and glanced about him, taking everything in, "I hope I have not kept you waiting you too long?"

Myah, responded, "Actually, no, Mr. Brookes. We have…"

"Guests and foreigners?" he questioned with eyebrows raised. "It seems that I am the last to know in my…" he quickly corrected himself as he felt Myah's steady gaze upon him, "This house."

Myah introduced Goliath, "This is Mr. Barka, a new friend." She spoke her next words deliberately, slowly and decisively, "Anybody who saves my son is a friend. Are you sure you will not join us, Mr. Barka?"

Jeremiah's eyes were like daggers. He scrutinised Goliath's face barely hiding his distaste at the Negro giant.

"My thanks, Ma'am," said Goliath courteously. "But, I must say, no."

"Very well then," burst out Jeremiah, "Let's eat."

The dinner progressed with very little talk. Naomi and Philip only had eyes for each other. Their love was clearly apparent for all to see. Hannah toyed with her food, throwing frequent, forlorn looks at Nathaniel who appeared not to notice.

Jeremiah was not quite the pig but his table manners were not the best and certainly resembled a nuzzling boar rooting for truffles in the wood. Myah, by contrast, carried herself with grace and dignity. Her bearing was poised and she was observant of the guests and did not miss a single nuance in the little chatter that ensued.

166

Once the meal was complete Jeremiah walked to the drinks tray, dismissing the butler to the kitchen, "Brandy, anyone? It's the good stuff from France," he proclaimed.

Unashamedly, Nathaniel pronounced, "Not unless it carries King George's seal."

Jeremiah's reply was a blank stare, so Nathaniel continued, "Port... if I may?"

Chapman smiled warmly. "I'll keep you company. There is nothing like some good aged English port."

Nathaniel acknowledged Philip with a thankful nod and smile at being backed up. Jeremiah shrugged and poured two glasses of ruby port before asking, "Sherry, ladies?"

Myah rose and waited for Hannah and Naomi to follow her, "Thank you Mr. Brookes but we shall now retire to the drawing room and leave you gentlemen to it, so to speak."

Chapman rose to his feet and bowed slightly as did Goliath and Jeremiah who were already standing. Nathaniel was not well enough to rise but touched his forehead as a mark of respect. Goliath stepped to the door and opened it, to let them out. He closed it and resumed his stance behind Nathaniel. Jeremiah now resigned to Goliath's presence dropped into his chair. He eyed Nathaniel, challengingly, "So my boy..." Nathaniel stiffened, "Have you rid the Welsh coast of all the smugglers and wreckers, yet?" He laughed cynically.

Nathaniel spoke in a measured tone, "Not quite... but I will," he finished decisively.

"I'll drink to that," affirmed Philip Chapman.

"Yes," said Jeremiah slowly, "And to getting yourself killed, too. Did you think of that Mr. Riding Officer?" he bristled accusingly.

"That's not my primary intention, I can assure you," continued Nathaniel evenly.

"Well, Sir, I have no need to remind you that you have promises to fulfil, not least to me and my daughter. You have not forgotten, surely?"

Nathaniel flushed guiltily at the mention of Hannah, "I would prefer to keep private conversations private, Uncle," he said abruptly. He turned to Philip, "No offence meant, Lieutenant Chapman."

"None taken," replied the lieutenant, "Do not give it a second thought."

Nathaniel, irked at his Uncle and somewhat embarrassed, put down his half-empty port glass and attempted to rise. Goliath came to his aid and supported him to the door. Jeremiah downed his brandy and looked after them silently fuming. Lieutenant Chapman, now wary of further conversation, rose, "If you'll excuse me, Sir. I will join the ladies." Jeremiah gave a curt nod and stood. He strode to the drinks table and poured himself another large brandy and scowled, blackly as Philip Chapman made his escape.

The following morning, the gentle rays of sunshine fingered their way through the half drawn curtains and caressed the bed, stroking Jenny's face. Nathaniel was at her side as Dr. Cunningham prepared his instruments and other medical equipment.

"Are you sure about this?" asked Dr. Cunningham.

"Apart from finding my father's murderers, to which I am sworn, this is the only thing that I *am* sure of."

Dr. Cunningham nodded and proceeded to wash his hands and forearms with alcohol. "The French may be a strange people, but their doctors lose less patients than we do during surgery."

"Just by washing their hands?" asked Nathaniel.

"No, by disinfection. At least that's what they claim. That's what this is for," and he passed the bottle to Nathaniel who scrubbed up and followed with an alcohol wash.

Nathaniel turned to Goliath, "You may wish to leave my friend."

"No, as you were there for me, so I will be for you and Miss Jenny."

Nathaniel smiled and stretched for the gauze and ether but Dr. Cunningham stopped him, "No, my friend. I'll take care of that."

"As you wish Dr. Cunningham."

"Certainly, Dr. Brookes," smiled the doctor.

Nathaniel reached forward and began to remove the bloodied dressings. Jenny's eyes fluttered open, "Nathaniel?" she said softly.

"It's all right, Jenny fach. The good doctor here will make sure you don't feel a thing, just relax and you will fall to sleep. We will do our utmost to restore your looks."

Jenny's eyes closed in acceptance and the two doctors began. The gauze and lint pad was drenched in ether and placed gently over her mouth and nose. She didn't fight it but breathed in deeply until her head fell back.

Nathaniel stretched out his hand and the nervous tremble vanished. He picked up the iodine, painted the site of the injury and picked up a scalpel, "Right, Doctor. Let us begin."

They worked together. They were meticulous and thorough. The necrosis was snipped away and the clean edges sewn together with tiny fine stitches that would fade to nothing in time. The line of stitching was smooth. There were almost certain that the operation would be a success as long as Jenny had good healing skin. Dr. Cunningham looked at Nathaniel over his glasses, "Good job. All we can do now is pray."

# Chapter Twenty-Four

## Miracles and Tears

The gentle afternoon sun warmed the garden with its loving light as Nathaniel and Philip sat together sharing some port. Nathaniel took a draught and sighed, his thoughts and mind with Jenny.

"When will you know?" asked Philip.

"We need to check that it's healing properly. But, we must leave it undisturbed for forty-eight hours and not let the operation site get wet. When the dressings are changed then we should then have some idea whether it has been successful, one way or another. We have done our best. I have high hopes. It looked as if we had done a good job, but then again, one never knows."

Philip swallowed and spoke tentatively, "If you don't mind me saying, she seems very dear to you, important... to have gone to all this trouble..." He raised an eyebrow quizzically.

Nathaniel gave a wry smile and chose his words carefully, "She has been... of extreme help to me, a good friend. And with her father gone, she has no one." Nathaniel took another sip of his drink.

Philip was sensitive enough not press Nathaniel further on Jenny and changed the subject. He continued in a more serious tone, "How is it really going, down there?"

"Not too good. The corruption is ingrained at all levels of society."

Philip grinned and added jokily, "Except the Church of course."

"Even the Church," responded Nathaniel with a smile.

"So, tell me, have you anyone you can rely on, if the situation becomes dire?"

Nathaniel thought for a moment, "I have Goliath. I can trust him with my life. And Mr. Pritchard is also able to exercise some influence on the dragoons stationed close by.

170

But it is not always guaranteed. He is often thwarted in his endeavours as he was in my father's day. It is very frustrating. This is a vicious war and people keep dying." Nathaniel checked himself. He could feel his anger bubbling to the surface again and his feelings of helplessness riled him. "What I can't understand is why we can never get the manpower we need? It's as if someone tries to block our every move, someone in authority. The local dragoons rarely turn out for us."

"Hm, the dragoons may not be of much help. It's the forty-first you should have at your back. From what we hear some of the dragoons have no interest in seeing an end to this bloody business."

"You are voicing my thoughts, exactly. The dragoons certainly drag their heels so to speak. I feel one or two of them may be in the smugglers employ."

Jeremiah entered the garden and overheard the last remark; he pronounced deliberately, "Every man must make his own fortune. That is my motto."

"What?" said Nathaniel aghast.

"I repeat, we all must do what we have to, to make a living."

"Even at the expense of innocent blood?" argued Nathaniel, shocked at his Uncle's words.

"Nobody is innocent," proclaimed Jeremiah arrogantly. "The Bible teaches us that."

"Sir, I take offence at that comparison," bridled Philip Chapman. "I will not be tarred with the same brush as common cutthroats." He rose from the garden seat and placed his glass of port on the garden table and nodded curtly at Jeremiah. He spoke quietly to Nathaniel, "If you'll excuse me, Nathaniel. I don't feel I can keep company with your uncle. I don't like his insinuations and will not enter into an argument. Forgive me," and he left the garden in something of a huff at the inference of a slur on his character.

Nathaniel turned to his uncle and said coldly, "Had you wanted to talk to me in private you could have asked. There is no need to deliberately offend our guests."

Jeremiah shrugged and asked baldly, "I need to speak

171

with you and I need to know. What are your intentions in respect of my daughter?"

"You do not mince your words do you?" observed Nathaniel.

Jeremiah considered and answered. "No. I call a spade a spade and expect others to do the same. Things do not seem to be running as they should or as expected from you, considering your promise before you left for that damned job." Jeremiah paused. Nathaniel remained silent. "Could I have your answer, Sir?" A note of petulance had entered his voice and his manner became agitated.

Nathaniel was unwilling to pursue the conversation and rose gingerly to his feet, clearly torn and still in some discomfort. "Rest assured you as her father will be the first to know, *after* I have spoken to Miss Hannah, of course. There are other more important things to concern me other than my future and marital status. These need to be attended to first."

Nathaniel strolled away rejecting further questioning and left Jeremiah impatiently drumming his fingers on the table. He grasped the port bottle and poured himself a very large glass, his temper was less than sweet, and he took a huge swallow.

Nathaniel, however, was in a dilemma and troubled. He struggled with what he perceived as his duty to his family and his promise to Hannah, and his very real feelings for Jenny. He entered the house and met with his mother who looked at him and instantly assessed his mood, "Come my son, we need to talk."

"But, Mother," he protested.

"I will not take no for an answer. Give me your arm and lean on me. We will adjourn to *my* sitting room where I know we will not be disturbed."

Nathaniel gratefully accepted her support and they walked on and into her private rooms. Myah opened the door and ushered her son inside, then closed the door firmly behind them. They did not notice Hannah coming down the stairs. She watched her Aunt and betrothed enter her Aunt's sitting room and tiptoed lightly down the stairs and paused outside the chamber.

Inside the very tastefully furnished room, Myah bade her son to sit, "Please, Nathaniel, sit. We need to talk."

Nathaniel groaned. He was not a man to express his inner emotions freely. He did not wish to upset his mother. He did not feel ready for such discussion and he was apprehensive of what she might say. He sat awkwardly, his eyes cast to the floor and fidgeted uncomfortably.

"My son, look at me." Nathaniel reluctantly raised his eyes to his mother's face. "I taught you from a little boy always to be honest, never to be afraid of your own feelings and that truth is paramount in all dealings with men, women and family."

"Yes, Mama." Nathaniel agreed, shamefaced.

"I blame myself. We should have talked of this more fully before, but I was uncertain whether or not I was right in my assumptions and when I last raised the question you avoided debate by leaving to take up your job as a Riding Officer."

Nathaniel studied his mother's face and the new lines that etched her face. She was tired of worrying that much he could see, and for that reason he felt guilty.

"Before you left, you gave a betrothal token to your first cousin, Hannah with a promise of marriage upon your return."

Nathaniel made to speak, and his eyes clouded with sorrow.

"No. Let me finish. I saw then as I see now that this promise was made not out of love or longing to spend your life with her but out of a stubborn duty that you perceived was due to me and to Naomi. You were afraid that without Uncle Jeremiah's protection that we would live a sad and poor life."

Nathaniel admitted, "That's right. I couldn't condemn you to a life of poverty. This was a way of securing your future and Naomi's future financially."

"My poor, poor boy. You are so misguided. I did not need that protection. Maybe, I should have spoken sooner, but now is the time... My Nathaniel," Myah paused and lifted up her head. She sat next to her son and took his hands. "You will not understand this and I do not want to explain to you now but I am not a poor person. I am a lady of means."

"Yes, because of Uncle Jeremiah," interrupted Nathaniel.

"No. Uncle Jeremiah is wealthy only because of *my* money and my financial backing. You do not owe Jeremiah anything. He owes us."

"What do you mean? ... I don't understand…"

"For the moment that is unimportant and I will explain fully at some point but first, and more importantly, I need to know, do you love Hannah?"

Nathaniel sighed and shifted uncomfortably in his seat.

Myah continued, "That gives me my answer, and I might add, I have never approved of families marrying within families; at some point it will result in bad blood. It is not wise or healthy. This I believe is what happened with Hannah's mother and her enforced marriage to Jeremiah. They were first cousins. On the other hand, I have seen the way you have looked after Jenny, the way your eyes glow when you talk about her, the way you are with her in her presence. She is the object of your desire, is she not?"

Nathaniel nodded dumbly. Myah patted his hand, "A mother knows these things. And all I want for you is your happiness. Hannah is a sweet girl but she is not for you and you need to tell her. She deserves that."

Outside the door, Hannah could just catch the words that were spoken inside. She looked at her naked hand. No one had noticed it was devoid of her ring. That had been her yardstick to measure by. Tears streamed down her face and she retreated back up the stairs to the safety of her room.

Myah continued, "I am afraid Hannah is not the most mentally stable. I do not know the effect this will have on her but she must know. Other suitors may then come calling. For her reputation not to suffer there must be a valid reason why the engagement is to be called off. This must be thought through, carefully. There is also the worry that her blood is tainted. Her mother, Julia, suffered with a debilitating mental illness that forced her at the age of thirty-three into an institution. No one could deal with her. Jeremiah tried. It was then he became very bitter. Finally, Julia took her own life. Hannah did not have the easiest of upbringings."

"I didn't know."

"It was all covered over. No one spoke of it."

"This makes it all the more difficult and awkward," responded Nathaniel. "What about Uncle Jeremiah?"

"Leave Uncle Jeremiah to me. And if you want proof of the lack of wisdom in first cousins marrying, you do not have to look far. I can give you many more examples of imbecile children born of such a union. This can be part of the reason as you will need a suitable heir to inherit when I am gone."

Nathaniel nodded unhappily still feeling the enormity of his quandary. Myah drew her son into her arms, "Happiness, Nathaniel. Happiness is so important. I had that with your father and I have you and Naomi as evidence. Don't let that slip through your fingers."

Nathaniel blinked back the stinging salt tears that threatened to overflow and held on tightly to his mother as he tried to reconcile himself to all she had said. He wondered when he would have the courage to speak to Hannah.


Jenny was sitting up in her bed, the exposed part of her face now clear of bruises. Her raven hair was well groomed and pulled away from her bandaged face.

"Well, Jenny, today's the day," announced Dr. Cunningham. He turned to Nathaniel and handed him a pair of scissors. "Dr. Brookes, your patient awaits."

Goliath and Myah stood at the foot of the bed and watched. Myah nodded encouragingly at her son, who took the offered cutters and turned to face Jenny who impulsively grabbed Nathaniel's hand, "Oh, Nathaniel, what if…?" Jenny exclaimed.

Dr. Cunningham interrupted, "Come now, my dear. No notes of pessimism now. In my long years of surgery I have never seen a more delicate touch than his. Have faith."

Jenny reached out to her bedside table and picked up a looking glass, which she placed on her lap, reflective side down. Nathaniel sat on the bed with Jenny and began to remove the bandages and gauze carefully. Jenny winced slightly.

"Try not to move, even if it hurts a little bit. There's nothing to worry about. There are just a few blood spots where it has dried and crusted on the dressing." Nathaniel took a pair of surgical tweezers and lifted the final piece of lint clear.

Myah and Goliath could only see Nathaniel's back. Jenny's face was hidden from them but they saw Dr. Cunningham's eyebrows rising. Before Goliath and Myah could step around to view Jenny's face she lifted the mirror, effectively covering her visage.

There was a small silence followed by Jenny in a tiny but broken voice exclaiming, "My God!" She slowly lowered the mirror and her radiant smile dazzled them all. Below the slight puffiness on her right cheek was a hint of a very fine red lined scar. "Oh my God!" Jenny repeated.

"Not to worry, my dear. In a few weeks the redness of the scar will be gone and it will continue to fade away."

Jenny burst into tears and flung her arms around Nathaniel and kissed him. Dr. Cunningham beamed at them over his glasses.

Myah's eyes spilled with tears of joy. She grabbed Goliath by the arm in her excitement.

"You have the hands of a healer," pronounced Goliath proudly.

"Jenny, you look beautiful," said Myah.

Nathaniel agreed, "You have always been beautiful, but now even more so," and he hugged her to him.

No one saw Hannah through the open door standing ramrod straight against the wall. She gazed in at the tableau in Jenny's room and couldn't fail to see Nathaniel's obvious affection for the young woman in bed.

Hannah's face paled and tears streamed down her cheeks. She choked back a cry and quietly left the scene, and returned to her room. All too clearly now things fell into place. She could understand Nathaniel's deference to her, his reluctance to spend time with her. Hannah picked up a piece of writing paper from her bureau. She dipped her quill pen into the ink and began to write. The words poured out of her and her tears mingled with the ink as she bared her soul to Nathaniel and absolved him from all blame. She broke off the engagement and enclosed her betrothal ring and sealed the letter with red wax. Feeling so much better and clearer in thought and mind than she had been for some time she knew what she had to do. She placed the letter inside the bureau drawer until it would be needed.

Later that day the family members gathered around the dining table for dinner. This time Jenny, now dressed and looking radiant sat with them at the table. Jenny was somewhat in awe of the lavish table décor and to being waited on by servants. Nathaniel was uncomfortable with having Hannah sitting on one side of him and Jenny on the other. He determined he would need to speak to Hannah soon, if not later that evening, then possibly in the morning. He would have to work out what to say to her to spare her feelings. He was somewhat surprised at Hannah's unusually bright appearance. She engaged in lively chatter with her cousin Naomi, when usually she would sit silently, only speaking when spoken to. Myah noted this and a worried frown crossed her otherwise calm features.

Jenny was somewhat out of her depth, dealing with the many spoons, knives and forks laid at her place mat on the table. Naomi caught her eye and would deliberately pick up the right utensils from the correct position for each course of the meal. Naomi subtly prompted Jenny as to which glass to use and when Jenny managed this feat with charm and grace that belied her lack of knowledge no one was any the wiser. It would be Jenny and Naomi's unspoken secret.

The meal was interrupted by the butler, who crossed to Nathaniel and spoke quietly, "A gentleman is asking for you in the hall, Mr. Brookes."

Nathaniel put down his napkin and questioned, "A gentleman? What gentleman?"

"A Mr. Pritchard, he is adamant that he needs to speak to you now."

Nathaniel rose from the table, "Do excuse me. I will try not to be long. Please continue with the meal."

Nathaniel followed the butler through the door and the table ignited with chatter again, only Jenny looked alarmed at the mention of Pritchard's name.

Nathaniel walked to the hallway where Pritchard waited, travel stained and weary, and with his hat in his hand; he was clearly eager to be somewhere else.

"Mr. Pritchard, what a pleasant surprise," greeted Nathaniel.

"Mr. Brookes. Please, pardon this intrusion."

"No intrusion, won't you join us?"

"No… no. Most kind, thank you. But, I must be off, really. I just dropped by to see how you were faring and to deliver some items that you left behind in your… er… sudden departure." He passed Nathaniel his carpetbag containing clothing and his medical bag. Goliath stepped into the hallway and waited silently at the foot of the stairs, followed by Philip Chapman who listened to the interchange.

Nathaniel received his property gratefully and placed the items on the floor, "Why, thank you, Sir. But, really there was no need as I plan to return before too long and resume my duties."

"Return?" exclaimed Pritchard, "Why? What on earth for? Do forgive me, I assumed…"

"Mr. Pritchard, my resolve is still set. I plan to finish the job; once and for all."

Pritchard paced nervously, his anger growing, "Have you taken complete leave of your senses, man? They killed your father. They have murdered all who have helped you. Why, your own life was hanging by a thread. Can't you understand that this is bigger than you, than all of us? Don't be a stubborn fool. Get out while you can. There will be no recriminations after all you have suffered."

"Mr. Pritchard, you knew my father and according to my mother I am not that different from him. Did you truly expect me to give into these threats? To drift away and whimper in a corner?"

Pritchard turned away to leave, his irritation overflowing and snapped, "Your father was a fool, a noble one, but a fool never-the-less. And you are the son of one!"

Nathaniel's eyebrows raised in surprise at the onslaught, "Sir! You forget yourself."

Pritchard sighed wearily and replaced his hat, "Fundamentally, I believe you are right. Your intentions are good. For too long now I have had to nurse one Riding Officer after another only to see them throw their lives away for nothing, for an ideal. We can never win against these unscrupulous criminals, their thuggery and the lackeys who are too cowardly to expose these rogues. You had an opportunity here, to leave and begin afresh. I am saddened for you, Nathaniel Brookes, although you are a most honourable man." Pritchard invited no more discussion. He simply turned and departed leaving the door wide open in his wake.

Goliath crossed to the door and closed it, "Well, that was big surprise."

Nathaniel felt his own ire, "He had no right to talk about my father in that manner."

Goliath ever the diplomat replied quietly, "He may be saying not throw life away; Want you step away from danger not intending to hurt father's memory. He your father's friend."

Philip Chapman pursed his lips in an attempt to restrain his own anger at what he had just witnessed. He was a man of manners and disliked the lack of respect displayed and, even more, he disliked Pritchard's attitude to solving the problem of ridding the coast of smugglers. He had broached the subject before and determined that he would speak to his superiors and bring his regiment to the coast and help fight the battle that had been lost for too many years. When an opportunity presented itself he would tell Nathaniel that he desired to stand behind him and watch his back.

Nathaniel removed his bags to the foot of the stairs and pronounced, "Come on Philip, let's eat." And they returned to the dining room.

# Chapter Twenty-Five

## Tragedy

The Brookes family were blessed with another delightful day of azure skies and golden sunshine and chose to enjoy the warmth of the garden. There was a flurry of activity around Jenny, seated comfortably in a chair removed from the house. Myah, Goliath, Naomi and Philip fussed over her whilst Nathaniel watched from the garden seat. Hannah observed the scene from an upstairs window her face etched in melancholy.

Myah leaned across Jenny and plumped up a pillow behind her, while Naomi wrapped a rich woollen shawl around Jenny's shoulders. Jenny inhaled deeply and asked, "What a heavenly fragrance, so delicate and pleasing; what is it?"

Naomi replied, "It is isn't it? But I have no idea what it's called. Mother?"

Myah laughed, "Forgive me, my dear, it has an unpronounceable French name."

"But it is in a very pretty bottle. It looks just like a real rose," added Naomi.

Nathaniel sat up sharply and his eyes gleamed as he heard what was said. Fear flickered in Jenny's eyes. Nathaniel pressed his mother, "Mother, where did you get it from?"

Myah answered carelessly unaware of the effect her words were having as she placed a rug over Jenny's knees, "It was a trifle. A gift from your uncle, from Mr. Brookes' last visit to Swansea."

Nathaniel frowned and stood up. Without speaking he left the garden and entered the house. He made his way to his mother's rooms and entered her bedroom leaving the door ajar. Hannah hearing footsteps crept from her room and peeped into Myah's bedchamber and watched Nathaniel. That is until she heard other feet mount the stairs and so she retreated into her own room but left it slightly open so that she could hear anything that was said.

Nathaniel, in Myah's room, looked about him slowly before crossing to his mother's dressing table. Surrounded by brushes, combs and other toiletries was the same rose shaped bottle that Jenny had described the Landlord selling at the Inn. Nathaniel picked it up and studied it, his face was a dark cloud and he exclaimed, "No! They must not reach my family. I will not have my loved ones tainted by goods from spilled blood."

Nathaniel marched out, his face a picture of determination and found Goliath had followed him, who asked, "What you going to do?"

"I don't know … yet. But, I have other things to settle here at home first."

"Ah! Jenny and Hannah. Have you made up mind?"

"You know?" said Nathaniel incredulously.

"It hard not to know. It plain you love Jenny," affirmed Goliath.

"I know. But, I am torn," he faltered.

"Between love and duty. Not good place to be," recognised Goliath.

The two men started back down the stairs and Hannah pressed her door shut and leaned against it her eyes working rapidly, flitting manically from side to side.


Nathaniel and Jenny walked through the secluded garden enjoying the last of the evening sun. They walked in step, their shoulders and hands almost touching; the silence between them accentuated by the song of the birds as they sang in the trees. Jenny's eyes glistened with tears. She could hardly bring herself to speak.

Jeremiah arrived in the garden and saw the two walking together. He watched them suspiciously and followed surreptitiously in their steps. Nathaniel and Jenny were completely oblivious to the interest their stroll was generating.

Jenny looked up at Nathaniel and swallowed hard. "This is an awful situation. I have come to …" she hesitated and took a deep breath and continued, "To love you like I never thought I could love anyone, but…"

Nathaniel interrupted her saying quietly, "But you know I am honour bound to Hannah."

"I know," sighed Jenny. "That is precisely the problem and she loves you. You know she does," continued Jenny.

"Yes. But my problem is that I love you. I love you, Jenny. You and no one else."

They stopped walking and Nathaniel turned her into him. He took her in his arms and crushed her small body to him. His lips burned down on hers in an open display of passion, passion that was doubly returned by Jenny. He held her close drinking in her fragrance and caressed her face and flowing hair. They kissed again gently, tenderly and lovingly.

Jeremiah glowered with rage as he watched and listened. His rage bubbled like that of a volcano about to erupt and he determined to damn all that his anger touched. He maintained his distance and fought to stop his fury from breaking out. Jeremiah stepped back into the shrubbery as the couple returned the way they had come.

"What are you going to do?" asked Jenny.

"I don't know. But, I know what I want. I have to pick the right moment, Jenny. Hannah is not in the best of health. I was going to speak to her later or in the morning but now… It may be best if I distance myself from everything; just for a while."

Jenny nodded her agreement, "I know, I understand, but don't leave it too long."

"I will tell her when I feel she is strong enough to cope." And they both stepped back indoors. Jeremiah's face was filled with fury.

It was later that evening after dinner was over that Nathaniel tapped on his mother's door.

"Come in."

She looked surprised when she saw her son's troubled face.

'Mother, I have made my decision. I have to return. I will return tonight to my post and finish what I have started."

"But, Nathaniel…"

"No, let me finish. I may not return. I hope I will, but I cannot promise and for that reason, I will not say anything to Hannah until I return, if I return. Her honour then will be intact. Look after Jenny for me. And bid farewell to Naomi and everyone. Goliath will look after you all."

"My son, are you sure about this?"

"I have to do it, Mother. Please." Nathaniel's voice was earnest.

Myah sighed and nodded her head sadly, "Very well. I don't like this but I will respect your wishes." She rose and embraced her son. "Farewell, come back alive."

Nathaniel's room flickered in candlelight. Grotesque shadows played on the walls as the candle flame sputtered and stretched. Nathaniel was frantically packing his bags when there was a knock at his door.

Nathaniel called, "It's open."

Goliath entered and looked surprised at the fevered activity. "We go somewhere?" he questioned.

"I have to return and finish what I started," replied Nathaniel.

"I be ready in minute," affirmed Goliath.

"No," argued Nathaniel. "I need you to stay here and watch over my family and look after Jenny."

"They are safe here, my place with you," Goliath responded.

"I don't think so," persisted Nathaniel.

Goliath continued, "Whatever evil threatens you and family has roots in Mumbles. It there we have to stop it."

Nathaniel stopped and surveyed his friend's earnest expression, "So be it then... to Mumbles. Together."

Nathaniel continued putting his things away. "I will meet you out front of the house with the horses, when you are ready."

"I be there. Need ten minutes." Goliath stepped out and returned to his room to pack his few belongings. He glanced around his haven of comfort and safety and stepped down the stairs to the hallway and outside to the steps of the handsome manor house.

The sun was just a promise as a pinkish glow lit the horizon. Nathaniel and Goliath both cloaked for travel left the front drive of the elegant house leading their horses, Jessie and Samson. There was hardly a sound on the cobbles in the early morning air. They stole away and didn't mount their steeds until they reached the road, which was deserted and wind torn. Once there they cantered off into the breaking light, their heavy cloaks flapping like the ragged plumes of ravens' wings.

They rode as if they were chasing the start of the day. Nathaniel threw frequent but subtle looks behind him as they ate up the miles. They approached the crest of a hill and Nathaniel leapt down and picked up Jessie's foot to examine her hooves.

"What wrong?" queried Goliath.

"Nothing really," replied Nathaniel. "Have you noticed we are being followed?"

"I had feeling but thought must be mistaken."

Nathaniel inspected the road ahead, "See that small copse of trees up ahead?" Goliath searched their path and nodded as Nathaniel continued, "We'll soon discover who our shy friend is. Come."

Nathaniel quickly mounted Jessie and they steamed off toward the trees to lie in wait.


Dawn was breaking and Hannah tossed in her bed. She sat up, threw back her bedclothes. Her eyes were open and staring. She swung her legs over the side and stepped up. Hannah grabbed her robe and left her room. She wandered across the landing to Nathaniel's room and tapped lightly on the door. Hearing no response she slowly opened his door and peeped inside. The room was in complete disarray with clothes strewn over an unmade bed. His carpetbag was gone as was his cloak and cocked hat.

Hannah retreated back to her room and sat woodenly in front of her dresser. She picked up a brush and began to vigorously draw it though her hair, scraping her scalp, brushing harder and harder. Her corn blonde hair flared out with static electricity giving her the look of a woman possessed. She dragged her locks into an untidy braid and stared at her face. A trickle of blood traced its way down her cheek from her scalp and dripped onto her nightdress.

Hannah cast down her brush and threw open her wardrobe door and selected her wedding gown, which had been worn by her mother many years before. She struggled into it without help and attempted to lace it up. Next, Hannah pulled on a pair of soft satin shoes and snatched a heavy headdress with a veil that sat on a shelf.

She carefully removed her sealed letter from her drawer and tossed it on the bed. She selected another piece of paper and her quill. She picked up a small knife and turned her arm up. Without flinching she sliced into her milk white soft flesh. Blood seeped from the wound. The quill dipped into Hannah's precious blood and she scrawled a name on the parchment, Nathaniel. The 'l' scratched along the paper and trailed off before she scribbled violently almost ripping a hole in the paper. She left this missive on her bureau desk in plain view for anyone to see. And then returned to her dresser and sat.

Hannah studied her reflection in the looking glass and patted her face with white powder. She hummed lightly and smiled demurely at herself. "With a hey and a ho and a hey nonny no," she sang. Hannah clapped her hands and laughed. She rose to her window and opened it. Hannah uprooted some flowers from her window box and clutched them to her before stepping out from her room. She closed her door firmly and ascended the servant stairs toward the attic.

Agnes, the maid, knocked politely on Hannah's door and waited a moment before entering. She glanced around the room that looked as if someone had ransacked it. She hastened along the landing and ran down the stairs to the hallway. Agnes progressed to the breakfast room and glanced inside. Hannah was not present. From there, Agnes dashed to the drawing room and again took a look inside. It was empty.

Now Agnes was really concerned and uncertain what to do. She ventured outside into the garden and searched about her looking for any sign of her young mistress. A magpie flew up squawking its chattering alarm call. One magpie alone was not a good omen. She heard a small sound above her and some moss and tiny stones plummeted onto the cobbled path. Agnes looked up and screamed.

Agnes' terrible scream permeated the air. Agnes screamed again whilst staring up at the roof of the manor. The strains of a song reached her ears, "Hey, nonny, nonny, hey nonny no."

The rest of the family and their guest, Philip Chapman, at breakfast stopped when they heard Agnes cry out. They put down their cutlery and rushed into the garden to see what was wrong.

"What's the matter, girl?" demanded Philip. Agnes pointed a wavering finger upward.

Jeremiah blustered as the last who arrived to the scene, "What on earth is the matter with the…" he looked up to see where Agnes was pointing to see his daughter, Hannah in full bridal gown balanced precariously on the top of the roof.

Philip demanded, "How can I get to her? Quickly…"

Jeremiah cried out, "Hannah! No! Hannah!" He bit hard into his lip and drew blood.

Before anyone could say anything else, Hannah tossed down her ragged posy and stretched her arms out as if to fly. She threw herself from off the roof to the unyielding cobbles below.

Jeremiah's agonised shriek rang out, "Noooooo!" Philip tried to grab him but Jeremiah slipped out of his grasp and ran to the broken body of his daughter. "Hannah, Hannah, no." He cradled his daughter's head in his lap.

Her eyes fluttered open and she whispered, "Hey ho!" But the spark of life faded from her eyes and her head lolled to one side.

Philip Chapman hurried to his side to try and prise him away from his daughter, "Mr. Brookes, please…"

"Let go of me!" roared Jeremiah. He ran his hand through his hair in abject misery and despair before bellowing, "Nathaniel Brookes! Wherever you are - you will pay with your blood for this; your own blood. As God is my witness." Jeremiah lay his daughter's head carefully down and rose. He turned to Myah and proclaimed icily, "I will have your son's head for this, Myah, family or no family. Nathaniel may have had a quest but now I have one, too, and with even more urgency. Rest assured I will track him down. His blood is mine," and he fled from the garden, turbulent emotions raged inside him. Myah stood still in shock and horror, her face was white and she bit her lip, struggling what to say and do.

The butler rushed to Hannah's still form and covered her body with a blanket. Myah, Naomi and the maid, Agnes wept as Philip Chapman took charge and instructed the butler, "Send for the Sheriff."

Naomi was frozen in shock. "I cannot believe it." Philip put his arm around her and Naomi buried her head in his chest and sobbed.

"Lieutenant Chapman," Myah addressed the young man tearfully.

"Ma'am?"

"Nathaniel... he must be warned and told. Jeremiah means what he says. He will kill him."

"I'll take care of everything. Worry not. I will go now. Where is Nathaniel headed?"

"Back to Mumbles, I believe, to finish what he started," cried Myah.

"Then I will after them all, now. By your leave." Philip kissed Naomi quickly and Myah took her daughter into her arms as the young officer left them to search for Nathaniel.

Myah spoke softly to her daughter, "Nathaniel left in the night without a word to anyone. Goliath went with him. I fear he may not return. All we can do is pray. Agnes you better tell Miss Jenny."


The wind was getting up and blew hard as a lone rider, swathed in a heavy cloak approached the copse of trees on the cliff top slowly and hesitantly. Nathaniel waited. He crouched low behind a stunted tree with his pistols at the ready.

Goliath held the horses some distance away. The rider walked tentatively into the clearing. Nathaniel broke cover and cocked both pistols. "Hold! Stand and identify yourself!" he shouted.

The horse back-pedalled in fear and the rider battled with the reins to calm the fidgety horse that was skittish in this ambush. The rider threw back the hood from the cloak and called out, "So, did you plan to shoot me or just frighten me to death?"

Nathaniel pulled up his pistols and exclaimed, "What in the name of God are you doing here, Jenny? Don't you know I could have shot you? Turn back"

"No!" Jenny was adamant and defiant.

"Please, listen to me. This will definitely end in blood being spilled and I don't want it to be yours," urged Nathaniel.

"All the more reason for me to stay with you. This is my home. Most of those I loved or knew have been killed. I have no intention of losing you, too."

"Please, Jenny. I could not bear it if you were harmed again," said Nathaniel mollified.

Jenny's response was to dismount and embrace him, "I do not wish to live without you." She turned her face up to him and stood on tiptoe to receive his tender kiss.

Nathaniel could see there was no dissuading her and reluctantly allowed her to remount and join him and Goliath on the journey back to Cliff Cottage. As the sun began slipping toward the horizon they cut a proud picture of three avenging angels silhouetted on the horizon. The sky was a dramatic blaze of red as they reached the top of the cliff path and surveyed the village below. Little was said and all were wondering what fate awaited them back at the cottage.

Ever watchful, with Nathaniel at the front and Goliath at the back they trotted carefully toward the cottage that had been rented from Lily. It is obvious from the state of the outside that vandals had wrecked what they could.

They dismounted and dropping the reins of their steeds in front of them so the horses wouldn't bolt, they entered and surveyed the damage. Nothing had been spared, furniture and crockery had all been smashed and someone had attempted to torch the place. Fortunately, the fire had not taken hold but had singed and scorched the walls. The stench of smoke filled their nostrils. Jenny opened the windows to help the flow of air through the house to try and clear the air.

Nathaniel set about trying to see what could be salvaged and Goliath went to attend to the horses. Fortunately, the stabling facilities were intact. There was even hay for the animals and water in the trough. Goliath made the animals comfortable and returned inside.

Jenny had checked the pantry and was surprised to find some food items remained. She remarked, "It will not match your mother's dinners but I will do what I can. There is flour for bread, even some mutton left hanging and potatoes…"

Goliath turned the splintered table back the right way up and with a sarcastic tone said, "You think someone try to tell us something?"

Nathaniel frowned, "They shouldn't be expecting us unless Pritchard has let slip to his men. And then the whole village will know our intentions."

"We must be on guard and watch," declared Goliath.

"Come," instructed Jenny, "Clear some space near the fireplace. Let's get the fire going. At least we won't have to go outside for kindling," she mused looking at the shattered chairs.

"Not all of them," ordered Nathaniel, "Some can be repaired and that's what we must do if we are to stay here."

"I'll see to the fire," exclaimed Jenny.

"But smoke give us away," remarked Goliath.

"I can't cook without a fire." Jenny looked at Nathaniel inquiringly.

"They'll know soon enough. We can't hide our presence forever. Build the fire," he commanded.

Goliath selected the least damaged items and using wood from the debris they began to try and repair some of the furnishings.

"You know, I don't know how we are fixed to stay here, with Lily gone. Did she have any relatives?"

"Not that I'm aware," replied Jenny as she began to clear the grate and lay the fire. "I think it was just her and David."

"Well, if not I will set aside her rent money just the same and it can go to any kin she has left."

Satisfied, they each undertook their tasks and soon a fire was burning merrily lightening the gloom in the room. Three chairs had been resurrected from the devastation and Jenny had made some flatbread and a mutton and potato hotpot. Enamel plates had been scrubbed and each sat down to their makeshift meal.

They ate in silence; a mantle of depression covered their shoulders. Twilight sank into night. Nathaniel pronounced "We'd best get some rest, tomorrow will come quickly enough."

Nathaniel and Jenny began to prepare some bedding for the night. Goliath offered, "I take first watch." The giant wrapped himself up and moved to the re-hung door to settle outside on the wooden verandah. "Will wake you in three hours," he said to Nathaniel.

Nathaniel nodded and flopped down on the blankets next to Jenny who sat staring at the fire hugging her knees. She bit her lip and finally asked, "I don't understand... why did you agree to marry Hannah if you did not love her?"

Nathaniel's expression revealed he was shocked by her outspoken manner and the brazen question. Jenny relented, "I'm sorry. I have no right to ask you that," she deferred lowering her eyes.

"No... no... You should know. I am not trying to dally with your feelings. I promise you. It was just... well, I felt it was expected of us."

"And since when do hearts follow the wishes and expectations of others," responded Jenny further emboldened.

"It was a matter of duty. My union with Hannah would have provided for my mother and my sister's future at least that was what I was led to believe."

"Not by your mother, I am sure."

"No. You are right. It was always Uncle Jeremiah that hinted at this. But always when we were alone, never in front of my mother. I truly believed we were beholden to him for our home and place in society. It seems I was wrong. My mother told me the truth of our birthright. We owe Uncle Jeremiah nothing. Now I have to find a way of setting things right without dishonouring Hannah's reputation. I fear I have shirked my duty there."

"It's difficult, I know."

They were interrupted by Goliath entering softly, "Someone come and not make big secret of it."

Nathaniel and Goliath picked up weapons. Jenny grabbed the poker and brandished it before her, getting used to the feel of it. "Don't you dare expose yourself in a fight. Get out the back where you won't be seen," admonished Nathaniel.

"No," argued Jenny. "My place is with you, both. I will stand at your side."

Nathaniel muttered under his breath, "Stubborn woman."

There was a sudden and rapid knocking on the door.

190

Goliath opened the door warily to reveal two women. They pulled back their cowls. It was Lady Caroline and her Lady-in-waiting, Martha.

"Mr. Brookes? Thank goodness I have found you. I wasn't sure if it was you or if someone else was in residence. We saw smoke from the chimney."

"And where ladies saw, so will others," advised Goliath.

"May we come in?" asked Lady Caroline searching around her anxiously.

"Lady Caroline, this is an unusual time for a visit. Please," Nathaniel gestured inside. The two women entered and saw the devastation that had been done to the cottage. As they came in view of the feeble lamplight Nathaniel saw the bruises marking the left cheek of Lady Caroline's face.

"I see that violence on women is a family trait," noted Nathaniel.

"I beg your pardon?" queried Lady Caroline.

"Sir James and his son, although his son would have marked the right side of your face."

Lady Caroline dropped her head slightly. "I am sorry to admit it but you are right. However, that is not why I am here. I must warn you. You are in danger, all of you. You are right, Goliath. They are already aware that you are here. There are plans afoot to ambush you and trap you as they did with the Pughs. They want you dead, Mr. Brookes. They want to purge the customs service of Riding Officers especially you. They say they will do for you in such a way that no sane man would ever take the job again."

Nathaniel and Goliath exchanged concerned looks appreciating the frightening knowledge that their fears were well founded.

"Well, with the element of surprise gone we can only rely…"

"On numbers," completed Goliath.

Nathaniel began to gather their belongings and hastily packed them. He glanced up at Lady Caroline, "Won't you be missed?"

"No. They have joined their wreckers. I can safely return home. They will be none the wiser."

"Unless someone else has seen you," said Jenny.

"That is so," agreed Lady Caroline. "We must hope and pray that God is on our side."

"Where do they hide out?" pressed Nathaniel.

"There is a cove… immediately below the Wreckers' Way. Do you know it?"

"I do."

"The cove is only accessible at low tide. It leads to the cave system but it is always heavily guarded."

"Thank you. Now go home and wait for assistance and I will take care of everything."

The two ladies pulled up their hoods and hurried away.

"Miss Jenny. She must go with them. They hide her away. No one think of looking for her there," said Goliath.

"I am not going anywhere. I am going with you. Besides they might not know I am back," decided Jenny.

"I'll not argue with you, we don't have the time," concurred Nathaniel. "Come we must hurry."

"Where we go?" asked Goliath.

"To the Customs House. We must hurry."

"What then we do?"

"Pritchard cannot refuse us a platoon, not this time. We must surprise them. Catch them unawares. Finish what my father started."

"But they many, we few."

"All the more reason for us to have surprise on our side. They won't expect an attack so soon. If we move now, we may have a chance. Catch the whole damn lot and end this iniquity."

"If not, we lose our lives," said Goliath sagely.

"All the more reason for us to be successful."

"Hope your bright thoughts right," muttered Goliath.

They gathered themselves together and watched Lady Caroline and her lady-in-waiting disappearing down the track to the village. They mounted their steeds and with firm resolve sprinted off toward the town and the Custom House. They did not see the lone rider traversing the cliff path some way behind them, nor did the rider see the group's departure. Jeremiah Brookes was on their tail and was headed straight for Cliff Cottage.

In righteous anger Jeremiah reined in his horse and

192

dismounted at the broken porch. He stormed inside and gave a cursory look around. He could see the wanton damage and havoc wreaked on the dwelling. He could also tell by the still smoking fire and dirty pots that they had not long left. He checked the ease and accessibility of his sword and pistol, dashed from the house, remounted and sped off toward the village.

Within a few minutes he had caught up with Lady Caroline and Martha. He pulled the horse in front of them, stopping their passage and leapt down to address them, "Forgive me ladies," he touched his cap, "I am I search of Nathaniel Brookes, the Riding Officer. I must speak with him on a matter of gross urgency." Jeremiah looked suitably earnest and sincere.

Lady Caroline replied, "Why, Sir. You have just missed him."

"May I enquire as to where he was headed?"

"I believe he has gone for reinforcements."

"Reinforcements? Then where…?"

"Wrecker's Way, to the caves I believe…"

Jeremiah jumped back on his steed and doffed his cap, "I thank you."

"You know how to get there?" questioned Lady Caroline, surprised.

"I believe I do, well more or less. I will find it. My brother rode this coast before Nathaniel."

"Then you are…"

"His uncle and we have important business to attend to. Farewell." Jeremiah turned his horse and rode back to the cliff path. He decided he would watch and pick his moment.

Lady Caroline shaded her eyes as she studied the stranger's back, "I hope I have done right," she murmured aloud.

"It was his uncle," reassured Martha. "What harm could there be?"

"I don't know," she mused quietly, "There was just something in the man…" She stopped and shrugged it off. "Come, we best hurry we want no more strange meetings out here." And the two women lengthened their step to return to the manor.

193

# Chapter Twenty-Six

## End Game

Jenny and Goliath remained on their mounts in the Custom House courtyard. Four armed dragoons were seated on horseback waiting patiently by the gate.

The door opened, Nathaniel, Pritchard and Sergeant Morris came out buckling on their swords. Nathaniel looked at the sparse troop of Dragoons, "We need more men. This is hardly enough."

"This is all we have," proclaimed Pritchard. "If we are to strike as you say, we must do it now. Surprise will be key in ending this damnable trade."

"We also need to send guards to Lady Caroline for her protection," insisted Nathaniel.

Sergeant Morris blustered petulantly, "We can't be everywhere and I hate to say it, but the thought of my trained dragoons against wreckers fills me with dread. We don't stand a chance! We are only eight, and one's a woman," he muttered disagreeably. "There are too many of them."

Pritchard scowled and reprimanded the sergeant, "Enough! Stop being defeatist. Let's be on our way. This is our one chance to end this skulduggery forever."

They all sat astride their horses and Sergeant Morris, together with his dragoons, led the way toward the cliffs.

Secreted in a copse watching the platoon's arrival was Jeremiah. He cursed softly under his breath and studied them as they manoeuvred their steeds to the dangerous track. The distance was too great to get a clear shot at Nathaniel with his pistol. He would observe in safety and then follow them down the path.

The mounted column rode in single file along the narrow path, led by the Sergeant. He was followed by two of his dragoons; Nathaniel, Pritchard, Jenny and Goliath were next. The last two dragoons brought up the rear. They soon reached the edge of the cliffs where a path cut down the side.

It was not too steep. Nathaniel noticed old furrowed ruts in the ground, "Wide enough for a small cart, I see," he observed.

"These paths are as old as the hills," rejoined Pritchard. "They have been used by the local fisher folk amongst others, for years."

"I'm sure," retorted Nathaniel.

They eventually arrived at the bottom of the cliff. The sound of thundering waves could be heard from a safe distance. The sandy cove was well protected from sight by a large outcrop of rocks a score of feet up the cliff face.

Sergeant Morris called back, "We will have to hurry. The tide may be out for the moment, but it can turn very quickly."

"You seem to be well acquainted with the tides, Sergeant," observed Nathaniel in an almost accusatory manner.

The sergeant didn't pick up Nathaniel's tone and responded, "Son of a fisherman turned soldier, Mr. Brookes. The sea salt still runs in my blood, though."

Morris dismounted and tied the reins to some driftwood that looked forlornly like flotsam from a wreck. He beckoned one of the dragoons across and ordered, "Stay with the horses. Keep your eyes peeled. No one must come up or down the path. Is that understood? You will be watching our back. It could mean the difference between success and failure."

"Yes, Sir," said the dragoon and acknowledged him with a nod before standing on guard with the horses. The rest of the company joined Sergeant Morris on the sand. They each drew their pistols and swords. Nathaniel glanced anxiously at Jenny, "Jenny I would feel more comfortable if you were to wait here," he advised.

"But, Nathaniel…" she protested.

The sergeant backed Nathaniel's instruction, "Mr. Brookes is right, Miss Banwen. This is no place for a woman."

Jenny reluctantly accepted what was said and picked her way back to the guard on duty. Goliath removed torches from his saddle pack. But Morris criticised the action, "We had better go without those. We don't want to announce our arrival." Goliath hesitated but Nathaniel caught his eye and shook his head as if to say, 'Leave them.' Goliath replaced them in his pack unwilling to throw them onto the sand.

The men hugged the cliff wall in single file and made for a low cave, well below the line of the watermark along the chalky cliff wall. The going was treacherous and slippery. Waves crashed below sending showers of water up and over the men, who stood stock still until it was safe to move. Once more, they gauged their passage against the large incoming ferocious waves on the tide. They finally reached the mouth of the cave even if a trifle wet, tasting the salt water on their tongues. The surf here exploded with greater ferocity and steely rain started lashing down whipping their exposed hands and faces.

Sergeant Morris turned to the others and commanded, "From here on, keep your voices down to a minimum. The echoes alone will surely give us away." He gingerly stepped forward and crept toward the rough rock hewn steps that climbed for a short distance just enough to clear the watermark in the caves.

They entered a wide space that contained a small boat, ropes, boathooks and several barrels and small crates. Nathaniel whispered, "Contraband?"

"Stores more than likely," responded Sergeant Morris with a knowing note in his voice. "They sometimes hide out for days even weeks. They would need supplies."

Goliath nudged Nathaniel and muttered suspiciously, "Can he see through wood?" Almost together, Nathaniel cocked his pistol as Goliath loosened his sword in its scabbard. In front of them a large wooden trunk lay half open with garments protruding from it, long thick cloaks, hats and scarves overflowed, predominantly a rusty coloured heavy woollen scarf caught Nathaniel's eye.

Up ahead, small brass tallow lanterns lit the way. The smell of those together with that of sputtering wax candles pervaded their nostrils, blending with the salty air and musty dampness of the dripping cave. Other pieces of flotsam and jetsam littered the tunnel floor, broken boards from ships' decking, nets from fishing boats, fragmented crab pots, splintered oars, rags and glass buoys used as markers. The group picked their way through the debris carefully and as silently as possible.

The tunnel twisted and turned for many yards but soon the sound of muffled voices drifted toward them. The sergeant hissed at Nathaniel, "Mr. Brookes, I would suggest you put your pistol away." He pointed at the rocks all around them. "Letting that off in here might not be a good idea, if you want to see the light of day again. The ricochet could take us all out as well as bringing rocks down on our heads."

Nathaniel scanned the cavern and understood what Morris implied and released the hammer on the pistol. He drew out his sabre instead. The company continued on as quietly as they were able. Nathaniel turned to speak to Pritchard but he had fallen to the back and was now the last man in the column. He appeared to be hanging back. Nathaniel's brow furrowed as he puzzled that fact, but now fully committed to their course of action, they collectively and slowly pressed on.

Goliath whispered, "I not like it. It seem we being herded to our death. It not feel right." Nathaniel was at a loss at what to say, he was feeling less than comfortable and now in his mind he questioned the wisdom of this act. His gut instinct was telling him he had made a mistake. But he had no chance to voice this or retrace his steps as they heard chatter in the distance. They paused and listened, before stealthily moving on.

The voices now seemed closer. The pounding waves that bellowed and cried outside sent an eerie distorted sound down the tunnels, like that of an alien being. They rounded another bend and Nathaniel gasped in surprise. The cavern in front of him was enormous, more like a cathedral than a cave with a huge vaulted ceiling of rock adorned with stalactites that stretched down to meet stalagmites stretching up from the ground forming colonnades that would challenge anything a human hand had ever built.

The dripping walls seemed to wink back at them as wet limestone reflected the light from a plethora of lanterns wedged into the rock. Barrels and boxes were stacked high along one wall and a large trestle table laden with food and grog sat in the middle of the cavern.

A dozen wreckers, including Silas, and others that had molested and stripped Jenny were sitting in a slovenly fashion around or near the table. A cry of warning resounded around the hollow from a sentry stationed on a pulpit like outcrop above them, the equivalent of a crow's nest on a sailing ship.

The disturbed wreckers all scrambled for their weapons. Nathaniel and Goliath prepared their swords and braced themselves for the attack but as Nathaniel gritted himself for combat a cold steel blade pressed against the nape of Nathaniel's neck and Sergeant Morris's venomous voice ordered, "Drop your sword, Sir."

Goliath immediately tried to swing his blade to protect Nathaniel but one of the dragoons bludgeoned him from behind. Goliath crumpled to the rocks, with a groan and blood oozed from the back of his head.

Nathaniel swung around, the rapier drawing blood from his neck. He faced the drawn swords of the Sergeant and his turncoat dragoons fully seeing for the first time the double game these fiends under the guise of the law actually were playing. His eyes scanned the rest of the band recognising the informant, Silas and other rogues who had striven to thwart him and escape him. His eyes lit on the merciless Charles who had mutilated his Jenny. His blood raged with anger and hatred and pulsed in his temple. He spat onto the sandy shingle floor, ridding himself of the taste of sour sweat, alcohol and salt that invaded his mouth and he felt the bile rise up as he recognised yet another, the profligate, Sir James Bevan.

"What's the matter, Mr. Riding Officer? Feeling lonely now?" asked the Sergeant in a mocking tone. The dragoons and wreckers erupted in cold cruel laughter. "Drop your sword. NOW!" The sergeant's shrill voice ordered.

Nathaniel was sandwiched between them. He had been led into a perfect trap. There was no alternative, his arm dropped and his sabre fell to the cave floor.

"And the pistol. Drop it."

Slowly and reluctantly, Nathaniel relinquished his firearm, which also clattered to the floor and the dragoon kicked it away and out of reach.

Sir James Bevan pushed forward through the ruffians with his son, Charles, at his side, "Welcome to our humble abode, Mr. Brookes." He stood challengingly his hands on his hips but spoke as if he was receiving guests to dinner at his own Manor House.

Nathaniel grimaced distastefully, "Sir James, I see that all my suspicions were correct. I note, also, that your sadistic son is here. Good. One haul will net all the rotten fish in one go," he pronounced with more confidence than he felt.

Charles snarled in anger, leapt forward and swung his left arm at the Riding Officer but Nathaniel blocked it and smashed his own fist into Charles' face breaking his nose and splitting his lips. Bright red blood gushed down Charles' mouth and chin. Nathaniel was unable to contain his delight and badgered Charles still further. "Ah! The spoiled brat is not used to being hit back. You see, Charles that's the disadvantage of striking a man rather than a defenceless woman."

Charles was frantic and angry. He fumbled for his sword but his father stopped him. "Hold!" he commanded. "All in good time. You will have your turn. But for now, I will relish this and I will not be rushed."

A scraping noise came from behind Nathaniel who turned to see a shadow detach itself from the wall and the darkness beyond.

Silas cried out involuntarily in awe, "Bloody hell, the smuggler Knight."

The figure stepped forward to face the assembled crew. His face as usual was swathed in a scarf, a heavy rust coloured one. He was covered in a long thick cloak, his hat worn low on his head. The wreckers muttered the Knight's name in admiration and with respect, touching their forelocks.

The Knight's voice, as always, was muffled but was immediately recognisable to Nathaniel. "Hold and let's make this quick! Step back, men. Let's make some room," the Knight ordered the wreckers who stopped in their tracks, moved back and watched the exchange. "This is all your doing, Nathaniel. I tried to stop you returning. You were safe. You could have walked away, lived a good life. I warned you. This is on your head. Your friends' blood will be on

*your* hands. Why wouldn't you listen? I told you to give up…
but no! You had to follow in your father's footsteps."

"I will do more than that Pritchard. I will see you hang for
your crimes against the Crown," retorted Nathaniel.

"I think not," rasped Pritchard. "Dragoons!" he shouted.

The Dragoons stepped forward and pushed Nathaniel
roughly to the middle of the cavern. One of them smashed his
mace into Nathaniel's back. His legs buckled and Nathaniel
dropped heavily to the floor onto his knees and in severe
pain. As the Riding Officer lay there Charles took his
advantage and delivered a swift kick into Nathaniel's
stomach. Nathaniel retched violently before wheezing
sarcastically, "How sporting, you couldn't face me standing,
can only kick a man when he's down!"

Charles twisted his face in snarling fury and made to kick
Nathaniel again, but this time the Riding Officer was ready.
From his kneeling position, Nathaniel caught hold of
Charles' foot and twisted it viciously. Bone cracked and
Charles fell to the rocky floor screaming in agony. He
continued to scream until at a nod from Sir James a cudgel
from Silas came down and knocked Charles senseless,
silencing his cries.

Pritchard addressed his band of cutthroats, "I will allow
you some sport. The tide will not return for some hours and I
intend to further your education for the duration. You can
have your fun."

The men guffawed in glee and gathered around him.

"Why…? Why Pritchard? Why would you do this?" asked
Nathaniel hoarsely, still winded.

"Why?" responded Pritchard superciliously. "For the
money of course. The gold, the power." He snorted, "Twenty
guineas a year for King and Country, no thank you, Sir! I
wanted more. And all these people wanted, was to continue
with their 'tradition'. Wrecking and smuggling is in their
blood; their way of life. I gave them that. I organised them to
do what they always did only in a better more efficient way."

The wreckers murmured agreement and listened to the
interchange with interest.

"And when my father tried to stop your murdering
ministry…"

"*Yes*, I did what had to be done. I had to protect what was mine. He was getting too close. One thing *is* true, I did like your father and respect him but he wouldn't stop. He wouldn't let it go, always needling, prying, investigating. He was a fool. And, the fool of a man has raised another fool, I see. So, what now, Riding Officer?"

Nathaniel looked up distastefully and held Pritchard's stare, "For a man with such big ideals I wonder why you hide yourself? Perhaps you thought it added an element of mystery or you were afraid that they would see you really for the weakling you are? You hide behind a mask to order murders and arson because you are too much of a coward to do the deeds yourself."

Pritchard moved forward with lightning speed and struck Nathaniel across the mouth, drawing blood. Nathaniel reeled and fell back but refused to let his eyes, now riveted on Pritchard, lose their gaze and they stayed locked on Pritchard's.

"So brave," Nathaniel goaded, "A real man would face me on equal terms."

Pritchard raised his arm to strike again but stopped as a commotion ensued from the tunnel. They all turned to see the entrance of the very last dragoon, who had remained on guard on the cliff path with Jenny. He had captured the pursuing, vengeful Jeremiah and he roughly pushed Nathaniel's uncle into the light. Jeremiah stumbled groggily, his face bloody and bruised, evidence from his cliff side tussle.

"Jeremiah?" roared Nathaniel in disbelief, as he began to weigh things up in his head.

The soldier tugged forcefully on a rope and Jenny was propelled forward. She lurched and tumbled onto the ground, her hands were tied in front of her. Nathaniel rose up in anger and swore vehemently, "You so much as…"

Pritchard interrupted, "What? What will you do? My men won't do anything they haven't already done to her."

Silas and a few others laughed lasciviously and made lewd gestures at Jenny who was terrified inside but displayed her resolute spirit by seeming to remain proudly defiant.

Pritchard turned to Nathaniel's uncle, "Ah, Jeremiah! How nice to see you again."

Jeremiah expostulated, "You! … Where exactly are we? What is this place?"

"This is where you make your money, Brookes. This is where it all comes from."

Jeremiah sneered, "I have no truck with you, Pritchard. Do as you like. I want him!" He pointed an accusing finger at Nathaniel and shoved his face in front of his nephew, the Riding Officer and hissed, "Because of you and your whore, my Hannah is dead! My sweet daughter, my only child." Jeremiah stifled a sob.

Jenny gasped and Nathaniel looked thunderstruck. They felt the blow of his words as if they had murdered Hannah themselves.

Jeremiah recovered his composure and fixed his eyes now black with hatred on Nathaniel. "I will tear you limb from limb," avowed Jeremiah. He lunged forward but two Dragoons held him back.

Pritchard roared, "NO! He's mine. And so are you Jeremiah Brookes. Bought and paid for, ten times over. You will do as *I* say."

Nathaniel blazed at Jeremiah, "What is he saying? Tell me that you were not involved in my father's death? Speak!" There was silence. "Tell me!" he shrieked.

"Of course he was involved," spat Pritchard.

"Liar," screamed Jeremiah.

"Liar? Who tried to restore the family business after your father drank away his fortune? You almost broke your back trying to save the business. And did your brother, Elijah try to help? Of course he didn't. All he ever wanted to do was to hunt down wreckers and smugglers, didn't he? While you slaved away… Your bitterness drove you, drove you to murder."

"His life was his own to live, his death was nothing to do with me," retorted Jeremiah. "He was my brother for God's sake."

"Yes, but Elijah managed to marry money. Something that eluded you, the one thing you didn't have!"

"Then it's definitely true. The money…I thought mother

may have been trying to salve my conscience... I wasn't certain..." muttered Nathaniel.

"Yes. The money is your mother's. She helped finance your bankrupt uncle and how did he repay her? By murdering her husband."

Nathaniel reeled at this admission and shouted, "No."

Jeremiah's denial chorused with Nathaniel in his refusal of the statement, "NO! That's not how it was."

Pritchard continued to strike like a deadly cobra and enunciated his words brooking no misunderstanding, "You paid me, Jeremiah Brookes, remember?"

"Yes, but to ruin his career as a Riding Officer, to turn him away from his path. To make him return to his family business, not to kill him" Jeremiah protested.

"Well, his career was ended, that's for sure," sniggered Pritchard. "I gave the order on your instruction, Brookes. And Black Bob and Silas here did the deed." Pritchard's laughter was like a razor in Nathaniel's heart but Nathaniel could see that he was outnumbered. He had to think quickly. Beyond Jenny, Goliath was showing signs of recovery. Charles, who was lying a few paces away, was also coming around. Nathaniel assessed the situation. He noted the knife tucked in Charles' belt. Nathaniel was in no doubt that it was the same one that had maimed Jenny months before.

Charles groggily struggled to his feet dragging his injured leg and winced painfully. He leered at Jenny, "Well, well, well. Look who's here? My favourite whore. What's more they fixed her face. A double pleasure for me when I ruin it again."

Nathaniel could bottle his rage no longer. He lunged at Charles and easily bowled him over because of his broken leg and ankle. In the tussle he managed to grab hold of the knife. The two wrestled fiercely, each trying to strangle the other amid the jeers and shouts of the scoundrels who watched in glee at this unexpected entertainment.

Nathaniel rolled on top of Charles and seemed to be gaining the upper hand, but Sir James attempted to come to his son's aid and kicked Nathaniel from off his boy. Nathaniel rolled away nimbly and came up in a fighting stance.

It was then that Goliath, who had been watching carefully, made his move. With the rabble watching the fight, Goliath swiftly attacked the two Dragoons in charge of Jenny and Jeremiah from behind and with an almighty heave he caught both of them and crashed their heads together. Their skulls cracked and both men sunk to the floor.

Meanwhile, Charles crawled away from Nathaniel snivelling like the coward he was. He hauled himself along on his arms, his broken leg trailing behind him. Sir James undeterred, advanced on Nathaniel, his sabre at the ready and he levelled it at Nathaniel's head who didn't think twice but turned the dagger, he'd wrested from Charles, and threw it swiftly. It found its mark.

Sir James' eyes opened wide in shock. He looked down at his chest to see the dagger buried in his heart. He tried to speak but no words would come. Blood frothed out of his mouth and he collapsed to his knees before falling forward thus pushing the blade in further, right up to the hilt. His eyes closed and a horrible rattling wheezed from him as he died.

Charles was now almost hysterical and screamed at the men gathered around, watching, "Kill him! Kill them all!"

Pritchard looked on coolly. He pointed at Nathaniel and calmly ordered, "Make sure he has no more weapons. Disarm him." Silas patted Nathaniel down and shook his head affirming there was nothing more.

Nathaniel glared at his uncle, who was trying to tear himself free from his restrainers. Nathaniel's eyes bored into Jeremiah who paused for a moment in his tussle with two dragoons. Nathaniel's look was harder and steelier than flint. He snapped, "You are worse than these criminal wretches around you. You have heartlessly abused my mother; our family, and now I discover you are at the back of my father's death. You are no better than a hissing serpent, which crawls on its belly. The lowest of the low," then he turned back to Pritchard, "And as for you... You disgust me."

Pritchard pulled out his pistol and aimed it at Nathaniel's head and curtly addressed Goliath who was slowly creeping forward, "Move another muscle and I kill him."

Goliath succumbed and offered no further resistance. He would not risk Pritchard's threat. Immediately, Silas, Black

Bob and three other thugs swarmed across and trussed both Nathaniel and Goliath up like condemned men. They were thrown on the ground not too far from Jenny who had been hauled to the cave wall and propped up like a rag doll her legs pulled apart and her feet staked.

Jeremiah was still struggling with his captors and gasping in fury. Pritchard strode over to him and slapped him hard across the cheek, drawing blood. "You made your bed, now lie in it!" Pritchard continued to needle the irate man; "You quite happily feathered your nest with the proceeds from these men's work. You asked no questions. You couldn't get your brother to finance you and so you chose to get his widow to do it under the guise and mantle of care after Elijah's savage death. You played her, and duped her. You got rid of him for your own ends and destroyed a family in the process. You are despicable."

"I will kill you for this," shouted Jeremiah futilely.

Pritchard scornfully replied, "Well, make up your mind. Please decide who you will kill first, me or him."

Charles hauled himself up, unsteady on his one good leg. He hopped across to his father and rolled his body over and grasped the hilt of the knife and tugged, withdrawing the blade from Sir James' chest showing no compassion for the loss of his father's life. "Thank you, Father," he muttered disdainfully. Clutching the weapon like some powerful amulet and parading it in front of him he hobbled across to Jenny and licked his lips. His excitement and the anticipation of what he was about to do grew as he played with his bloodied dagger. He smirked and rasped hoarsely, "I believe you two have met before, have you not?"

Jenny tried to back peddle toward Nathaniel but could not manage the movement with her hands tied. Charles had now tipped over the edge of reason and he laughed insanely, "So nice of them to fix you up for me."

With a mighty heave, Jeremiah finally threw off his captors and charged toward Nathaniel. Goliath squirmed on his back and thrust out his foot, which caught Jeremiah's leg and sent him flying into Pritchard.

There was an explosion as Pritchard's pistol went off. The noise reverberated painfully around the cavern. The men blocked their ears and cried out in pain. The stench of gunpowder filled the air. There was a huge rumble then dust and loose stones rained down from the unstable rock walls. The falling stones were followed by larger rocks and the ground trembled.

Wreckers and Dragoons looked around and upward in fear and tried to dodge the falling boulders. Black Bob gazed up fearfully and raised his arms to shield his face as a monstrous chunk of rock came crashing down and smashed him to the floor crushing his chest. Charles was thrown off balance. He stumbled and lost his grip on his knife, which skidded and stopped on the cave floor between him and Jenny.

Suddenly, a burst of lights and a flash of red and white appeared at the cave entrance and a voice shouted, "Forty-first! Chaaaarge!"

Philip Chapman and his Forty-first Foot erupted into the cavern. Their bearskin hats made them seem larger than life, throwing the wreckers into disarray. Fixed bayonets and swords clashed in the smugglers' retreat. Every sound was amplified in the confined space. With every blow and scream more stones were dislodged. The smell of clashing steel, which sparked, blood and fear permeated through the cavern.

Jenny and Charles both lunged for the knife at the same time and their heads butted together. For a second or two they were both disorientated and in their dizziness they both missed the knife. Jenny threw her bound hands over Charles' head as she leapt on his back and pulled the rope against his throat. They fell backwards. Charles landed on top of her and jarred the air from her lungs as his full weight almost flattened her. He screamed with the pain in his leg and attempted to slip away but Jenny exerted more pressure on his neck with the rope and wrapped her legs tightly around his waist. "Like it tight, do you?" she spat. "Like it rough, eh?" She drew on every last ounce of strength to forcibly restrain her sadistic tormentor. His face began to turn blue as he gasped for air but Jenny continued to squeeze. His one good leg drummed a terrible tattoo on the ground as Jenny carried on wringing the life out of him. Charles rasped his last and fell limply against her. Uncertain whether or not this was a ploy, Jenny pulled on the rope once more completely crushing his windpipe. She then struggled to free herself whilst all around her the battle raged.

Philip raced to Nathaniel and Goliath and quickly freed them by slicing through their bonds. A stalactite came crashing down and impaled one blackguard stealthily creeping along the sand and shingle floor, who was about to pounce on one of Chapman's men.

Philip shouted, "Fetch Jenny and get out of here before the whole cliff buries us under."

"No, Pritchard must hang for this!" roared Nathaniel.

Goliath reached Jenny and threw Charles' dead body away from her like a broken puppet and tried to protect her from the falling rocks, taking a couple of blows on his arms and shoulders in the process.

Jeremiah and Pritchard grappled together for their lives in the middle of the cavern as if pit in hell itself. Pritchard unsheathed a hidden blade and slashed Jeremiah across the throat who gurgled grotesquely as his life force spurted out like a crimson tide and Nathaniel's Uncle, his eyes wide with disbelief and horror, dropped to the ground dead.

Nathaniel approached Pritchard through the surrounding madness and called his name, "Pritchard!"

Pritchard slowly backed away from Nathaniel and crashed into a duelling couple, Silas and one of Chapman's regiment. Pritchard angrily pushed Silas away and right into the soldier's awaiting bayonet. Silas was eviscerated. He clutched wildly at his abdomen with his intestines spilling out and gave a croaking death rattling cry before he slumped down on the ground as a boulder fell and pinned his groaning body to the sand.

"Pritchard!" repeated Nathaniel, his voice strong and resolute in the mayhem around them. He stood proudly, a majestic figure of righteous morality, a towering force for good.

Pritchard had nowhere to go. He picked up an abandoned sword from the shingle floor and charged Nathaniel bellowing as he ran. Chapman alerted Nathaniel with a warning shout; "Nathaniel!" and he tossed his sabre into the air, which the Riding Officer neatly caught.

The swords clashed but the battle was one-sided. Nathaniel was the superior swordsman, fitter and faster. His reactions were like lightning. Within a few parries and lunges, Nathaniel had disarmed Pritchard, who still refused to raise his hands in surrender.

Nathaniel growled at Pritchard, "I keep my promises... you will hang!"

Pritchard's face reddened with fury; he flew at Nathaniel with his bare hands. Nathaniel's sword was of no use in close quarter combat so he dropped it and it clattered to the floor. The two men grappled together, each trying to gouge out the other's eyes, their hands clutched at each other's throats trying to choke the life out of them. All the while, in this pit bull brawl they were surrounded by treacherous falling rocks.

With a sudden powerful thrust Nathaniel pushed his opponent backward and managed to tear off Pritchard's heavy scarf disguise and with it the top buttons of the custom man's shirt popped open revealing Nathaniel's father's ring hanging on a chain around his neck. The sight of this drove Nathaniel into a blistering rage. Oblivious to the ever-increasing dangerous situation, Nathaniel kneed Pritchard viciously in the groin and was rewarded to see his opponent go down.

Pritchard pleaded for his own life in a snivelling, cowardly fashion, "No! For God's sake, no! Please, Nathaniel."

"I'll show you the same mercy you showed my father," blazed Nathaniel and he leapt on Pritchard. His hands tightened around the Knight's neck, his knuckles turned white with the power and force he exerted.

Philip Chapman thrust off a swarthy ruffian and struck him down, who was now mortally wounded. Philip glanced across at Nathaniel who was throttling the life out of Pritchard. He finished off the wrecker with a single thrust of his blade and dashed to Nathaniel. "Nathaniel, don't! If you kill him like this you'll be no better than him."

Nathaniel screamed back, "He murdered my father. He must die!"

"That's as may be, but not by *your* hand!" reasoned Chapman. "You must see."

Tears of rage and sorrow flowed from Nathaniel's eyes but he relinquished his victim and dropped despairingly to his knees. Pritchard collapsed to the ground, choking and gagging. Chapman extended his hand and helped Nathaniel back onto his feet. The wreckers were now either all dead or captured.

"Can we leave now, before this becomes our tomb?" requested Chapman, looking about him as the stones still rained down.

Nathaniel nodded, yes; wearily and too out of breath to speak.

Chapman ordered one of his men, "Shackle the prisoner." But, Pritchard, however, may have been beaten but he was not defeated. With one last surge of strength he grabbed the Welsh Foot soldier's musket and charged at Nathaniel from the back yelling like a banshee. Without batting an eyelid, Philip Chapman smartly parried the bayonet and decisively ran the villain through with his sabre. Pritchard looked amazed and in incredulity that his charmed life was being cut short and staggered forward before tumbling to the ground and all movement stilled. The king of smugglers was dead.

"Hurry quickly!" shouted Chapman, alerting his men. The remaining solders with their captives hurried to the entrance of the cave as rocks showered down burying the broken and bloodied corpses in their den.

Nathaniel was the last to reach the cave entrance before a final rumble dislodged the last boulder. He looked back as it came hurtling down sealing the entrance to the cave forever. He felt it was just and it was right. He turned to Philip and looked at him warmly with thanks, "You were right in there, and I thank you. I am forever in your debt, Sir. But what I don't understand is how you came to be here."

"Let's get to safety and I will explain, although I think you have more to tell me than I you."

The two men scrambled up the path to the cliff top and the waiting company.

# Chapter Twenty-Seven

## Farewell

Philip Chapman assembled his men. The surviving wreckers were suitably bound and restrained. He gave the order to march them to the Custom House and place them into detention until they could face a court of law. The troops moved out smartly in spite of the bloody battle they had endured and were gratified that they had not lost a man.

Jenny sat on the grassy cliff top to recover her strength and sensibilities. Nathaniel turned and faced his friend. He looked at Goliath with admiration and shook his hand with obvious love and affection for the big giant. "Without you at my side, I would never have succeeded. I owe you my life, my friend."

Goliath smiled warmly, "And I you, Nathaniel. I proud to have served you. But now, it's time, I wish go back, return."

"Return?"

"Home. My life not here."

"But, I had hoped..." he stopped, "No, of course. I must not be selfish. You have your own life."

"And you have your Jenny."

Nathaniel stretched out his hand and gently pulled Jenny to her feet. He took her in his arms and crushed her to him. His lips caressed her fragrant hair and he whispered, "My love. I never want to let you out of my sight. I want you at my side, to come home to every night as my wife."

"Oh, Nathaniel," breathed Jenny and she turned her face up to him, her eyelids closed over those sparkling green knowing eyes that had seen so much sorrow and were now ignited with hope and she waited for his kiss. He enfolded her in his arms, passionately, protectively and pressed his lips against hers with fire and love; an urgent kiss that then became gentle and tender. Goliath nodded and smiled. This was good.

The trio made their way to where the foot soldiers had

tethered their horses after taking them from the beach. As they walked Jenny nestled herself against Nathaniel's shoulder as if afraid that someone would snatch him from her. He lifted her onto her mount and the valiant three trotted off down the cliff path to the Custom House after the battalion.

They drew up outside to see Lieutenant Chapman emerging from the Government building. He hailed them, "Nathaniel. The scoundrels are under lock and key with no chance of escape. Four of my men are on duty. They will not let you down."

"Who is in charge here, now?" asked Nathaniel.

"There's only Thomas Lloyd. He is the acting Head of Customs. There is no one else. He was as shocked and staggered as we all were to discover that Pritchard was the infamous Knight. Thomas is an honest man."

Nathaniel dismounted and shook Philip Chapman's hand, "Thank you, my friend. If it wasn't for you...."

"No thanks needed. I have been itching to join this war and now I have, I will apply for the regiment to watch the coast until such a time that all ships have safe passage in these waters."


Nathaniel and Goliath faced each other on the docks. Nathaniel extended his hand, which Goliath shook warmly. Both men stood silently for a moment remembering all they had been through before they spontaneously embraced and hugged each other. Neither man seemed to want to let the other one go.

Goliath held Nathaniel's gaze after they released each other and he murmured, "Thank you."

Nathaniel smiled at his very good friend and whispered, "God speed. If ever you decide to return, you know where to find me."

"That I do," rejoined Goliath. "But, as you have your Jenny so I have my Aleka, at home and waiting, I hope."

Nathaniel nodded in understanding. Goliath picked up a small bag and mounted the shore gangway to board a sailing vessel moored at the quayside. He proudly strode up to the ship and turned taking one last look at Nathaniel. The Negro giant gave a small wave and disappeared into the bowels of the ship as the gangway was lifted.

Nathaniel watched the ship as it steamed out of the harbour. He remained there for some minutes well after the boat had sailed from view. He sighed and turned slowly away. His stride gathered pace and he lifted his head with pride and made his way to Jessie waiting at the Harbour Master's Office. He thrust his hat firmly on his head, his cloak swirled behind him and the Riding Officer trotted away from the sea and back toward the town and the Custom House.

As he made his way through the town, people smiled and doffed their caps. No one shunned him or drew away from his greetings. People were polite and personable. The contrast in the local's behaviour was enormous. Nathaniel and Jessie soon clattered to a halt outside the Custom House and he entered with a flourish. Thomas looked up, "Mr. Brookes, Sir. Orders have arrived for the new Riding Officer set to patrol from Mumbles Head to Swansea and along the Gower."

"And what of the Bristol Channel?"

"As you predicted, Sir. That stretch will have another rider."

"It is well."

"I still can't believe it, Sir. To think we worked for years believing the Crown couldn't afford us any more men. And that Mr. Pritchard was at the back of everything."

"And now, we have the coastline better protected and an honest man to take the reins of responsibility here," smiled Nathaniel.

Thomas blushed, "I don't think I will fill your shoes, Sir, Mr. Brookes."

"Thomas, Pritchard had us all fooled. There is no blame laid at anyone's door. I have to return to my family and resume my medical career. My time here is done. You are an excellent administrator and will serve the Crown and your country well."

"We will miss you, Mr. Brookes."

"I won't be far away. There is need of a doctor here and I intend to fill that post."

Nathaniel gathered his final papers together and stepped toward the door, which opened gently revealing Lady Caroline and her maid, Martha.

"Lady Caroline," he said surprised.

"Mr. Brookes, I am so glad to have caught you."

"Yes?"

"I know you are moving on but I had to thank you. Thank you for saving my life. If it hadn't been for you I would have been condemned to a miserable existence for as long as my husband let me live and now…"

"Now, you are your own woman. What will you do?"

"The Manor is mine. I have been left well provided for and reaped the reward of returning the contraband stored and hidden at the house. I thought I might look toward improving the lot of women in the area. I intend to open a school and teach young girls and women who want to learn."

"An admirable occupation, I am sure."

"I just have to get over the prejudice of some of the men. But, I think I can manage that. Martha here is to be my first student." She smiled and extended her hand, "Good luck, Mr Brookes. We will not forget you. If ever you return you will always be welcome at the Manor."

"That may be sooner than you think, but not as a Riding Officer."

"In that case, until we meet again," smiled Lady Caroline.

Nathaniel bowed courteously and opened the door to show them out. He was now certain that he was leaving Swansea and Mumbles in better shape than he had found it. But now, now he had to return to his mother's house and Jenny. Nathaniel felt he had a good life ahead of him. He had plans to make for his and Jenny's future and with that thought in mind he bade farewell to Thomas and left the Customs House and the employ of the Customs Service.

# Chapter Twenty-Eight

## Four Years Later

The day was glorious and the gentle summer sun beamed down. Its warmth spread over a pretty thatched cottage with its own fragrant country garden, sitting at the edge of Mumbles. The garden was alive with laughter as two toddlers played happily with each other and their grandmother, Myah, who laughed delightedly at the youngsters' antics and chatter. Although Myah's hair was a little greyer, her face was more relaxed, and her mouth seemed ready to burst into a smile at any opportunity. The laughter lines around her eyes were a strong testament to this.

She giggled as the two children darted around her legs, nearly pulling her to the grass, "Enough now children. It's time to let Grandmama gather her breath." The toddlers ran around, chasing each other and Myah made her way onto the patio where Naomi and Jenny were now sitting.

A tray of drinks for the family were placed on the rustic table and the two young mothers chattered happily together. Jenny poured them each a cool glass of cordial and they sat and watched the little ones play.

"Ah me, I am ready for this," said Myah taking a long draught, "I'd forgotten how exhausting young ones can be."

"Imagine how much harder it will be when they are older and can run faster," laughed Jenny. "At least I can still catch Bart now he's just started to run. He is fast on his feet for one so small. The older he gets the more difficult it will be. I can see him running rings around me."

"He's already doing that to me now!" exclaimed Myah. "And his chatter... He is very advanced in his talking, for one so young."

"I know, Sarah-Jane is the same. I wonder, Jenny how do you think they will turn out? What do you think they will be?" asked Naomi.

"I am happy to have him grow up healthy and strong. I

will let him be whatever he wishes. I do not intend to impose my will on him."

"Then you are wise," agreed Myah. "Children need to be nurtured and grow up in a household of love. But, they also need to make their own mistakes. That way they will learn."

"Well, whatever they decide, I am sure we will encourage and support them. They have a long way to go yet," declared Naomi.

The toddlers were chasing each other around. Bartholomew was pretending to ride a horse and making clicking noises with his mouth. They both tumbled into the small sandpit and rolled around giggling. Myah sighed and pronounced philosophically, "What will be, will be. Now, I will go and fetch some more glasses. I am sure the men folk will be home soon. They will need some light refreshment before dinner."

Myah retreated indoors to get the glasses. Naomi turned to Jenny, "Ah, Jenny, if only life could go on like this. I would never complain about anything ever again."

"I understand. It must be hard for you, never knowing if you will be sent to another part of the country or even abroad, such is the life in the military."

"I know. That is why we must make the most of each blessed moment that we have with family especially on days like this. Where is Nathaniel? Time travels on. He left before dawn broke."

"As you and I both know, babies will come when they are ready and not before. It is the third time this week he has been called to Mrs. Boyce's house. I should imagine her husband Elwyn is more than tired of running here for Nathaniel at every little twinge or practice contraction."

Myah returned with two tall glasses and settled them on the tray before joining the children in a game in the sand pit. Laughter filled the air and the two young mothers watched their offspring affectionately, contented that they were safe and happy.

The sound of a horse cantering along the country lane assailed their ears and soon Philip Chapman rode into view. He dismounted and tied his horse to the garden gate and bound over it in a single leap. "I hope there's some for me.

It's just what I need after that ride." He leaned across kissed Naomi as his little daughter scrambled out of the sandpit and came running up.

"Daddy!" exclaimed Sarah-Jane, happily.

Philip scooped up his baby girl and swung her around before depositing her back on the grass. She chuckled and toddled back to her cousin, Bartholomew.

"Any wreckers, Captain Chapman?" Naomi asked her eyes twinkling brightly.

Philip grinned boyishly, "No, Mrs. Chapman, not a one in sight."

"I had thought Nathaniel would have returned by now," said Jenny a small frown creasing her face.

"I'm sure I saw the buggy anon as I made my approach to the cottage. It could be Nathaniel," pronounced Philip.

As he spoke the noise of a small buggy and horses' hooves drew nearer. The little wagon slowed as Nathaniel drew up and left his carriage at the garden gate. He jumped down and joined the family, his heart bursting with pride as his eyes lit on Jenny and his small son.

Chapman raised his glass, "Ah, Dr. Brookes! And how was your day today?"

"Mrs. Boyce was finally delivered of an eight pound healthy baby boy and it couldn't be a better day. In fact, we must all wet the baby's head with a toast." He reached out for a glass of cordial that Jenny had poured. "To Mrs. Boyce and baby, Geoffery."

They all raised their glasses and drank before Bartholomew shook himself of sand and ran to the family and then dived at his father's legs demanding to be picked up and placed on his shoulders.

Nathaniel placed a loving and protective arm around Jenny's shoulders and asked his son, "So, Bart. What do you want to be when you grow up?"

Bartholomew screwed up his face and thought for a moment before announcing in a small voice, "A Riding Officer."

.